One wish granted. Ryan Weiss for a master. My best friend under the influence, and still no sign of Oliver. I could handle this. I would not panic, and I would not freak out. That was my mantra as I made my way through the party and out to the Weisses' front porch. And that was what I told myself when I realized it was dark outside—even though it had been morning when I'd made my fourth wish.

I will not panic, and I will not freak out.

A gust of wind whipped across the porch, chilling my legs—my long, model-skinny bare legs. Oliver had said that his appearance changed based on what his master needed or wanted him to be. Did that mean I'd turned into Ryan Weiss's fantasy girl?

Gross.

Focusing on the place where I'd last felt my magic—somewhere under my rib cage—I concentrated hard on being myself again. My real self. Nothing happened.

And without Oliver here, there wasn't a thing I could do about it.

OTHER BOOKS YOU MAY ENJOY

LINDSAY RIBAR

the FOURTH WISH

speak

An Imprint of Penguin Group (USA)

SPEAK

Published by the Penguin Group

Penguin Group (USA) LLC

375 Hudson Street

New York, New York 10014

USA * Canada * UK * Ireland * Australia

New Zealand * India * South Africa * China

penguin.com

A Penguin Random House Company

First published in the United States of America by Kathy Dawson Books,
an imprint of Penguin Group (USA) LLC, 2014
Published by Speak, an imprint of Penguin Group (USA) LLC, 2015

THE LIBRARY OF CONGRESS HAS CATALOGED THE KATHY DAWSON BOOKS EDITION AS FOLLOWS:

Ribar, Lindsay.

The fourth wish / by Lindsay Ribar.

Pages cm.—(The art of wishing ; book 2)

Summary: "When eighteen-year-old Margo McKenna becomes a genie, she must figure out how
her new powers work, deal with having a master who attends her high school, and try to graduate
with her new secret under wraps—all while learning what 'forever' really means when
your boyfriend is a centuries old genie"—Provided by publisher.

ISBN 978-0-8037-3828-7 (hardback)

[1. Wishes—Fiction. 2. Magic—Fiction. 3. Genies—Fiction. 4. Theater—Fiction.
5. High schools—Fiction. 6. Schools—Fiction.] 1. Title.

PZ7.R3485Fou 2014   [Fic]—dc23   2013038555

Speak ISBN 978-0-14-751003-7

Printed in the United States of America

1 3 5 7 9 10 8 6 4 2

the FOURTH WISH

Chapter ONE

There was only pain, at first—the pain of my magic breaking me into a collection of atoms, getting ready to make me into something new. It was painful, but I knew it was necessary.

I just wished I could make it happen *faster*.

With that thought, the magic inside me sped up and exploded outward like a supernova—and the pain vanished, leaving relief in its wake, coupled with a strangely soothing sensation, like minty feathers on my skin.

I opened my eyes.

Just seconds ago I'd been standing with Oliver on the stage of the empty Jackson High auditorium. Now there were people everywhere. Girls with wobbling heels and smoky eye makeup, boys with baggy pants and gelled hair, all walking around with plastic cups in their hands and shouting at each other over the too-loud music.

None of them was Oliver.

One of the girls bumped into me, sending me stumbling.

I felt my ankle turn a little, and I realized I was in heels, just like she was. Why was I wearing heels? The last time I'd done that was in *Guys and Dolls* back in sophomore year. The girl turned and raised an eyebrow at me, like she was waiting for me to apologize. When I didn't, she gave a dismissive shrug and turned away again, back toward the crowd.

"Fine, be that way," I muttered—and immediately snapped my mouth closed. The voice I'd just heard wasn't mine. It was higher, and softer. More ingénue than leading lady.

I looked down at my hands. My fingers had become longer and thinner. The Big Dipper–shaped constellation of freckles on my left arm was gone. There was pale pink polish on my nails, instead of my usual bold greens and reds and purples.

I had to find a mirror, stat.

Around the corner was a door marked with a taped-up paper sign that said BATHROOM!!! in orange marker, but there were three people already lined up to get in. So I pushed open the next door, and found myself in a very adult-looking bedroom, with a mountain of coats on the bed and a full-length mirror in the far corner. Pausing just long enough to turn the light on, I made a beeline for the mirror.

My breath caught. The girl staring back at me was *beautiful*.

My magic had created a new body for me, exactly as Oliver had told me it would. Gone was the real Margo McKenna—short and flat-chested, not beautiful by any means, but firmly on the prettier side of average—and in her place was someone new. Long blond hair that framed high, sharp cheekbones. Milk-pale skin marred only by a tiny mole just above red-painted lips. Big brown eyes accented by dark, sexy makeup . . . and a tall, thin body wrapped in a short black dress.

It was like the weirdest fitting-room experience ever. And it would only get weirder from here. There was a reason I was in this place, wherever it was, and a reason that I looked the way I did. All of this was happening because someone had called me here.

I was a genie.

Which meant I owed that someone three wishes.

As if on cue, there came a tug just behind my rib cage—not quite painful, but very persistent. I knew instinctively that this was a call, and that I was supposed to follow my magic to its source. But then what?

I'd had nightmares like this, over and over throughout most of junior high, before I'd conquered my stage fright: It's the opening night of a musical, and I'm supposed to play the lead . . . only there haven't been any rehearsals, and I don't know my lines.

And just like in the dreams, there was only one thing I could do.

Wing it.

I shimmied through the crowd, across the living room, up a flight of stairs, and into a bedroom at the end of the hall.

I peeked in. Three girls and one guy were in the middle of playing "Carry On Wayward Son" on Rock Band. The walls were covered with posters of Tenacious D, this supposedly hilarious band whose jokes I'd never found particularly funny. Another girl sat on the bed, chatting with two guys.

But the one who'd called me was the boy lingering a few feet behind the Rock Band players, playing air-guitar along with the song, rocking out like he was imagining himself on stage at Madison Square Garden or something. The door creaked as I pushed it farther open, and the boy turned around to face me.

Ryan Weiss.

Out of seven billion possibilities, I'd ended up bound to someone I actually knew? That couldn't be right. But my magic surged, and I felt its approval like a cool breeze on a humid summer day. *First contact has been made,* it seemed to say. *This is the person you're supposed to meet.*

He was holding my red guitar pick between his thumb and forefinger, which was exactly the way I'd held Oliver's silver ring when I'd wanted to call him.

I drew in a sharp breath, remembering.

"How will I know what my spirit vessel is?" I ask.

Oliver smiles at me. "You'll know."

The snippet of memory flitted away as fast as it had appeared. When had that conversation happened? I needed to find Oliver. This was moving too fast, and I didn't know what to do next, and he was the only one who could—

Before I could even finish the thought, there was another sharp tug in my chest, and my magic dropped three pieces of knowledge right into the front and center of my consciousness:

First, I was not allowed to leave until I answered Ryan's call properly.

Second, a proper answering of the call involved telling Ryan that he'd summoned a genie and was therefore entitled to make three wishes.

Third, I'd waited long enough. It was time for me to act.

"Hey, shut the door, would you?" said the girl on the bed— which was when I realized that I knew her. Jill Spalding was one of my fellow seniors at Andrew Jackson High. She was also in the cast of *Sweeney Todd* with Ryan and me—our high school musical, which was due to open in just over three weeks.

"Sorry," I said, and stepped all the way into the room. Ryan's eyes were now fixed on me, and a predatory smile spread like syrup across his face. Apparently I wasn't the only one who thought my new body was hot stuff. I could practically feel—almost *hear*—how much he wanted me.

This pleased my magic immensely.

It did not, however, please *me*.

"Hey," he said at last.

"Hi, Ryan," I replied.

That creepy feeling of desire spiked as I said his name— that was when I realized I was hearing his thoughts. Oliver had been able to hear my thoughts, too, back when he was my genie, bound to me. Only the thoughts about wanting, though. The thoughts that might eventually turn into wishes.

But unlike Oliver, who'd been able to pluck thoughts from my head as easily as reading a book, I wasn't getting much of anything from Ryan. There was the insistent sense of *I want you,* and a distinct image of a slice of pie, accompanied by what looked like a beer can, but it was gone before I could make any sense of it.

He gestured toward the TV. "You want to play next?" he asked. I felt, very forcefully, that he wanted me to say no.

"Uh . . ." I bit my lip, trying to decide, but after a few seconds, pressure began to build behind my eyes. Answer. I had to answer truthfully. My magic demanded it.

"No, that's okay," I said at last. The pressure receded instantly.

Ryan's smile broadened. "Cool."

"Carry On Wayward Son" ended, and the four players congratulated one another and handed their instruments to Jill and her boys. But when one of the girls tried to give Ryan her plastic guitar, he just waved her away.

"But it's your turn," said the girl, her voice unmistakably flirtatious. "You said you wanted to play Pearl Jam next."

Ryan barely even looked at her. "I can play later," he said.

The girl shrugged, but slipped the guitar strap back over her head. "Two turns for me, then," she said.

"So what's a girl like you doing in a place like this?" said Ryan, giving me an obvious once-over as the opening lines of "Bad Reputation" blared from the TV speakers. Oh god, he was actually flirting. He had *lines*.

"Just hanging out," I replied, managing a smile somehow.

"Nice," he said, grinning like I'd just delivered a great joke. "So what's your name?"

A name. Right, I needed a new name. I couldn't exactly call myself Margo, not looking like this. Maggie, like my parents called me when I was little? No, I needed something completely different. And there was that pressure behind my eyes again, threatening to grow into very real pain if I didn't answer soon.

"Amber," I said, picking something totally random. "My name's Amber."

The pressure receded again.

Well, that was interesting. According to Oliver, questions asked by a master required immediate and truthful answers— yet my new fake name seemed to work just fine. "Hey," I said, "ask me where I'm from."

"Uh, okay," he said. "Where are you from?"

"I was born in Sweden, and I grew up in Alaska, but I moved here last year because I got tired of it being cold all the time."

Once again, my magic seemed satisfied. Not just satisfied, actually. As I pulled Amber's story out of thin air and told it to Ryan, I could actually feel it becoming true.

"Ask me how old I am," I told him, bouncing on the balls of my feet.

"Uh. How old are you?"

I waited just long enough for the pressure to start building, then said, "Twenty-one."

This time, when the pressure receded, it left a tingle of impatience in its wake. I was playing games, and my magic wanted me to tell Ryan what I was, and why I was here.

The sooner I did that, the sooner I could leave and find Oliver.

"So listen, Ryan," I said. "I need to talk to you. In private, if that's okay."

His eyebrows shot up. There was that *I want you* feeling again. Then he cut a glance toward the people playing "Bad Reputation," and it faded a little. Indecision played over his face.

But I knew how to make him decide for sure. I reached out and grabbed his hand, letting him feel the magic pooled in my fingertips.

"Holy hell," he said, jumping back a little. "What was that?"

"Magic," I said simply, holding my hand up and waggling my fingers at him.

"Magic," he repeated. His eyebrows knitted, and I could sense him wanting something. I just couldn't tell what.

"Yes," I said. "There's . . . let's call it a business contract I need to discuss with you, and it involves magic. Which is why I'd prefer to go somewhere private."

"A contract." His desire for me waned a little as he repeated the word. "Uh, if you say so. How about my parents' room? There's just coats in there now."

"Perfect."

"Hey, guys, I'll be back in a few," Ryan announced to the room at large. Rock Band Girl turned around to give him an exaggerated pout. He brushed past her as we left, and I was pretty sure I saw him pat her butt. Ew.

As we headed downstairs, some guy I didn't know almost crashed into me. I pressed myself against the wall and watched him lumber upward, clutching a red cup in each hand. "Nice party," I said dryly.

"Not bad, right?" said Ryan. "I mean, they're usually way killer, like way more than this, but this one was last minute. The 'rents decided to skip town for the week, so I got some people to come over for drinks and some tunes, and before you know it, everyone invites everyone else, and blam! Party! Guess that's just how it goes, huh?"

"Guess so," I agreed, even though I'd never experienced such a thing before. Impromptu parties seemed like the kind of thing that happened in movies, not in real life.

He opened the door to the coat room, and I flipped the light on. No way was I about to let mood lighting play any part in this conversation. This was going to be strictly business.

"You don't have a drink," he said suddenly. "You should have a drink. We still got some mixers left, I think, if you want something girly. Or are you a beer chick?"

"I'm good, thanks."

"Whatever," said Ryan with a shrug, and sat on the bed. He patted the space beside him, looking far too eager. "So, what's this about a contract?" He tried to make the word sound sexy this time, but failed miserably. Somehow I managed not to laugh at him.

I sat down, leaving plenty of space between us. "Here's the thing." Then I paused. This was it. I'd been cast in my role, and my magic had written the script. All I had to do was deliver my lines.

"I'm a genie, Ryan. I am here to grant you three wishes."

He blinked, and was silent. I didn't have to be a mind reader to know that this wasn't what he'd been expecting. His jaw worked, and I could practically see him wondering how he was supposed to react.

So I went on: "Do you remember the red guitar pick you were holding upstairs?"

His brow creased, and he dug into his pocket and produced the pick. "This one?" he said, holding it up so I could see.

"That one," I said. "When you picked it up, just like that, between your thumb and your first finger, it called me to you."

"And then your hands," he added doubtfully. "They were all weird."

I nodded. "Yes, and then my hands were weird. What you felt was my magic. The same magic that will grant your wishes, when you make them."

"Magic. Yeeeah." He looked askance at me, like he was struggling to reach a decision. After a moment, his lips twisted into a smirk. "Prove it. Magic me up some more beer. There's only like two sixers left. Simon's usually in charge of booze, but he didn't even show tonight, so . . ."

I tensed at the sound of Simon's name, but was relieved that he wasn't here. The last time I'd seen him, he'd unwittingly put Oliver and me in life-threatening danger.

"Ryan," I said patiently, "I can't do anything unless you wish for it. But why don't we talk about it first, so that—"

"Oh, wait, no," he said, his eyes lighting up as he cut me off. "I got something way better. I wish for that stage manager girl to fall, like, balls-to-the-wall, crazy-ass in love with me! You know that girl? Naomi Sloane?"

My heart leaped into my throat. Of course I knew Naomi. She was my best friend. And she liked Ryan even less than I did.

"Yes," I said quickly. "But before you decide for sure—"

Then my magic was surging forward from wherever it had hidden itself, knocking the breath right out of me. It didn't matter that he hadn't made up his mind. He was touching the guitar pick, and he'd already said *I wish*.

I tried to clamp down on it, but it was too powerful, just like when I'd turned into Amber, and my deep breaths became gasps, and I was going to explode, I couldn't handle it, I couldn't control it—

Colors burst like fireworks behind my eyes. My fingertips burned hot and cold and hot and cold until they turned numb. My vision went white. I couldn't breathe.

Then it was over. I blinked myself back to reality, taking in the room, the bed, the pile of coats—and Ryan sitting next to me, looking at me like I'd just started speaking in tongues.

Apparently my magic didn't need my input before it granted my masters' wishes. Good to know.

"So?" he said. "Where is she?"

"I don't know," I replied truthfully. Maybe she wasn't at the party. Maybe she was so far away from the party that the wish hadn't reached her. I was pretty sure wishes weren't constrained by distance, but I could hope—

The door swung open. In walked Naomi Sloane, pointing a finger directly at Ryan. "Ah-ha," she said. "Quimby said he saw you come in here. Wait, who are you?" This last was directed at me, along with narrowed eyes and a suspicious expression.

"Amber," I said, nervous under the weight of her gaze. If anyone here could see through my magical disguise, it would be Naomi. We'd known each other approximately forever.

"Well, Amber," she said, in a tone that mocked without malice, "I have to talk to Weiss here. So, do you mind?" She jerked her thumb over her shoulder toward the door, making her meaning perfectly clear.

"But you don't even——" I snapped my mouth shut. Sure, *I* knew how much Naomi disliked Ryan, but I wasn't me right now, at least not in her eyes. As far as she was concerned, I was just an obstacle standing between her and the private moment she obviously wanted to have.

I stared at her, held in place by indecision even as my magic gently nudged me toward the door. My magic wanted what my master wanted. And Ryan very much wanted me to leave.

"I don't even what?" asked Naomi. She'd made her way over to Ryan by this point, and was squeezing his shoulder in a way that could have passed for platonic . . . at least until you looked closer.

Ryan, for his part, was clearly finished contributing to the conversation. He was staring slack-jawed up at Naomi, and the overwhelming *I want you* feeling was back, stronger than ever. Only this time, it wasn't directed at me.

The Naomi I knew would never touch Ryan like that——and Ryan, who'd just witnessed *magic,* for heaven's sake, appeared to have forgotten all about me. I wanted to hit the pause button and talk some sense into both of them, ask them what the hell they were thinking . . . but I couldn't. Not without more information.

My magic had gone dormant inside me once more, and now that Ryan didn't want me around, I wasn't obligated to stay. Which meant I was free to find Oliver and start asking him some serious questions.

Chapter TWO

One wish granted. Ryan Weiss for a master. My best friend under the influence, and still no sign of Oliver. I could handle this. I would not panic, and I would not freak out. That was my mantra as I made my way through the party and out to the Weisses' front porch. And that was what I told myself when I realized it was dark outside—even though it had been morning when I'd made my fourth wish.

I will not panic, and I will not freak out.

A gust of wind whipped across the porch, chilling my legs—my long, model-skinny bare legs. Oliver had said that his appearance changed based on what his master needed or wanted him to be. Did that mean I'd turned into Ryan Weiss's fantasy girl?

Gross.

Focusing on the place where I'd last felt my magic—somewhere under my rib cage—I concentrated hard on being myself again. My real self. Nothing happened.

And without Oliver here, there wasn't a thing I could do about it.

So I started walking. Unlike my real body, Amber's body was inclined to walk toe-to-heel, which made me feel uncomfortably flighty. But I pushed the feeling aside and kept going. Once I reached the nearest main road, it would only be a twenty-minute walk home. I had no idea what time it was, but it must have been late, since the roads were practically empty.

The first time I saw headlights, I thought about flagging down the approaching car and asking for a ride. But I didn't. Not because the idea of hitchhiking freaked me out—although it did—but because the last half hour had proven how completely out of my depth I was, and this was the first thing I'd encountered tonight that I actually knew how to deal with. I might not have the slightest idea how to use my magic, but I could damn well get myself home without help.

The car passed without slowing down. My hair and my dress fluttered in its wake, and then the road was empty again. I kept walking.

Both my parents' cars were in the driveway, and all the lights were off, which meant they were probably sleeping. That was a relief . . . until I realized I didn't have my keys. No pockets, no backpack, not even a purse. Nowhere to put a key, even if I had one.

But as soon as I thought it, a little shiver jolted through me, and something shifted against my skin. The skin of my left breast, to be exact. Where I'd only felt fabric a moment before, there was now something small and metal tucked into my bra.

So my magic wouldn't turn me back into my real self, but it was perfectly willing to give me a key to my real house? Yeah, that made a lot of sense.

I unlocked the front door, disabled the alarm system, and slipped my shoes off once I got inside. Usually I left them by the front door, but not tonight. I didn't want my parents waking up and finding some stranger's stiletto heels on our shoe rack.

Hell, I had no idea what they'd do tomorrow when they found the same stranger sleeping in their daughter's bed. My mind flashed to a movie I'd seen on TV once, where some kid-wished to be an adult, then woke up the next day looking like Tom Hanks. I didn't remember much of the actual plot beyond that, but the look on his mom's face had stuck with me. The idea of my own mom looking at me like that made my stomach churn.

I locked my door, just in case.

And that was it. I was home, standing in my own room, surrounded by my own things. My modest collection of books. My not-so-modest collection of CDs and vinyl. My dresser and my laptop and my posters.

A rustling of cloth made me jump. Peering curiously at me from just inside my closet was a little gray tabby face, attached to a long, lithe feline body.

"Hey there, Ziggy," I said softly, bending down to pet her.

But she flattened her ears and hissed at me.

She didn't recognize me at all.

I froze, horrified, and Ziggy darted around me, right for the door. Finding it closed, she reached one paw into the space underneath, like she might be able to tunnel her way out. I thought about making her stay until she got used to me, but dismissed the idea almost immediately. What if it didn't work? What if she spent the night yowling and hissing and trying to claw my eyes out?

I unlocked and opened the door. Ziggy disappeared into the dark hallway.

Without bothering to change out of Amber's party dress, I pulled my blankets over myself. Ryan Weiss and my stupid cat be damned. Right now, all I wanted to do was sleep. Surely Oliver would find me tomorrow.

My limbs felt like anvils when the knock on my door woke me up. I started to mumble something about how it was the middle of the night and couldn't I just sleep in peace—but a familiar brightness behind my eyelids shut me up. Daylight. I'd just fallen asleep. How could it be morning already? Had I really been that exhausted?

"Margo, honey, are you in there?" My mom's voice, punctuated by another quick knock. "I didn't hear you come home last night. Are you okay? We really should talk about this."

Those last three words, spoken in a tone that hovered between sympathy and anger, were like a splash of cold water over my head. I sat up, my blankets fell away . . . and there was the dress. The black, shiny cocktail dress whose bed-induced wrinkles had left soft impressions on pale skin that wasn't mine. Crap.

I reached up to rub the sleep out of my eyes, and my fingers came away smeared with dark makeup. Fingers that weren't mine. Makeup that wasn't mine. Double crap.

"Margo?" called my mom. "You'll be late for school. And why is your door locked?"

I couldn't answer her, not with Amber's voice sounding so different from my own. But she wouldn't go away unless I said something.

Channeling my inner ten-year-old, I hunched over and gave a loud, obnoxious cough. "I'm sick," I said, warping Amber's voice to sound as nasally as possible. It didn't actually sound too far off from my normal fake-sick voice.

Another moment of silence stretched between my mom and me, and I filled it with one more halfhearted cough.

"You were sick yesterday, too," she said sternly. "Too sick to go to school, but apparently well enough to stay out all night without even calling to check in. Or answering your phone, for that matter."

Was it really only yesterday that I'd ditched school to spend the day with Oliver? It already felt like a different lifetime.

"Sorry," I said in the same nasally voice, and coughed again. Another moment of silence. I couldn't believe this. I was supposed to be learning how to be a genie, and instead I was pretending to be sick so my mom would leave me alone.

"Fine," she said at last. "Behave like that if you want, Margaret. I'll see you when I get home from work. But don't think you're getting off without talking to me." Her footsteps moved away down the hall, and I let out a slow sigh of relief.

She'd sounded strict in a way that she hadn't since she'd remarried Dad nearly a year ago. Usually she was too busy being in love to bother being a responsible parent.

A moment later I heard her car pull out of the driveway, followed by Dad's, and only then did I heave myself out of bed. Ten minutes later, freshly scrubbed and smelling of shampoo, I dragged out my favorite pair of jeans and started to tug them on. That was when I discovered the crucial flaw in my getting-dressed plan.

None of my clothes fit.

Aside from being far too tall, Amber's body was entirely the wrong shape for my wardrobe. The only things in my room that would fit me were my bathrobe and my fuzzy green turtle slippers—the former because it was one-size-fits-all, the latter because they were slip-ons. Even Amber's feet were bigger than mine.

I debated putting the little black dress back on, but that would just be sad. And kind of gross, since it still smelled faintly of smoke. So I put on my bathrobe and slippers, then headed back over toward my bed, where I kept my guitar. If anything had the power to make me feel more like my real self, it was playing music.

But before I could reach under my bed and retrieve the case, I felt a sharp tug, like a fish hook had lodged in my rib cage. A call. Far stronger than the one I'd felt last night at the party. So strong that my breath hitched against it.

It pulled me forward, off the bed and toward the window. Fear washed over me. Was I supposed to step through the window? Fall to my death? Try to fly? I didn't know, but the pull was so strong that all I could do was stumble forward.

Everything around me went gray.

Chapter THREE

There was nothing. No sound, no light, no touch, no walls and no sky and no floor, nothing at all but me and an endless expanse of gray. But I kept moving forward, pulled by the call.

I saw the bedroom a split second before I stepped into it—and then, with a rush of air and breath and magic, my slippered feet skidded to a halt on a hardwood floor. Plastic Rock Band instruments were everywhere. Jack Black leered down from a Tenacious D poster on the wall of a room that smelled vaguely of unwashed socks. And sitting in a desk chair, wearing a ratty brown T-shirt, was Ryan.

"Killer," he said, looking down at the red guitar pick, which he held between his thumb and forefinger. Then back at me. "I am totally killer!"

"You are?" I said. That probably wasn't the response he was looking for, but I couldn't help it. I reached out, trying to see what he was thinking, but his thoughts were still a tangle of white noise, just like last night. "Is that good?"

"Um, obviously." He jabbed two fingers at his own chest. "I, Ryan Weiss, am the actual master of an actual freaking genie. That kind of equals killer, am I right?"

I couldn't remember if I'd said the word *master* to him last night. But my magic was prickling at me to answer his question, so I forced a smile, got my thoughts in order, and said, "You're right. Very killer. So, hey, when I left last night, Naomi was—"

"She just left a few hours ago," he said, with the most self-satisfied grin I'd ever seen. "I said she should skip school with me, but I guess she's not into that. But still. Great job with that wish. Instant results. I dig that."

I blinked stupidly at him. "You mean she spent the night?"

Using his heels to swivel his desk chair back and forth, almost like a victory dance, he said, "That's totally what I mean."

"Did you guys . . . ?" But I couldn't bring myself to finish the question. Asking the question meant getting an answer, and I didn't want to hear him say it out loud. "Never mind."

He smirked at me. "That chick. I swear."

"Yeah, she's great," I said quickly, before he could go into detail. I had to take control of this situation, and I had to do it fast. Smoothing my features into what I hoped was a businesslike smile, I said, "So, do you have a second wish? Is that why you called me? Because I could grant it right now, if you want."

A desire surged forward from the static of his thoughts, but I couldn't tell what it was. "No," he said. "Just got a question. How long is that Naomi-being-in-love-with-me wish gonna last?"

I had no idea how to respond to that—until, less than a second later, my magic deposited the answer into my brain. "Since you didn't specify a time limit, the wish will last indefinitely."

Ryan's eyes narrowed. "Huh," he said, obviously displeased. "Okay, then I want a do-over so I can make there be a time limit. Like, in case it gets old and she starts stalking me or something."

My magic bristled just beneath my skin, adding a strangely indignant feeling to the certain knowledge that I couldn't do what he wanted. "Sorry, Ryan my darling," I said, and was surprised when the words didn't sound patronizing. Casual flirtation sat comfortably on Amber's tongue. "No refunds, no exchanges."

"But that's not fair," he said.

"Fair or not," I said, "those are the rules. I have to play by them as much as you do."

"Fine," he said, swiveling around so he was facing his laptop. He grabbed the mouse and clicked a window open. "The cave guys said you can't fix a wish after you make it, but I still figured it was worth a shot. Everything's worth a shot, right?"

"Right," I said automatically, before my magic could force me to answer. "Wait. The cave guys? Who?"

He looked over his shoulder at me, like he was trying to figure something out. But he didn't answer. "So, I screwed up one wish," he said. "Which means my other ones need to be real good." He scrolled down the page.

I leaned forward to see what he was looking at, but he clicked the window off before I could see, revealing a You-Tube video, paused in the middle. I recognized it immediately as the animated opening sequence of that old TV show *I Dream of Jeannie*. On Ryan's screen, the cartoon Jeannie the Genie was mid-dance, with her hip thrust out to the side and her hands in a weird yoga-ish pose above her head.

Ryan looked back just in time to catch me frowning at the image. "She's hot," he said with a laugh. Then, after a slight pause, "You were hot too, last night. How come you're dressed like my mom?"

"Because it's stupid o'clock in the morning, and I wasn't expecting you to call," I said, crossing my arms over my chest, like that would somehow block his view of my wet hair and kitten-printed bathrobe. "What's it to you?"

"I just expected you to be hot again, that's all." He shrugged in a way that made his disappointment clear, then reached over and clicked Jeannie's window off.

My magic tugged at me, and I could sense it offering to put

me back into the kind of clothes Ryan had been expecting to see—or, alternatively, into Jeannie's revealing little outfit— but I shoved it away as quickly as I could. I'd never been the sort of person who dressed up just to impress boys, and I certainly wasn't about to change that now. Not for him, anyway.

"So deal with it," I said through gritted teeth.

"Feisty," he said. "Nice. So, yeah, two wishes. Any suggestions? I mean, what would you wish for?"

To turn into myself again. To have a better grasp on how to use my magic. To find Oliver. But I didn't want to say any of those things to Ryan. They would make me look weak, and that was the last thing I needed.

On the other hand, I had to answer truthfully. After a few seconds in which I didn't answer, the pressure of my magic started building up, fast enough that I panicked and blurted out something that was very true indeed: "Right now, I'd wish to be pretty much anywhere but here, and bound to pretty much anyone but you."

Ryan's whole body seemed to tense up, and I took an instinctive step back, throwing my hands up and smiling widely. "Kidding!" I lied. "Totally kidding!"

He rolled his eyes. "Dumb question, I guess. I mean, you're a genie. You're all magic and stuff, so there's nothing left to wish for. Unless—wait, am I supposed to wish you free? Like in *Aladdin*?"

I nearly choked. "No," I said quickly. "You're not supposed

to wish me free." What I didn't say was that wishing me free would kill me.

"Oh, good," he said, grinning. "Then I don't have to waste one."

"Nope," I said.

"So I guess you can go now," he said, apparently satisfied. "I'll call you later, okay?"

"Later?" I asked as dread coiled through me. "When's later?"

"Whenever I want," he said smugly. "I mean, I'm your master, right?"

"Right," I replied, feeling increasingly uncomfortable. I had to put a dent in this *I'm your master* thing, stat. "Although I'd prefer it if you'd refrain from calling me unless you have something *useful* for me to do."

He narrowed his eyes, like a challenge. "Or else . . ."

I shrugged and gave him my best enigmatic smile. "I'm a genie, Ryan. A being whose power you cannot even begin to comprehend. If you think there isn't an 'or else' attached, you are sadly mistaken."

It was a bluff, of course; if he challenged my assertion with direct questions, my illusion of actual power would collapse like the house of straw in front of the Big Bad Wolf. But he didn't. He just rolled his eyes again and said, "Fine. Whatever. Be gone, all-powerful immortal being. I have wishes to plan."

I rubbed my hands together, willing the buzz in my fingertips to swell into something bigger so I could get back to my room the same way I'd gotten here . . . but now that Ryan wasn't wanting anything at me, my magic lay dormant again, unresponsive to my will.

"What are you waiting for?" said Ryan, obviously annoyed. "I said see you later."

"I'm not waiting for anything," I said evenly. "Call me if you think of another wish."

And then, like a totally unmagical girl doing the worst Walk of Shame ever, I slunk out of his room and closed the door behind me.

As bad as walking home in party clothes had been, walking home in my bathrobe and slippers was a zillion times worse— not in the least because it was mid-morning and there were cars everywhere. As I trudged down the sidewalk, I pictured every single driver rubbernecking at me.

At least none of them would recognize me.

A couple blocks away from Ryan's house, I heard footsteps behind me, running. Assuming it was a jogger, I moved politely over to the edge of the sidewalk so he could pass. But then a female voice called, "Hey, there you are!"

I tugged my robe tighter and whirled around, nearly tripping over my unwieldy slippers in the process. A little ways behind me, rapidly approaching and obviously out of breath, was a girl I didn't know. She wore artfully ripped jeans with black cowboy boots and a leather jacket. A wide streak of bright purple accented her short black hair, and a diamond stud glittered in her nose. Suddenly I felt even more self-conscious.

"Sorry," I said as she drew closer. "You've got the wrong half-dressed, turtle-slippered blonde."

She glanced at my slippers. "Turtles. Cute. But what happened to your shoes?"

"Nothing," I said irritably. "Sometimes I like taking my turtles out for a walk, okay? Look, I'm not a huge fan of blowing people off, but I'm not exactly in a new-friend-making mood at the moment, so best of luck finding whoever you're looking for, and nice to meet you, and have a great day, and good-bye."

I waited for her to turn around and leave, but the worry on her face just deepened. Her voice turned soft and plaintive. "Wait. You really don't recognize me?"

I froze. Looked just a little bit closer at the nose-ringed girl—and that was when I saw them. Her eyes. Bright green. Dark lashes. The shape of them . . . the way they were looking at me . . .

"Oliver," I whispered, my heart suddenly certain even though my brain was still catching up.

The girl nodded. "Long time no see," she said, with a slight tremor in her voice.

His voice. Of course. Ever since last night, I'd been watching for the Oliver Parish that I knew—the tall, shaggy-haired, hoodie-clad boy who'd been a sophomore at my high school for a few months earlier this year—even though he'd told me, *explicitly* told me, that he reinvented himself for each new person who found his vessel. But being told was very different from actually seeing it.

The curved hips. The feminine clothes. The chest. *Oh god,* I thought. *My boyfriend has boobs.*

But all I said was, "You look different."

His face twisted into a smirk—the kind of smirk that looked far more natural on this girl's face than it would have on Oliver's. "So do you," he said, raising his eyebrows like it was our new little in-joke.

I tried to laugh, but it came out choked. That was when his smirk faded, leaving an expression of alarm in its wake.

"Oh," he said. "I didn't realize—hold on a second. I'll shift back." He took a deep breath, and the air around him shimmered. And there, in place of the nose-ringed girl, was Oliver, with his kind face and soft lips and bright, bright green eyes.

He took a step toward me, but tentatively, like he was afraid I'd say no. That was what did it. Not the gesture itself, but the hesitation of it. The reluctance to make the first move. It was so familiar, so irritatingly and adorably *him,* that I practically fell into his arms.

Our bodies pressed together, but I was taller now, almost as tall as he was, and I fit against him strangely. I couldn't make this new body relax into his, like my real body had done.

"I'm so sorry, Margo," Oliver said, clutching me tightly. "I thought you'd know it was me."

"How?" I asked, pulling away so I could see his face again. "How would I have known? You looked completely different."

He raked a hand through his dark, shaggy hair. "Sure, yeah, but didn't you see my magic?"

I shook my head; I hadn't seen anything but a poster child for every indie rock band that had ever existed.

"Seriously, you didn't? Like an aura or something, sort of whitish and glowy?"

I shook my head again. "I'm supposed to see auras now?"

"Just mine," he said with a secretive smile. "It's a genie thing. You have it, too. That's how I recognized you. You glow."

"I glow," I said flatly. "Great. What else? Do I trail pixie dust in my wake?"

"No," he said. "And it's just a little bit of a glow. Not a big deal, just—"

"Just the difference between recognizing you and thinking you were a total stranger," I finished. "And I didn't even know to look for it. Well, hey, I'll just add that to the giant pile of things I don't know, huh? Like how to turn back into myself, or how to get home without having to walk a million miles, or how not to get bound to people like Ryan goddamn Weiss, the biggest douchebag *ever,* who used a wish to bang my best fr—"

I stopped cold. *Naomi*. I'd been so caught up in the details of my own magic, and all the things I didn't know how to do, that I'd nearly forgotten what Ryan's wish had done to her.

"Your best friend?" said Oliver, looking suddenly wary of me. Probably because I'd been yelling. "What happened?"

I closed my eyes, balling my hands into fists as I made myself breathe. "What happened," I said, "was that Ryan made a wish. She fell in love with him, and she spent the night, and they . . . they did stuff. And in case that's not bad enough already, Naomi *hates* Ryan, plus she has a boyfriend, and I know she never would've cheated on him without that stupid wish. So. My first question is, how do I fix Naomi? Second, how do I get Ryan to make good wishes instead of crappy ones? Third, how do I read his mind? I kept trying, but all I get is static. Oh, and fourth question—"

"Margo, calm down," said Oliver, reaching out and putting a hand on my shoulder. "One thing at a time, okay?"

"Calm down?" I said. "I spent a whole night in a stranger's body, hiding from my parents, granting wishes for Ryan Weiss, watching Naomi throw herself at him, with no idea where you were, or how to be myself again, or why it was nighttime, or . . ."

My throat was suddenly thick with tears, and I couldn't finish. Oliver wrapped his arms around me again, pulling me close.

"I'm so sorry," he said, his voice quiet and soothing. "I would have been there last night, except nobody had picked up my vessel yet. No vessel, no master. No master, no body. My ring didn't bind itself to a new master until about half an hour ago, and when that happened, looking for you was the first thing I did. I swear. I'm just thankful I knew where you were going, otherwise it could have taken a lot longer."

"You knew where I was going?" I asked. "How? I didn't even know."

"You said you wanted to come back to Oakvale. I told you it was a bad idea, but you wanted to."

"I never said that."

"Yes, you did," he said. "Right before you threw your vessel back into the real world. That's why it landed in Oakvale. I don't know why it picked Ryan's house—maybe it's the exact center of town or something—but it did. We waited for hours for someone to pick it up. You cried. A lot."

He peered closely at me, like he was waiting for the story to jog my memory. But I was more confused than ever.

"Did you say the real world?" I asked. He nodded. "As opposed to what? Where were we?"

He looked uncertain, like he was trying to figure out if I was messing with him. "You really don't remember?"

I shook my head numbly. Apparently now I was the sort of person who went around losing her memories. Awesome.

"I took you to the Between. I thought we could stay there

for a bit, and I could show you how everything works. Give you a chance to adjust, you know? But you freaked out and ran away. You said—" He paused abruptly. "Wait. What *do* you remember?"

I shook my head again. "Nothing. I mean, I was on the stage at school, and then I went with you, and then I was at Ryan's. What happened? What did I run away from? What were we between?" I cringed, suddenly embarrassed. "Did I really freak out?"

"Only a little," said Oliver with a smile. "And we were between . . . well, everything. The space between everything and everything else, like I told you before. We were—oh, wait. We *were* until you said that, and then . . . ohh. You don't remember because you didn't want to, and you don't *remember* not wanting to remember. That explains it."

"Um, no, it doesn't. What are you talking about?"

"I'm talking about . . ." He bit his lip, running a hand through his hair again. "Okay. The Between. Just now, Ryan called you from your house to his, right? And the call pulled you through that gray space?"

I nodded; my short trip through that airless, soundless, empty space was still uncomfortably vivid in my memory. "That's the Between?"

Oliver nodded. "It's kind of like a portal. A shortcut to wherever you want to go. But it's also whatever you make it. It does what you want. And when you were there with me, you wanted to forget having been there, so it made you forget when you left."

I stared at him. "So . . . I did magic on myself that I don't remember doing?"

He nodded, looking uneasy. "I think so. It's the only thing that makes sense."

"No, it doesn't make sense." I knew I sounded desperate, but I didn't care. "*Nothing* makes sense."

Oliver slid his hand down my arm, and for a second I thought he'd try to hold my hand. Instead, he simply touched his fingertips to mine—and that was all he needed to do. Our magic connected, and we *sparked*. There was no other way to describe it. It was like electricity, flowing from me into him and him into me and back again.

Feeling like Maria at the dance in *West Side Story,* I brought our hands up higher, right between our hearts. I stared at them, marveling at the intensity of this thing we shared.

"Margo, I know you want answers," he said, voice lowered almost to a whisper. "It's new, and it's scary, but you'll be fine. You just need to learn how everything works. And I'm going to teach you, because I love you, and because you're damn well smart enough that teaching you magic is going to be the easiest thing I've ever done." He smiled. "And because it's the least I can do for the girl who saved my life."

"I did kinda save your life, didn't I?" I said, waggling my eyebrows at him.

"More than 'kinda.'" He grasped my hands tightly, suddenly looking very serious. "Margo, I never thought I would survive . . . him."

Xavier, he meant. The genie who'd meant to kill Oliver, just like he'd already killed every single other genie in the world, by hunting down their vessels and wishing them free. He would have succeeded if not for my fourth wish, which had set Xavier free, destroying him in Oliver's place.

It didn't escape me that Oliver wouldn't say his name.

He went on: "I had a century and a half to get used to the idea that one day, he'd show up and wish me free. I made my peace with it a long time ago. I was expecting it. I probably even deserved it. But then you came along and——"

"Deserved it?" I said, somewhat alarmed. "What do you mean?"

He blinked at me. A second passed. Then he shook his head, laughing softly. "Nothing. I'm just being melodramatic. The point is, without you, I wouldn't be here. And there's no way I can even begin to repay you for that."

I shrugged, as a blush crept across my skin. "Give me a twenty, and we'll call it even. Seriously, you don't owe me anything." I paused. "Although you did mention something about teaching me how to use my magic . . . ?"

"So I did," he said. "Are you ready?"

"Way past ready," I said. "Show me the ways of the Force, Obi-Wan."

"Yes ma'am," he said, giving my fingers a quick little squeeze before he broke our connection. "First things first: We're getting you out of here. The fast way."

"Jumping, right?" I said. "That's what you called it?"

"Yup," he said. "It's not technically jumping, though. It's more like . . . well, just walking. Through the Between."

I blew out a breath and steeled myself as best I could. "All right. Bring it on."

Chapter *FOUR*

Oliver clutched my hand firmly in his, telling me to pick where I wanted to go—anywhere in the world—and concentrate only on that. So I pictured my bedroom, then nodded to tell him I was ready. We began to walk.

And then I was surrounded by empty, blank gray. Even the floor—no, that wasn't a floor. It wasn't *anything*. Except for me and Oliver, there was nothing there but a void.

"Oliver," I said, squeezing his hand. Or at least, I thought I was squeezing. I saw his hand in mine, and I felt something hand-shaped, but it had all the substance of a cloud. It felt like touching a ghost.

"You're okay," came his voice, soothingly even. "Keep picturing where you want to go. Keep walking."

"But how can I—"

"Don't think. Just do it. I'll follow you."

So I walked. Even though I couldn't feel myself move, or feel ground beneath my feet, I walked. I wanted to hide my head, to pinch myself until I woke up. Or, at the very least, to remember what had happened the last time I was here.

And then—

"It's not working, Oliver. I can't see." My voice is tight, my words clipped.

"It'll be okay. I promise. Just relax. The door is right here. Just concentrate on seeing the door, and you'll be fine." He's the only thing I can see in this place. Everything else is formless, depthless gray. There's no gravity, no color, no touch, and definitely no door.

"You relax. This is all your fault. Oh god, I'm gonna be sick. I'm gonna . . ."

My entire body rebels against the total absence of sensation. I've never felt so horrible in my entire life, not even when I had the flu in junior high and couldn't get out of bed for two days.

"I need to go home," I realize out loud. The sound of my own voice is a fragile comfort, but I cling to it. I keep talking. "Back to Oakvale. I don't want to remember this. You hear me? I want to fast-forward. I want to forget this ever happened."

Oliver's eyes widen. "Not Oakvale, Margo. You're not ready. Start somewhere new. There're too many things that can go wrong——"

"More wrong than this?" I cry. "Screw you. I'm going home."

"Margo, please . . ."

But before he can say anything else, I take the too-solid object in my hand—the flat, red piece of plastic that now holds a piece of me inside it—and I throw it as hard as I can. It lands in an empty bedroom. I try to follow it there, back out into the real world, but my magic won't let me.

So I sit, curling myself up as tightly as I can. I watch. I wait. I try not to cry, but I end up crying anyway.

I went still as the realization sank in: That was what I'd done last time. I'd freaked out and run away, just like Oliver had said. I looked at him for confirmation, but if he knew what I was thinking about, he didn't let on. He just smiled and said again, "Keep walking."

After a few more seconds, my bedroom appeared before me: a hazy image behind a veil of gray. I stepped through, and my feet landed on carpet.

I breathed deeply, savoring the sweet feeling of air filling my lungs. I felt like I hadn't breathed in years.

"Your house?" Oliver said, eyeing the room suspiciously. "Isn't there somewhere we can go that's less—"

"It's fine. Nobody's home."

"That's not what I . . ." He bit his lip, uncertain, but then shrugged. "It's okay. We'll stay here for now. Easier to learn new things in familiar surroundings, right?"

"Sure? I guess so?"

"Speaking of which, you did well just now. With the jump. Was it easier this time? Not that you remember last time."

"I do remember, actually. I thought about wanting to remember, and I did." I hunched my shoulders a little, embarrassed. "Sorry for throwing a tantrum."

Concern clouded his face. "It wasn't a tantrum. You panicked. It was my fault; I should've warned you what it would be like."

"Still," I murmured, remembering the very un-Margo-ish way I'd yelled at him. The way I'd cried. "I can't believe . . . I never do that. Never."

Except that I had.

"Once in your life won't kill you. Everything gets easier with time, even crossing the Between. It'll be second nature soon enough."

"Good," I said firmly. "Then let's start the clock right now. I need to turn into myself again, and I need to make Ryan wish Naomi back to normal. Oh, and how do you do the mind reading thing?"

Looking sort of taken aback, Oliver said, "You can't just make someone wish for what you want. It doesn't work like that. If you want him to fix her, it's up to you to talk him into it. There aren't any shortcuts."

"Mind reading's a shortcut," I said. "Right?"

"It can be, if you know how to use the information you find," said Oliver. "But those are skills that come with time and practice. You can't rush it."

Time and practice. I didn't like the sound of that. How many wishes like Ryan's would I have to grant before then?

"Sorry," Oliver added.

"No, it's fine," I said morosely. Kicking off my turtle slippers, I sank onto my bed and extended one leg out toward him. "And since you asked, what happened to my shoes is that none of them fit anymore. Amber's feet are enormous compared to mine. Does turning into myself take time and practice, too?"

"It shouldn't," he said with a grin. "In fact, that's a perfect first lesson. Let's turn you back into Margo."

"Yes, please," I said.

"Right," he said, rubbing his hands together. "Well, it's easy, kind of like jumping. You just think of who you want to be, and step back into it."

I stared at him. "Okay, you just said 'easy' and 'jumping' in the same sentence. Error message. Does not compute. Reboot. Try again."

"Okay . . ." His eyes darted around my room, like it might give him a hint about where to begin. It didn't seem to help.

"How do *you* do it?" I asked. "Show me. I'll follow your lead."

"You sure?" he asked, his brow furrowing. "You didn't seem too happy seeing me as Gwen last time . . ."

Gwen. A female name for his female body.

"I'm sure," I said.

Oliver shimmered, and then Gwen stood before me again, with her nose ring and purple streak and jeans that clung snugly to her hips. "Still sure?" said Oliver, in Gwen's light alto.

I made myself nod. "But I still don't get it. You were Oliver, and now you're . . . not. What are you doing to make that happen? How did you learn? Did . . ." I hesitated—but only for a second. "Did Xavier teach you?"

Back in the early 1800s, Xavier had granted Oliver's fourth wish in exchange for his human life—the same as Oliver had done for me just yesterday. Back then, Oliver's name had been Ciarán, and Xavier had called himself Niall. They'd been friends at first . . . and then more than friends, apparently, though I wasn't sure exactly how much more.

By the time I met Xavier, though, he'd gone straight-up Knife-Wielding Bad Guy.

As soon as I said his name, Oliver's entire body seemed to close off. He shot me a dark look that made Gwen's face almost unattractive. "He said I'd be better off figuring it out on my own, so that's what I did."

I thought that was a pretty mean thing to do, but Oliver's tone didn't exactly invite commentary, so I just said, "Ah."

He ran a hand through Gwen's purple-streaked hair. "It was just so long ago. And I've never had to explain it before. But let me see. Hold on."

He shifted back into Oliver, then paused thoughtfully. Then shifted back into Gwen. Then Oliver again. It was dizzying.

"Hmm," he said.

"Hmm?"

Oliver slid onto the bed, right next to me. "It's like . . .

like flexing a muscle, almost? Hold out your arm. Palm up. Here." He slid his index finger in a straight line from my wrist to my elbow. "That's where I feel it. Right there, just under the skin. Imagine there's a muscle there—a muscle you didn't have when you were human—and flex it."

"*When I was human,*" I said. "I'm not human anymore."

Oliver hesitated. "Well, I'm no scientist, but I'm pretty sure this"—he shifted into Gwen again—"isn't how humans work." He paused. "Margo, are you okay?"

For a moment I just blinked at him, letting my brain catch up with what shouldn't have been a major revelation. Oliver had talked several times about his human life, as opposed to his life as a genie. It simply hadn't occurred to me, until this moment, to think of myself in the same terms.

"I'm fine," I said firmly.

Oliver shot me a worried look, like he was trying to decide whether or not to believe me. Which was fair, since I didn't know if I believed me either. I wasn't human anymore, *and* I wasn't Margo anymore.

Well, at least I could fix one of those things.

"So, flexing?" I said.

He nodded. "Just under your skin. I mean, I'm not sure it'll feel the same for you, but . . ."

I imagined the invisible muscle, just like he'd said . . . and my magic filled in the rest. A cool, tingly feeling washed over me, cell by cell. My eyes flew open, and I practically leaped up off the bed, looking eagerly down at myself. Sneakers, jeans, and a faded Olive Oyl T-shirt: all things I owned. But even better than that, I was back in my own body. Right down to the calluses on my fingers and the constellation of freckles on my arm. I was me again.

"I did it," I whispered.

I looked up, and he was standing there with hands outstretched, like he was ready to hold me up if I fell over. But when I spoke and my own voice came out, he lowered his hands, a cautious smile spreading over his face.

"Margo," he said, eyes shining.

"You bet," I replied, taking a deep breath with my very own lungs. "Oh, that feels awesome. This body is my favorite, favorite body."

"Would it be horribly uncouth of me to say that it's mine, too?" asked Oliver. He stepped closer, touching our fingers together again. Our magic sparked, just like before—and something inside me sparked right along with it.

When I pulled him down for a kiss, it felt even better than drawing that first breath after crossing the Between. One of his hands moved to my lower back, and the fingertips of the other grazed the back of my neck. A soft, minty sensation, like magic, began to spread over my skin.

This was how Oliver and I were supposed to fit together. This was the reason I'd made the fourth wish. This was the real me.

"You're flickering," said Oliver. His mouth was inches from mine, and he was still holding me tightly.

"I love the way you kiss me," I said. My skin felt warm. "What's flickering?"

He pulled away a little. "Margo. Focus. I mean you're starting to shift back."

The thought of shifting back sent a jolt of adrenaline through me. I could feel my magic reaching out to undo what I'd just done—to shift me back into Amber. I clenched my stomach again, and my magic receded. I remained myself. But just barely.

"There you go," Oliver said, after a moment. "Knew you could do it."

I responded with a groan, pressing both hands against my stomach. The effort of keeping my magic in check was like doing sit-ups in gym class, but two hundred times worse. "It doesn't want me to be myself. Why? What am I doing wrong?"

"Nothing at all. That's just how it works. You became Amber for your master, so whenever you aren't actively using your magic to be someone else, Amber's who you'll revert back to."

"Oh, awesome," I said. "Just for the record, you know, I didn't turn into Amber on purpose. You made it sound like you actually get a choice, but my stupid, defective magic did it for me."

"It's not defective. It's just new. You're operating on pure instinct now—brand-new instincts, at that—but once your brain and your body catch up with those instincts, you'll learn how to keep your magic under control. Same as I did."

I nodded, trying to be comforted. I could do this. I *would* do this.

"Wait, though," I said. "That means you're *trying* to be Oliver right now. And if you weren't . . . ?"

He ducked his head a little. "I'd be Gwen."

"Ah," I said. "She seems . . . interesting."

"Of course she is," said Oliver, plopping back down on the edge of my bed. "She's me."

I rolled my eyes. "I didn't say 'sexy and adorable and a really good kisser.' I said 'interesting.' I'm talking about her, not you. Where'd she come from, anyway? Who's got your ring now?"

"Someone nice," he said.

"Someone I know?" I asked.

"Someone way nicer than Ryan, anyway," he said, like he hadn't heard me. "What are the odds you'd get someone like that, your first time out? Seriously. Did he really use a wish to sleep with Naomi?"

My shoulders sagged, and I sat down on the floor, drawing my knees up to my chest. "He wished for her to love him. The sex part was collateral damage."

He let out a low whistle, sliding down to join me on the floor. "Ouch," he said. "Although it could be worse. Love wishes are way easier to deal with than sex wishes. They leave more room for free will. Whatever Naomi did with Ryan, she still did it of her own volition, not because the wish forced her."

Well, that was something, at least.

Just then, I heard a car pulling into the driveway. Running to my window, I muttered a curse under my breath. "My mom's home," I said. "It's not even noon, and she's home from work. What the hell?"

"Watch it," said Oliver. "You're flickering again."

"Crap!" I said, backing away from the window and clenching my stomach. "Double, triple, quadruple crap. Am I okay now?"

"Yes," he said, looking anxiously toward the window. "But we should go." He held out his hand.

"Go where?" I asked.

"My apartment," he said. "Wherever. Anywhere but here."

"Yeah, and then my mom'll come upstairs and find me missing," I said. "I can't do that to her two days in a row. Besides, she'll start thinking something's up if I don't start acting normal again."

"Normal?" he replied, blinking. "But I thought . . . when you made that wish . . ."

"You thought what?"

Out in the driveway, the car's engine turned off.

"I thought we'd . . . I don't know, really. I guess I thought we'd run away together. See the world. Make a clean break between your old life and your new one."

For a moment I was silent. Suddenly, a lot of things made sense.

"Oliver," I said carefully, "I didn't jump into my bedroom for the 'familiar surroundings.' I came back here because I *live* here." When he didn't reply right away, I went on: "I'm eighteen. I'm not even finished with school yet. I'm in a play that opens in three weeks. I've got a family. You knew that."

"I did know that," he said.

"I made a fourth wish to save *your* life," I said. "Not because I wanted to give up my own."

"Oh." A moment passed as he absorbed this information. Below us, the front door opened, then closed again. He managed a small smile. "In that case, you'd better stay and I'd better go. Don't want your mom catching you with a boy in your room, right?"

Relief flooded through me, and I leaned up to give him a quick kiss. "I'll see you tomorrow, okay?"

"Same time, same place," he said. "I mean, same place being here, not the sidewalk."

I shook my head. "I have school tomorrow, and then rehearsal. How about afterward?"

"You're going to *school*?"

I raised my eyebrows.

"I mean, it's just that your magic's still unstable, and—"

"And I'll handle it." He looked like he was about to protest, but I cut him off: "Seriously, Oliver, I'll be fine. I won't flicker in front of my teachers."

The stairs began creaking; my mom was seconds away from my room. I made a shooing motion and mouthed the words "Please go!"

"Bye," he whispered, and vanished.

When my mom knocked on my door, and then let herself in without waiting for my reply, she found me lying on top of my covers, nodding along to an old P!nk album. I acted surprised to see her.

"Aren't you supposed to be at work?" I asked, sitting up and turning the music down.

"Aren't you supposed to be at school?" Mom held up a white paper bag. "I took a half day to bring my favorite daughter some chicken soup. I hear that's a thing parents are doing these days."

I wanted to ask if it was Anti-Flickering Chicken Soup, but stopped myself just in time. "You haven't done that since I was about four."

"Then it's about time I did it again, don't you think?" She looked around, like she was trying to decide something. "I should get a tray."

"That's okay," I said, exaggerating a groan as I got to my

feet. "I'll come downstairs. I was starting to go stir crazy up here anyway."

She settled me in the kitchen with a bowl of soup, which was fresh from the deli and still hot, and poured some dry food into Ziggy's dish before making a turkey sandwich for herself. As I ate, I clenched my abs as hard as I could against my magic. I refused to be the sort of person who flickered at the lunch table.

"Where did you go yesterday?" said Mom, without any pre-amble.

I was prepared for this. "Emergency play thing. Didn't you get my voicemail?"

"There wasn't a voicemail," she said suspiciously.

Putting on my best exasperated face, I heaved an enormous sigh. "Stupid phone. It does this all the time. I'm so sorry; I thought you knew where I was."

"Your dad and I called you. Three times."

And I'd have known that if I'd checked my phone—which I hadn't done since I'd shown up, as Amber, in the middle of Ryan Weiss's midweek boozefest. I cringed. "Seriously? God, I'm sorry. Big theater, loud music, you know . . . but I should have checked."

Mom seemed slightly mollified by my display of contrition, but she still shook her head as she took a bite of her sand-wich. Then she reached over and touched something I hadn't noticed before: a thick envelope, sitting on the table between us. "This came yesterday, by the way," she said. "I'm guessing you didn't see it."

The envelope had my name on it. And the return address . . .

I grabbed it and tore it open. Right under my name, right at the beginning of the first paragraph, was a word I'd waited years to see. *Congratulations,* it said. I skimmed the rest, but it was hardly necessary. That first word told me all I needed to know.

"I'm in," I said, suddenly numb. I stared at the letter. "NYU let me in."

Mom's eyes shone with pride, and she gestured at the fridge with her sandwich. "Consider me not at all surprised. That's why we're having cake after lunch. With ice cream."

"Cake?" I said. "We weren't supposed to have cake till I heard back from all ten schools."

Ten schools, including several Ivy Leagues. On the night before mailing out my application to Harvard, I'd actually lit a candle and said a prayer to the college admission gods. It seemed like twelve million years ago.

"I didn't want to wait," said Mom, shrugging. "Besides, this is the first one. The first one's always the most special, even if it's not the school you end up going to. And your other letters should arrive this week, too, so. . . ."

I wondered if NYU offered a major in being a genie. I could

take classes in how not to flicker in front of people. I could minor in shapeshifting.

"What's wrong?" said Mom. "I thought you'd be happy."

"Nothing," I said quickly, forcing my face into a smile. "Cake. Awesome. Shouldn't we wait for Dad, though?"

"There'll be enough left for your dad later. But all those college visits, all those applications? That was just you and me. Not to mention I paid all the application fees," she added with a laugh. "So let's just make it the two of us for now, okay?"

That was the moment it hit me. If I hadn't panicked in the Between and run back to Oakvale, I might not be here right now. I might have taken Oliver's advice and gone somewhere completely different, Thailand or Alaska or Guam or something, and Mom would be none the wiser. I wouldn't have answered when she'd knocked on my door that morning. She might have called the police by now.

I got up and hugged her, as tightly as I could.

She said something as she hugged me back—but I didn't hear what it was. The constant dull ache in my abs had suddenly flared. I hissed before I could stop myself.

"You okay?" said Mom.

Mumbling something about not feeling well, I fled to the first-floor bathroom, locked the door, and only then did I let my magic overtake me. In a matter of seconds, I was Amber again.

I'd done it. I hadn't flickered in front of my mother. I'd controlled it long enough to get somewhere safe. And after a moment of rest, I could go back to being Margo.

Focusing on the hidden place just under my skin, I called my magic again, forcing it to shift me back into myself. It was easier this time. A lot easier.

"You okay, sweetie?" came my mom's voice from the other side of the door.

I smiled at myself in the mirror above the bathroom sink. "Yeah," I said. "Yeah, I think I'm gonna be fine."

Chapter FIVE

After a full night's sleep as Amber, I shifted easily back into Margo. I ate a bagel and drove to school. I went to my locker and got out my books for math and French, all the while wondering if anyone could tell that I'd changed. That there was magic chafing at my insides, trying to shift me into someone else. But nobody paid me any more attention than usual.

Score one for me.

But when I walked into the calculus classroom, my sense of victory dissolved like so much smoke. Simon Lee, the only human witness to my fourth wish, was sitting alone at his desk—and when he saw me, his eyes practically bugged out of his head.

"Dude." He twisted toward me, gripping his desk so hard that his knuckles turned white. "You're alive."

"Of course I'm alive," I said, pausing cautiously just inside the door. "Should I not be?"

"You disappeared," he whispered. "Right there on the

stage, and there was all this fire and then Shen was gone— wait, no, Xavier was his real name?—then Xavier was gone, and you just faded away, and Oliver was just acting like oh, no big deal, this is totally normal, and it was *not totally normal at all*—"

"Shh!" I hissed, looking out toward the hallway. I darted over to the desk next to Simon's, within whispering distance. "Okay, definitely not normal, but I don't want everyone to hear about it, okay?"

"Okay," he said meekly.

"You haven't told anyone, right?"

He paused, just long enough for visions of YouTube videos to dance menacingly through my head. "No," he said. "I thought about it, but no. I mean, who would believe me?"

"Good, okay," I said, letting out a huge breath of relief. "Just . . . just keep it that way, yeah?"

"Sure, if you say so," he said uncertainly, and then lowered his voice again. "But dude, what the hell was that? What happened?"

I cast one more glance toward the doorway as I debated how much to tell him. "I wished Xavier free, so *he* wouldn't be able to wish *Oliver* free. That's what happened."

Simon narrowed his eyes curiously. "And wishing a genie free means killing them. Hence the fire." I nodded. "But the thing where you disappeared . . . ?"

Another glance at the doorway. "That was because I had to

use a fourth wish. The first three wishes are free, but if you need a fourth . . . well, there's a price for that, you could say. That's why I disappeared."

"A price?" he said, obviously wanting me to explain further. But I just pressed my lips together and nodded, so he tried a different question. "Why didn't you let me do it? I'd've totally made that wish for you. I know you heard me say so."

"I know," I said, smiling tightly at him. "And I appreciate it, but it was something I had to do myself."

The confusion on Simon's face only deepened, but he nodded anyway. "Well, hey, as long as you're okay."

"Totally okay," I said, with the sunniest smile I could muster.

"Good," he said. "So, listen, did you hear about—"

But before he could say anything else, the classroom door swung open again and my best friend walked in. Naomi Sloane held her books in one hand and a Starbucks cup in the other, as stylish as a movie star in her perfect makeup and designer dress.

She frowned when her eyes landed on me, and I froze. She knew. She could tell I was different. She knew it was me at the party, that I'd been the one to make her fall for Ryan, that I only looked like Margo because I was trying to.

But then she turned to smirk at Simon. "You owe me five bucks," she said.

Ah.

Her aloof gaze and chilly tone weren't about my being a genie—they were about the fight we'd had.

Simon seemed to shrink a few inches as Naomi swaggered across the room and loomed over his desk. "No, I don't," he said uncertainly. Naomi just raised an eyebrow.

"What's going on?" I said.

Since Simon was busy rifling through his pockets, Naomi turned back to me. "We had a bet."

"I gathered as much," I said, trying very hard not to sound as tetchy as she did. "A bet about me?"

"I said you were just out sick." Naomi jerked her thumb over her shoulder. "But Lee here was convinced, number one: That you died. Number two: You faked your own death and ran away with nothing but Oliver Parish and a single suitcase full of hopes and dreams. Number three . . . What was number three, Lee?"

"Gtkennnpinvj," he muttered.

"Sorry, what was that?" said Naomi, cupping a hand to her ear.

He shot a worried look at me. "Number three was getting kidnapped and murdered by an evil genie." I drew in a breath, but before I could say anything, he continued hastily: "And it wasn't hopes and dreams, okay? Give a dude some credit. It was a suitcase full of lacy stripper underwear. Thongs and stuff."

I felt my face go hot. I did not want Simon thinking about my underwear. Maybe a month ago, when I'd still thought he was the hottest boy in school—he liked to call himself the Asian Johnny Depp, and he definitely wasn't wrong—but now? No way.

"You said hopes and dreams, Lee," said Naomi, leaving no room for argument. "Fork over the cash."

He thrust a five-dollar bill at her, looking distinctly annoyed. Apparently satisfied, Naomi pocketed the money and headed for her seat, just in time for the rest of the tiny class to start trickling in.

Simon leaned toward me again, speaking in a loud whisper. "What I *was* gonna say, before my money started mysteriously disappearing, was did you hear about Naomi and Ryan Weiss?"

Naomi's jaw dropped open, and she reeled back like she'd been slapped. I was just as taken aback. How the hell did Simon know about that? Hadn't Ryan said that Simon wasn't even at the party?

"No," I said firmly. "I didn't hear anything. And whatever *you* heard, you should probably keep it to yourself."

Simon blinked at me; clearly that wasn't the response he'd been expecting.

"Um, thanks, McKenna," said Naomi, shooting me a perplexed look.

I just shrugged. Nobody spoke; everyone was waiting to see what would happen next. But nothing did, unless you counted Simon and Naomi pointedly ignoring each other as they dug their textbooks out of their bags.

When Mr. Morton walked in moments later, he was faced with what was probably the best-behaved calculus class in the history of his career.

Five minutes into class, a folded piece of paper landed on my desk. I shot a questioning look at Simon, and he nodded at the note, raising his eyebrows. I unfolded it.

Sorry, it said. Only said that cuz she was mean 2 u first. Are u guys besties again now? Pls clarify.

I was pretty unclear on that point, too. She was mad at me because she thought I'd ditched her over the weekend to go play a gig at a club in New York State, and I wasn't sure she was ready to forgive me.

So the next time Mr. Morton turned to write on the blackboard, I swiveled around and smiled at Naomi, just to see what would happen. Not only did she smile back, she also gestured toward Simon and rolled her eyes. Like we suddenly had an inside joke about him.

Yup, besties again, I wrote back.

His reply: Oops. My bad. Thot I was defending ur honor.

Stifling a laugh, I wrote: Aww. You wanna be my bestie too?

He read the note, then looked up and fluttered his eyelashes at me.

"Mr. Lee," came Mr. Morton's exasperated voice, making me jump. "This is calculus, not Flirting 101. Save it for the playground."

Simon dropped his jaw dramatically. "We're getting a playground?" he said. "Best senior year ever!"

Forty-five minutes is a long time to sit in a calculus classroom on the best of days. But when you're spending every second of that trying very hard not to turn into someone else, forty-five minutes feels like forever. Especially when you start at seven thirty in the morning, and especially when your abs are still sore from the day before.

By eight o'clock, I couldn't think about anything but the pain. It was like when you need to pee so badly that you're one hundred percent sure you're literally going to explode. Except worse. And magical. And unless I could relax, just for five seconds—just for *one-fifth* of a second—I was going to die, right there in the calculus classroom.

I squeezed my fist around my pencil, like that might help somehow. It didn't. I tried taking long, deep breaths, like my mom did when she wanted to calm down. That didn't help either.

Then I saw something out of the corner of my eye.

Simon. Staring at me with wide, frightened eyes.

"What?" I mouthed, as apprehension curled through me.

He looked like he was about to say something, but Mr. Morton got there first: "Mr. Lee, Miss McKenna, unless you're discussing a matter of life and death, please finish your—"

"Actually, Mr. Morton," I interrupted, "I feel kind of sick.

I had this stomach thing yesterday, and I'm still a little—I mean, can I go to the nurse?"

He narrowed his eyes, like he was trying to decide whether or not I was lying. Then he shrugged and wrote me a pass. I grabbed it and my books, then dashed out of the classroom. But not before Simon said, "Someone should go with her and make sure she's okay."

Crap, I thought, and picked up my pace. But he caught up with me anyway, a few yards down the hall.

"Nurse's office is the other way," he said.

"Bathroom," I said, pointing toward the end of the hall. It was so close. It was *right there.* All I had to do was lock myself in a stall for a few minutes . . .

"Dude, you need to throw up?" asked Simon, keeping pace with me. "Should I get a teacher?"

"No, don't get anyone. I'm fine."

I tried to move past him, but he moved with me, blocking my way. "If you're fine, then tell me what I saw back there."

Clenching my stomach as hard as I could, I said, "What *did* you see?"

"You . . . changed. I dunno. Like you were you, then you were someone else, then you were you again in, like, a split second."

In other words, I'd flickered. Right in the middle of the classroom. And I hadn't even noticed. Crap, crap, infinite crap.

"Really?" I said, raising my eyebrows and infusing my tone with disbelief. "That sounds a little . . ."

"Crazy," he said, shaking his head. "I know. Never mind. I'm probably just seeing things. I swear, ever since what happened in the auditorium, I've been . . . never mind."

"Yeah, tell me about it," I said. "But seriously, I have to—"

"If you ever wanna talk about it," he said, sounding desperate. "You know, all the wishes and whatever. I'm here, okay? I mean, I wouldn't mind having someone to talk to either, is the thing, being that I got stabbed and stuff, and I figured, since you were there . . . you know."

Of course. Simon had almost been killed that day; it was my third wish that had saved him. I wasn't the only one whose life had changed. But what was I supposed to do about that now?

"Plus I have something of yours," he continued quickly. "I found it, and you should come over so I can give it back, and—"

"Simon." I looked him squarely in the eyes, trying to ignore how guilty I was starting to feel. "I'm very sorry about what happened to you. Xavier actually stabbed me, too, one time, and we'll definitely have to compare stories. But not now, because I really, *really* need to go to the bathroom, and you have to get out of my way."

He stepped to the side, looking hurt. I tried not to care.

Once I'd finally locked myself inside a stall, I let the muscles in my abdomen relax. In less than a second, my magic flooded through me and over me, and my skin changed and my hair changed and my height changed and my clothes changed and it felt so damn good I could have died happy right there.

I leaned my forehead against the cool metal of the stall, bracing myself with my hands, not even caring what kind of invisible unsanitariness I might be touching.

This was the worst plan ever. Oliver was right; I had no business coming back to school while my magic was still so unwieldy. If I was going to make this work—and I damn well *was* going to make this work—I had to start taking things slower.

New plan of attack, then: I'd go home. I'd catch up on my homework. And in between math problems and reading novels and writing paragraph-long essays in French, I would sit in front of my mirror and time myself. I'd see exactly how long I could go without flickering.

And today was Friday, which meant I had the entire weekend to practice. Maybe by Monday, I'd be ready to tackle school again for real.

But that still left one very important problem.

We had a rehearsal tonight.

Chapter SIX

Jackson High's official policy was that you couldn't participate in any after-school activities on school grounds if you'd been absent from school that day—but Miss Delisio's drama club policy, which always trumped the school's, was that if you missed more than two rehearsals in a row, you were out of the play. And I'd already missed both Wednesday and Thursday nights.

Sure, I was one of Miss Delisio's favorites—plus I had a lead, so I'd be really hard to replace only three weeks before opening night—but I wasn't going to risk losing my role unless I absolutely had to. Besides, we weren't scheduled to work through any of my big scenes that night, so I'd probably be okay.

Probably.

A full afternoon of trying not to flicker, with varying degrees of success, had yielded a very useful piece of information: The more I ate, the longer I was able to be my real self. Especially if what I ate included a lot of sugar and caffeine.

Which was why I showed up at the theater armed with an enormous roast beef sandwich, a thick piece of leftover apple crumble, and a giant thermos full of sugared-up coffee.

I also showed up half an hour early.

Sliding into an aisle seat in the first row, I dropped my bag on the floor and pulled out my sandwich. The sound of crinkling paper practically echoed in the cavernous space as I unwrapped it, but I didn't mind. It made the theater feel slightly less ominous.

I hadn't expected it to feel ominous.

The last time I was in this room, I'd made a wish, saved Oliver's life, and turned my own life upside down. There was the pit—the place where Xavier had stabbed Oliver, and later Simon, with a switchblade. There was the stage itself—the place where Oliver had collapsed, bleeding, in my arms.

Distracted by the onslaught of too-recent memories, I wolfed my food down in no time at all . . . which left me empty-handed and all alone in the room where Oliver had almost died. Maybe coming early hadn't been such a good idea after all.

Taking a quick look around to make sure I was truly alone, I jumped into the Between, and then back into my bedroom. I knew my parents weren't home, so jumping straight to the kitchen probably would've been safe, but I wasn't about to risk it. Besides, I'd jumped into my room once before. Doing it a second time felt like starting a routine, and routines were good. Routines were *me*.

I went downstairs and rooted around in the fridge, methodically pulling out tangerines and cold cuts and cheese and leftover potato salad, tucking them all into a plastic grocery bag until I was sure I had enough food to keep myself safe. I took a deep breath, getting myself ready to jump again.

Then I looked at the clock above the stove. Rehearsal was going to start in less than ten minutes. Which meant the auditorium would be crowded with people by now, and I couldn't exactly materialize in front of them.

Giving myself a mental pat on the back for thinking ahead, I altered the plan. I'd jump into one of the dressing rooms instead. Nobody used the dressing rooms until we started rehearsing in costume, and that wouldn't happen for another week, so today they would be empty.

Or so I thought.

A soft gasp came from behind me as I landed, and I whirled around. In the middle of the room, halfway between me and the door, were two people, arms around each other in such a way that it wasn't hard to guess what they'd been doing. One of them was looking right at me, and his face was a mask of disbelief.

It took me a minute to find my voice. "Hey, Simon. Um. Wasn't expecting to see you here. . . ."

The second person disentangled herself from his arms and turned to face me. *Even better,* I thought, as I saw who it was.

"Margo?" said Vicky Willoughbee.

Vicky, a mousy little sophomore at my school, had been Oliver's master before me. She'd made a wish that forced people to think she was the greatest thing since cheeseburgers. I was one of the few people the wish hadn't affected. It had even snared Miss Delisio, the director of *Sweeney Todd,* which was why Vicky had been cast as Mrs. Lovett: the part that should have been mine.

But I'd made my peace with that, more or less, after she'd confessed that she knew she didn't deserve the part. I'd even promised to give her acting lessons at some point.

Vicky's eyes darted from me to the door, then back again. There was no way I could have gotten in without her seeing me, and we both knew it. I saw recognition begin to dawn on her face, and I racked my brain for any excuse that could explain what had just happened. I'd been hiding in the closet. I'd climbed in through a window. I'd—

"You're one of them," said Simon, before I could organize my thoughts. "You're one of them. Like Shen. You're—no, stay away from me!"

I realized I'd started to move toward him, and abruptly froze, stunned. Setting down the bulging bag of food, I held my hands up. "It's just me, Simon. I'm not gonna do anything to you."

"But you're . . ."

"A genie," Vicky supplied softly, looking at me with nothing more than guarded curiosity. Her experience with genies had been far gentler than Simon's.

"Wait, how do you know about genies?" asked Simon, eyeing Vicky suspiciously.

"From Oliver," she said, waving an impatient hand at him before turning back to me. "Are you really . . . ?"

"She just appeared out of nowhere," said Simon. It sounded like an accusation. "Have you always been one of them? Is that why you and Parish hooked up? Why didn't you tell me?"

"There wasn't anything to tell," I said sharply.

I was trapped. They knew. I wasn't me anymore, and they *knew.*

Then again, if anyone had to be around to witness my second screw-up of the day, at least it was these two——the only two people in school, besides Ryan, who already knew that genies existed.

Forcing my voice into a calmer version of itself, I continued: "It's kind of a recent development. Remember how I said there was a price for making a fourth wish?"

Simon looked even more confused. Then it seemed to click. "No effing way," he said.

"Yes effing way," I replied.

"Huh?" said Vicky.

Simon turned a lantern-bright grin on her. "Margo killed

the bad guy, and she had to use a fourth wish to do it, and it turned her into a *genie*. Right?" he added, looking at me for confirmation.

"You killed someone?" asked Vicky, clearly horrified.

I started to say that it was a wish, which wasn't exactly the same thing, but Simon spoke first. "The bad guy," he clarified. "She killed the bad guy. After he stabbed me."

"Wait, *what?*"

"I'll tell you later, Vicks," said Simon. "Dude, Margo, what kind of magic can you do? You gotta show me."

But before I could answer, Naomi's voice rang out from the auditorium: "All actors, please report to the theater! Rehearsal will begin in exactly one minute!"

Relief flooded me, and I shook my head. "Not now. But please, promise me you guys won't tell anyone."

"Of course not," said Vicky, her eyes wide.

"Duh," said Simon. "Hey, you should come to my place after rehearsal's over."

I squinted at him. "I have stuff to do tonight."

"Sometime this weekend, then. Come on, you totally have to. Besides, I have that thing I've been wanting to give you."

"What is it?"

He shook his head, dark eyes shining. "I can't believe you haven't figured it out. Just come over. Just for a little while. I won't try anything funny, I promise."

Vicky rolled her eyes, which made me pause. In all the fuss

over my interruption, I'd somehow managed to forget what it was that I'd interrupted.

"You guys," I said slowly, pointing first at her, then at him. "You're, uh . . . you were . . . just now?"

"Kissing," said Simon, grinning like a loon as Vicky blushed. "Lip-on-lip action. Hookin' uuuuup."

"Shut up," said Vicky, who looked awfully pleased.

"Right," I said, edging past them toward the door. "Lip-on-lip action. I, yeah, definitely had no idea you guys were . . ."

"Wait," said Simon. "You forgot your . . . what is that, dinner for six?"

He gestured toward my overflowing grocery bag. A banana and a half-empty jar of Nutella sat temptingly on top.

"Dinner for *me*," I said, darting over to snatch it up.

Suspicion had returned to his eyes. "That's a lot of—"

"Genies eat a lot," I said curtly. I had no idea if that was universally true, but since I was currently fifty percent of the world's genie population, I figured my personal experience had to count for something. "But we should get going. Don't want to be late!"

I fled, leaving a perplexed Vicky and a worried-looking Simon behind me.

I found a seat in the audience, took a long sip from my coffee thermos, and focused all my energy on not flickering.

The good thing about that night's rehearsal was that I had a lot of downtime. The bad thing was that most of the scenes we worked on were Judge Turpin's—which meant I spent a lot of time staring at Ryan Weiss.

The fact that Ryan had been cast as Turpin was annoying, since he was almost as terrible an actor as Vicky—but not exactly surprising, since he had a pretty good voice and could hit low notes that most boys my age couldn't dream of hitting. So at least listening to him sing wasn't a completely horrible experience.

Only now, from my spot in the front row, his low notes weren't the only thing I could hear. White noise underscored everything he sang, a constant current of wanting that I couldn't begin to decipher. Finally, when I couldn't take it anymore, I gathered my stuff and moved a few rows back. Then a few more, then a few more, until I finally reached a point about halfway back, where his thoughts were out of my range.

When Miss Delisio gave us a ten-minute break, Ryan hopped off the stage and made his way up the aisle toward me. I braced myself for the moment his thoughts intruded on my own again.

"Hey Margo, what're you staring at?" he said as he drew close to me. "You want a piece of this?"

"Uh," I said.

"No, she doesn't," said a voice. Naomi slid into the seat beside me, uncapping a Snapple bottle as she smiled mirthlessly at Ryan. "Nobody wants a piece of that."

Ryan grinned. "Know what I think, Naomi? I think *you* do."

"You wish," said Naomi. But the comeback lacked her usual venom, and she was close enough that I could see spots of color forming in her dark cheeks. She was blushing. Ryan was actually making her *blush*.

Ryan laughed to himself and continued up the aisle, the white noise of his thoughts growing fainter as he left us behind.

I studied Naomi, who was suddenly focusing very hard on drinking her iced tea. She looked like she was trying to compose herself; I took a moment to do the same, clenching my abs as tightly as I could. There would be no flickering. Not in front of Naomi.

After a moment, I said, "Is it just me, or is Ryan being even more of a dick than usual?"

"Not just you," she said. "So, where *did* you disappear to this week? And why'd you leave early today?"

"I was sick," I lied smoothly. "Stomach thing. You won the bet, remember?"

"Then why was Lee acting so weird about it?"

I shrugged. "How should I know? He's Simon. He always acts weird."

"Hm."

"So, the thing with you and Ryan—"

"There's no thing," she said.

"Really? Because I heard—"

"There's no thing, and I don't want to talk about it."

". . . Okay."

I took a sip of my coffee. Naomi sipped her iced tea.

Then she sighed, shifted in her seat so her whole body was facing me, and said, "Okay, McKenna. Are you ready to tell me why you ditched me last weekend, or not?"

Ah, yes. The gig she thought I'd played at that club. The one Xavier had played instead, posing as me. The one Simon had filmed and posted online. I wanted to talk about that night even less than Naomi wanted to talk about Ryan—but I had to tell her *something,* even if it wasn't the whole truth. I didn't want to go back to fighting with her.

"I didn't ditch you," I said. Her eyes narrowed, but I continued before she could argue: "Think about it. You drove me up to the South Star Bar in time for the gig, right?"

She nodded.

"We got there and the bouncer wouldn't let us in. Said the opening act was already inside. We went around back and heard this horrible singer through the window."

"Then we left," she supplied, sounding impatient. "I know. I was there for all that. Then you and Oliver Parish went off together and you didn't show up to sleep over until way later than I thought you would . . . and then, the next morning, there's a YouTube video of you. Playing a gig. At the South Star."

She spread her hands wide, as if to say, *That's all the incriminating evidence I need.*

"The video's a fake," I said. "Just ask George. He'll tell you I didn't come back and play a set. I promise."

I pointed at George the Music Ninja, our musical director, who was currently leaning against the stage and talking with Callie Zumsky, who was playing Johanna. George was the super-talented lead singer of this band called Apocalypse Later—and the one who'd invited me to open for them at the South Star last weekend.

And the one who, thanks to Xavier and his stupid pretending-to-be-me thing, now thought I was a talentless hack who should probably never be allowed to perform my own material on stage again.

"Or I could ask Lee. He's the one who took the vid in the first place." Cupping her hands around her mouth like a megaphone, she shouted, "Hey, Lee!"

Crap, crap, crap. I'd been betting on Naomi not wanting to bother George, but I hadn't thought about Simon. . . .

Simon came running, as most people do when their stage managers yell their names. "What's up, dude?" he said, kneeling backward in the seat in front of Naomi.

"Nothing," I began—but Naomi cut me off:

"You know that vid you took of McKenna at the South Star?"

Simon's brow furrowed, and he glanced at me. "Yeah, why?"

"McKenna here is saying it's a fake," explained Naomi.

"Whereas *you* told me you uploaded it yourself. So which is it, Lee? Spill."

Simon glanced at me again, and I widened my eyes in a caricature of fear. Fortunately for me, Simon was not only quick on his feet, but apparently really good at taking hints. "It was a fake," he said, heaving a dramatic sigh.

Naomi's eyes narrowed. "Explain."

"Someone hacked my account," said Simon. "Uploaded that thing while I was asleep, I guess."

That thing being a video of Xavier, wearing a pitch-perfect copy of my body as he screeched out pitch-very-imperfect excuses for songs. Songs that some people, Simon and Naomi included, now thought were mine.

Naomi didn't look convinced. "Then why'd you say it was your vid?"

Simon looked sheepish. "I dunno. I guess I didn't want everyone to know I got hacked."

"Oh, yeah, because that matters so much."

Drawing himself up, Simon gave her an affronted look. "It matters when you have as many YouTube followers as I do. I mean, have you seen how many views I get on my *Doctor Who* fanvids? People go nuts over those things."

I bit my lip to hide a smile. I owed Simon big-time for this one.

"Fine, fine, whatever," said Naomi, rolling her eyes. "Let

me just get this straight. You have no idea where that vid came from?"

"Nope," he said. "And I took it down as soon as I could."

"And you weren't at the Apocalypse Later gig?"

Simon glanced at me again. "Nope. I was planning on going, but had to do a family thing instead. Listen, d'you mind if I go? I really have to piss."

Naomi waved him away. It was all I could do not to applaud his performance as he left. I'd just been hoping he wouldn't give me away; instead, he'd gone above and beyond to cover for me.

"See?" I said, trying not to look as giddy as I felt.

But Naomi just gave me a wry smile. "See what? That Simon Lee's a horrible liar and there's something that *both* of you are keeping secret from me? Come on. Even if he's not the one who posted it, that's still you in the video."

Okay, so maybe Simon hadn't done as awesome a job as I'd thought.

"Naomi, I . . ."

"Whatever." She shook her head, took a swig of her drink, and stood up. "Forget I even asked."

"Naomi, listen," I said, grabbing her wrist. She looked down at me in surprise. I wasn't usually a wrist-grabbing sort of person, and she knew it. "Okay. Yes. Something happened that night. Everything got messed up, and it's . . . ugh."

She sat down again. "What happened?"

Both her face and her voice had gone soft around the edges. In the space of one simple question, she'd turned from Scary Stage Manager Naomi into Best Friend Naomi—the person I'd shared secrets with for as long as I could remember. Suddenly, it seemed so wrong that Simon and Vicky knew about me, while Naomi was still clueless.

I'm a genie, I thought, willing the words in my head to find their way up my throat and out of my mouth.

"Um," was what came out instead.

Naomi's lips quirked into a half smile. "'Um' was what happened?"

"It's kind of weird to . . ." I trailed off, watching as Simon joined George and Callie over by the stage. "You know this morning, when Simon said that thing about getting kidnapped by an evil genie?"

Naomi smirked. "That kid. He's such a nerd sometimes."

Sometimes was an understatement, but whatever. Taking a quick breath, I said, "He wasn't far off, is the thing."

Her gaze grew sharp. "I don't follow."

"Genies. That's what happened." My tongue was growing thick and clumsy with nerves, but I kept talking. "There was this shapeshifter who could make himself look like me—"

"A shapeshifter or a genie?" said Naomi impatiently. "Which one?"

"Both," I said quickly. "I mean, not like one-of-each both. Like one guy who was both. This guy was the one you saw in Simon's video. He made himself look like me, and he took my place, and he played those horrible songs to make everyone think I sucked."

Silence stretched between us, even amidst the echoing chatter that filled the auditorium. I fought the urge to avert my eyes, or to fidget, or to do anything else that might give her permission to write me off as a liar.

Finally, she licked her lips. "So," she said, "a shapeshifter genie stole your identity just so he could ruin your reputation as a singer?"

Her tone was measured. Neutral.

"It wasn't just about that," I said. "It was a warning. He could get to me anytime, any way he wanted, and that was how he proved it, and . . ."

Naomi was still listening, but her eyebrows slowly bunched together, and I started to realize that this story was far more complicated in hindsight than it had seemed while I was living it. Plus our break would be over any second.

"Listen," I said. "There's a lot more to this than . . . I mean, there's stuff that . . . it's this whole big thing. And I want to tell you. But maybe not here? Or, like, here but not *now*? Like if you want to stay and talk for a bit after rehearsal . . ."

I realized I was babbling, and made myself stop. Silence again. Naomi blinked. I waited.

I hated waiting.

"Okay," she said at last. "You—I mean—yeah. Okay, we'll talk after rehearsal."

And with that, she got up and headed back for the stage, leaving me alone with nerves skating over my skin.

"Ready?" I said.

Everyone else had left, and Naomi had somehow convinced Miss Delisio to leave us the keys to the building. She'd settled herself in the middle of the front row, and was watching me with eyebrows raised, waiting for me to fill in all the blanks left over from two hours before.

The second half of rehearsal had given me enough time to think about exactly how I wanted to tell her this, and also enough time for one very important thing to occur to me, which was this: Telling her wouldn't be enough. I was going to have to show her.

Which was why I was standing in the pit in front of her, more like a performer than a friend, rubbing my hands together like the friction would help me work up the nerve to do what I'd planned to do.

"Ready," said Naomi.

"This is going to be weird," I said.

"I can handle weird," she said. "What I can't handle is you not telling me what the hell's going on."

So I told her. By disappearing from the pit, and reappearing up on the stage.

"Ta-da," I said, waving down at her.

But Naomi didn't hear me. She was too busy letting loose with a string of curses as she clutched the arm rests of her seat.

I waited for her to calm down. To her credit, it didn't take long.

"What did you do?" she asked. "You were just down here. Now you're . . . not."

I crouched down and hopped off the edge of the stage, making my way across the pit toward Naomi, trying not to let on how fast my heart was racing.

"What I just did was magic," I said. It was easier to say, somehow, after having just done it. "Because . . . well, because I'm a genie, too. As of, like, the day before yesterday."

Her mouth worked, like she was trying to find the appropriate response and failing completely. It was oddly calming to watch—mostly because I was pretty sure it meant she believed me.

"Want to hear the rest?" I asked, sitting gingerly in the empty seat beside her.

She squirmed in her seat, and for a second I was sure she was shying away from me. But then she nodded firmly and said, "Yes."

So I started from the beginning.

The only thing I left out was Vicky's wish, since that was Vicky's story to tell, not mine. But other than that, I told her everything, beginning with the day I'd found Oliver's ring in the girls' bathroom and accidentally bound him to me, and ending with the fourth wish I'd made in this very room just two days ago.

She stopped me now and then to ask questions. Once I'd answered them all, she sat quietly, letting my story sink in as I fidgeted nervously beside her.

Then she said, her voice slow and deliberate, "You? Are an idiot."

"For making a fourth wish?" I said, smiling at her bluntness. That was just one of many reasons why I loved Naomi. "Yeah, no kidding. That was probably the stupidest thing I've ever done in my life. I barely thought it through, and—"

"Um, no," she said, giving me a withering look. "I meant you're an idiot because this has been, like, the main focus of your life for weeks now, and it apparently never occurred to you that maybe you should *tell me*."

"Oh, it definitely occurred to me," I said. "But I didn't think you'd . . . I dunno . . ."

"You didn't think I'd, what, believe you?" she said. "Geez, McKenna."

My face heated up. "Well, that, a little. But mostly I didn't want to give Oliver's secret away, you know?"

"Sounds like it's your secret just as much as his."

"Well, maybe now it is," I said. "Not before, though."

"Yeah," she said slowly, and pursed her lips at me. "So what's it like, anyway? I mean, you have to grant wishes now, right?"

I nodded.

"And you have a master? Like, someone who's in *charge* of you?"

I nodded again. "In charge of my magic, anyway."

She frowned, curling her lip ever so slightly. "Still. That doesn't seem right."

I shrugged. Right or not, that was how my magic worked.

"Who is it?" she asked.

Ryan, I thought . . . but I didn't say the name out loud. Something in the sharpness of her eyes, or the twist of her lips, said she still didn't know what to think of my bound-to-a-master situation. Or how much to judge me for it. If she found out that the very first wish I'd granted had made her fall for Ryan . . . well, I had a feeling that wouldn't exactly tip the scale in my favor.

Besides, I'd just dumped a whole lot of information on her. If I were her, finding out about that wish would send me right over the edge.

So I lied: "Someone you don't know. He's not from around here."

"Hm," she said. "Well, as long as he treats you nice, I guess."

Nice wasn't exactly the word I'd have chosen—but before I could decide whether or not to tell her so, her phone rang. She dug it out of her bag, making a face when she saw who it was, but answered it anyway.

"Hey, can I call you back in a few?" she said, and then paused. Smiled and rolled her eyes. "No, I promise I will. Fifteen minutes." Another pause. "Okay, ten. Just don't jump off a bridge before then, okay?"

She clicked her phone off, and I said, "The boyfriend?"

"The sister," she replied, gathering her stuff and standing up. "So I actually do have to go. But make no mistake, McKenna—this conversation is far from over."

Chapter SEVEN

Telling Naomi the truth had been no easy task, but the worst was behind me. And if that wasn't enough of a relief, I was almost home—which meant that in a few more minutes, I could let my magic relax until morning. Well, if I wanted to. I still planned on being my real self for as long as I could.

My parents were home, but they were too busy cuddling in front of the TV to pay me much attention. I stopped in for a quick "Hi, school was fine, rehearsal was great, no I'm not hungry," and then went up to my room.

Oliver wasn't there yet, so I booted up my laptop, put some music on, and flopped down on my bed, just to rest my eyes for a second.

"Is this a bad time?" came Oliver's voice, jerking me awake. When had I fallen asleep?

A quick glance at my computer clock told me that half an hour had passed. Turning down the volume on Jeff Buckley's voice, I said, "Ever hear of knocking?"

It was Amber's voice that came out. I looked down at myself. Sure enough, I'd shifted back—probably when I'd fallen asleep. And I knew I hadn't locked my door. Awesome.

"I've heard of it," he said. "I've also heard it makes noise, and I didn't know if your parents were home."

"They're right downstairs, and you're making noise just by talking. Seriously, get a cell phone or something, so you can at least call first and—" I made myself stop. I was rambling, and I sounded a lot angrier than I meant to. Sure, I was jumpy and uneasy and kind of annoyed with the world—but that was my own fault, not Oliver's. "But whatever," I said, shifting quickly back into my real self. "Come here."

He obliged, crossing the room and giving me a kiss. "Sorry I woke you up," he said. "Rough day at school?"

"Kinda," I said, fiddling with the hem of my shirt. "For the half an hour I was there, anyway."

"Only half an hour? Why?"

"It was nothing," I said. My cheeks went pink. "I just . . . I sort of . . . flickeredinmathclassandSimonsawmeand . . . um." Oliver's eyes went wide. "It's fine, though! Simon knows, but he won't say anything. And Naomi and Vicky, too."

"All three of them?" he said faintly. "Three individual people saw you flicker?"

"No, no," I said. "Only Simon. And Vicky found out by accident. Naomi knows because I told her."

This didn't seem to make Oliver feel any better.

"She's my best friend," I said firmly. "I tell her everything. And it's not like she's gonna go around blabbing."

"If you say so," he said uneasily.

"But on a different note," I said, "can we please take a moment to acknowledge that I made it through three whole hours of rehearsal without flickering once?"

Oliver grinned. "Did you really? How?"

"Strong coffee, eight billion pounds of food, and a will of steel." I raised my arms, like Evita addressing her public. "I am a rock star."

Oliver lifted me up into a bone-crushing hug; I laughed as I hugged him back, pressing my face into his hoodie and hoping it would muffle the sound enough that my parents wouldn't hear.

"You are a rock star," he said, when he finally put me down. "Did you know it took me weeks to figure out how to shift back into myself? And months before I could hold it for any length of time. Meanwhile, here you are, going to rehearsal like it's any other day, with nobody the wiser. You're . . ." He trailed off, shaking his head.

I grinned. "Exceptionally talented?"

"I was going to say exceptionally stubborn."

"Not untrue," I said. "But hey, speaking of rehearsal, guess who's a complete douche-canoe?"

Oliver pursed his lips. "Not me, I hope."

"Obviously you," I said, punching him lightly on the arm.

He tried to look hurt, failed, and opted for rolling his eyes instead. "Or, more believably, Ryan Weiss."

"What'd he do?" asked Oliver.

"Well, listen to this," I said, plopping down onto my bed. "Simon knew about him and Naomi sleeping together. And I'm two hundred percent sure Naomi wouldn't have told Simon something like that."

"So Ryan's telling people," he said wearily, sitting down next to me. "Not cool."

"No kidding, right?" I said. "Naomi was *pissed*. I mean, not that I blame her. And she started blushing at rehearsal when he talked to her. Like, seriously blushing. Naomi doesn't blush for *anyone*. It's just so . . . icky."

He shot me a look. "What did she say when you told her about the wish?"

"Um, nothing. I didn't tell her. But hey, there was something else, too. It's been bugging me since yesterday, but I just put my finger on it like an hour ago. So, okay, the first night I talked to Ryan, his reaction was pretty much what you'd expect. Like, 'No way, magic is real?' and all that. But when I saw him again yesterday, he was talking about the rules of having a genie like they were old news. He even called himself my master, and I'm pretty sure I never said that word to him."

Oliver shrugged. "It's not much of a stretch. The 'master' thing, I mean. It's sort of common sense."

"Sure," I said, "but what about the rest? Like this. He asked if he could have a do-over on his wish, and I said no, and he didn't even get mad. He was just like, 'Oh, the cave guys said it doesn't work that way, but whatever, I tried.'"

Oliver's eyes narrowed. "The cave guys. He said that?"

"Yeah. Why, does that mean something?"

"Ali Baba's Cave," he said with a sigh. When I responded with nothing more than a blank look, he stood up and began to pace. "It's a website. Sort of a haven for nerds with a thing for Middle Eastern mythology. Religious arguments, role-playing games, fan fiction—you name it, it's there."

"Middle Eastern mythology," I said. "Which means *Arabian Nights*–type stuff."

"Which means genie stories," finished Oliver. "I've had quite a large handful of masters who've found their way to that site, so a lot of people on the message boards actually know what they're talking about. Here, let me just show you," he said, darting over to my open laptop.

Within seconds, he'd pulled up a gaudily designed website full of animated shooting stars, curvy female silhouettes not unlike Jeannie's, and oil lamps with thick smoke coming out.

"Let me just log in," he said, clicking on the top of the screen. "You can't get to the boards without an account."

I watched over his shoulder as he typed the screen name CKelly0603, followed by a password.

"Who's C. Kelly?" I asked.

"Me," he said, turning around just long enough to flash me

a grin. "Ciarán Kelly. That was my full name, back in the day. And the numbers are my birthday. June third."

"June," I said. "That's, what, Gemini?"

"Yup. And just for the record, that whole thing about Geminis having multiple personalities?" He shimmered into Gwen, only to shift immediately back into Oliver. "Total myth."

I snickered.

"Here you go," he said as the word *Welcome* flashed briefly across the screen, then disappeared in a dramatic puff of smoke. "Ali Baba's Cave. If you go to the 'Life Is Magical' forum, that's where people talk about real magic. And I use the term *real* very loosely. You want the chair?"

I shook my head. He turned back around and scrolled down to the forum he'd indicated . . . only it wasn't called "Life Is Magical," but instead "Lyfe Is Magyckal." Okay, then.

It was exactly what Oliver had said it would be: threads upon threads containing discussions of magic. Some were about spellcasting, and others were about magical beings like witches and vampires and werewolves. Some—many, in fact—were about genies.

And one of those had been started by someone named TenaciousRW. Had to be Ryan. I pointed it out to Oliver, and he clicked. I leaned closer to read over his shoulder.

Subject: FOUND A GENIE!!

HEY, ABC HOMIEZ. SAY YOU FIND A GENIE AND SHE SAYS

YOU GET 3 WISHES. USED 1 ALREADY (DRUNK, LOL) BUT 2 LEFT. WHAT DO I DO?!?!

There were no replies. Oliver clicked on Ryan's screen name to see if he'd posted anywhere else, but all he found was a series of short posts in a forum called "The Cave Openeth."

"Role-playing game," said Oliver dismissively.

I shook my head. "I didn't know Ryan was a nerd. I mean, a nerd who can't spell, but apparently that isn't an issue here. Or it *is* an issue, and that's why nobody replied."

"Maybe someone contacted him directly," said Oliver. "You know, private message or something."

"Maybe," I said doubtfully. I couldn't imagine anyone reading Ryan's post and still wanting to have anything to do with him.

Oliver gave me a sympathetic smile. "You really don't like him, do you." I shot him a look. "Okay, yeah, understatement of the year. Just curious, though: Do you dislike him as much when you're Amber?"

The question confused me, but only for a moment. "Ahh," I said. "You mean, did I fiddle with Amber enough to make her not hate him?"

Oliver had told me once that he did that for every master he had—fixed himself so he automatically enjoyed the company of whoever his master was. He'd called it a precaution; I'd called it a magical bike helmet.

"I'll take that as a no," said Oliver. "But you can adjust her whenever you want. It's not too late."

"No," I said. "I don't want to change the way I think, just for his sake."

"Fair enough," said Oliver.

"You really do that with everyone you're bound to?" I asked. He nodded. "Did Xavier do it, too?"

Oliver's face went dark, and he looked away. At first I thought he wouldn't answer, but after a moment: "He was the one who showed me that trick in the first place."

The words sounded like they'd been pried out of him with a crowbar. So I swallowed any other questions I might have had, and settled for saying, "Huh."

"Hey!" he said, brightening again so quickly that it gave me momentary mental whiplash. "What do you say we take a break from all this Ryan stuff for a while?"

His smile had taken on a suggestive edge, and I felt a blush starting to creep across my face as my mind filled with images of Oliver's hands on my waist, Oliver's lips on my neck, Oliver's head on my pillow. . . .

"Got anything in mind?" I managed.

"Well, I was wondering if you were up for exercising your magic a little."

"Exercising?" I echoed, my shoulders slumping as images of fingertips and kissing gave way to images of treadmills and yoga pants.

"Yeah," he said. "I want to show you something cool."

"I like cool things," I said. "What is it?"

"First, a question. On a scale from one to ten, how much do you like concerts?"

"Eleven," I said with a laugh. "You've met me, right?"

"Thought so." He grinned and held out his hand. "Let's go."

I took his hand, and we jumped at the exact same time. A few seconds of agonizing airlessness later, we were back in the real world. And I was standing in a dark room, big and crowded and reeking of beer. All the people around me were clapping.

On the stage was a group of guys, adjusting keyboard stools, checking guitars, and grinning at one another. I didn't recognize them.

The applause started to die down, and a bearded guy stepped up to the center mic and said, "Thanks!"

As the room quieted, the first notes of a song floated through the venue. Keys first, high and clear, accompanied by a slow, velvety percussion beat. The bearded guy nodded along to the rhythm, adjusted the guitar slung across his back, and then began to sing.

The words were simple, and his voice was growly. Pure. Honest. He sang about bones and blood and bullets, all set to a strangely hopeful melody—and when he said something about holding someone's hand, Oliver reached out and held mine.

Then the percussion kicked into high gear, and the singer's voice opened up. All I could think was, *Thirty seconds ago, I was in my bedroom.*

I blinked back tears.

"Who are they?" I asked, leaning close so Oliver could hear me.

"No idea!" he said. "But I like them!"

"They're amazing," I agreed.

Oliver leaned down and said, "I figured we could just hop from venue to venue until we found something good. You wanna stay here?"

"Hell yes!" I said. "Where are we, anyway?"

"I forget the name," he said. "But it's somewhere in Austin."

"Holy . . . As in, like, Texas?"

"As in Texas," he said, and turned back toward the stage, his face shining, his hand still clutching mine.

I could go to Texas whenever I wanted to. I could go *any-where.*

"We could do this every night, you know," said Oliver.

"God, yes," I said.

"Every day, too, if you ran away with me," he added, with a waggle of his eyebrows. "We could go to Japan and Australia, find all the best places to see shows . . ."

But he trailed off as my face fell.

"Never mind," he said, brightening again. "But seriously, isn't this awesome?"

"It seriously is," I said.

The applause died down, and another song began, even better than the last one. I leaned against Oliver and he slung an arm around me, and there we stood: two anonymous people in a crowd, thousands of miles from home, listening to an amazing band whose name we didn't even know.

Just listening.

Chapter EIGHT

"Diego," said Naomi, as she examined her reflection in the mirror, "is turning twenty next month."

"Oh yeah?" I said, from my Best Friend Perch on the store dressing room's tiny seat. "Is he doing anything cool?"

Diego was the guy she'd been seeing for a few months now—a college guy I'd never actually met because he was "busy" all the time.

"Just the usual frat-boy gathering. I haven't decided if I'm going. I just think it's funny that you always make fun of *me* for liking older guys."

Ah, so that was what she'd been getting at.

Naomi had spent the past hour trying to find the perfect jeans, all the while steering the conversation back and forth between the normal and the magical. Which was to say, between her life and mine. And every time she brought up my stuff—my magic—she accompanied it with a wary sort of side-eye, like she was ready to absorb a small measure of new information, but not too much, and not too fast.

That was the look she was giving me now.

"Well, I think what's funny is that you used to think Oliver was younger. And boring," I added, which made her grin. "Honestly, the age thing is way less of a big deal than I thought it'd be. He doesn't act old, you know? And it's not like he can go out and find anyone his own age."

"True," said Naomi, twisting herself around to inspect her backside in the mirror. "What do you think, McKenna? They look good in front, but do they make my butt look flat?"

I snorted. "Nothing could make your butt look flat."

"Good," she said, nodding as she continued her critical examination. "I'd have to get new sandals, though."

"Don't you already have like twenty-seven pairs?" I said.

I had exactly three.

"Oh, at least," she said. "But I don't have any orange ones. And this cut definitely requires orange sandals. I'm thinking low heel. Maybe a wedge."

I nodded. Naomi understood how to wear clothes like kittens understood how to be adorable. There was no point in questioning it. "Then we'll hit a shoe store next," I said.

"Ah, but which store? That's the question." She stripped off the new jeans, which I dutifully clipped back onto the hanger, and slipped into the skirt she'd worn here. "The other question is, what do you guys do together? Like, when you're not being all magical at each other? Or is it all magic all the time?"

She side-eyed me again as she opened the dressing room door.

"Well," I said, "we went to a concert last night."

"Cool."

"In Texas."

She blinked. "Oh."

"And we're probably going to another one tonight." My fingertips tingled with anticipation. I didn't know where we'd end up this time; Oliver wanted it to be a surprise.

"So . . . that's just something you can do now, huh?" she asked, looking strangely suspicious. "Go wherever you want, whenever you want?"

"Almost whenever," I said. "I still have real-life stuff to plan around. School. Rehearsals. Shopping trips with my bestie. You know."

"Yeah," she said, still looking a little uneasy. But before I could figure out why, a loud chime came from Naomi's yellow sunflower purse. She took out her phone, pressed a button, and made a face. "It's Kris. Wedding trouble again. It's the dress this time."

"Wedding?" I echoed blankly. Kris was Naomi's older sister, who, much like Naomi herself, always had a boyfriend. But this was the first I'd heard about a wedding.

For a second Naomi looked completely confused—and then she laughed. "I totally forgot to tell you, didn't I. Kristina got engaged on Tuesday."

Well, that explained it. Naomi and I hadn't been speaking on Tuesday.

"Who's she marrying?" I asked, trying to remember if I'd heard anything about Kris's latest relationship. "Wait . . . not the guy with the horrible mother?"

Naomi nodded. "Jared. He's the wussiest thing I've ever met. Twenty-five years old and never learned to stand up to his own mother. Now, apparently, she wants Kris to wear her tacky old wedding dress. Kris said hell no, because *obviously*, but Jared's saying maybe she should just do it."

She held out the phone so I could see the text for myself.

"Gross," I said, absolutely meaning it.

"I know, right? Ugh, I can't even think about it too much. It just makes me want to——" She cut herself off, shaking her head and forcing her face into a smile. "Anyway. Shoe store! Let's go."

"Um, you should probably pay for those jeans first, yeah?" I said, grabbing her as she headed for the exit.

She looked down at the jeans she held, as if seeing them for the first time. "Oh. Right. Sorry, my brain is . . . ugh. Whenever she tells me something new about this guy . . ."

"Gotcha," I said, and steered her toward the registers. "Hey, tell you what—why don't I get those for you?"

"As in buy them for me?" she asked, side-eyeing me again. "Why?"

"Because your brain is ugh, and because I can. Watch." I

turned out the pockets of my old, faded jeans, and she raised her eyebrows, like she wasn't sure what she was supposed to be looking at. "Empty, right?"

She nodded warily.

I tucked my pockets back in. "Abracadabra. I have sixty dollars in my front left pocket." And then I reached into the pocket in question and pulled out three crisp twenties. "Oliver did that to buy us sodas last night. It was the coolest thing I'd ever . . ."

But I trailed off as I saw the look on her face. She did not look nearly as impressed as I'd hoped she would.

"Where'd that come from?" she asked.

"Thin air," I said. "The ether. The void. I have no idea."

This time she turned her side-eye on the money in my hand. "You can't just create stuff out of nothing."

I grinned. "Maybe *you* can't."

"I'm serious. That's just physics."

"I guess magic trumps physics, huh?" I said.

A woman gave me a weird look as she walked by, but didn't say anything. I wondered what she thought we were talking about.

"Seems like cheating to me," said Naomi uncertainly—and then straightened, lifting her chin a little. "Well, either way, I can't have you enabling my spending habits, McKenna. I'm buying this myself."

And she marched off toward the registers, leaving me

more than a little confused. Using magic wasn't the same as cheating.

, Was it?

That weekend, Oliver and I went to San Francisco for a singer-songwriter festival, to London for a pop concert, and to a city in Indonesia, where we saw some sort of traditional dance performance whose name I couldn't remember.

And when we weren't traveling, I did homework, like a normal human person. I wrote an essay and studied for a chemistry test. I listened to Naomi vent about Kris's dress and the fiancé and the mother. I even watched a couple movies with my parents.

It was exhausting—in the best possible way. It was also proof that I could totally do this. I was one hundred percent capable of living a double life.

Well, as long as I had enough caffeine to keep from flickering.

When I arrived at school on Monday, armed with a giant thermos of coffee and a bag of chocolate-covered espresso beans in my pocket, Simon was waiting. "You," he said, pointing his cell phone at me, "are a hard woman to connect with."

"I am?" I said.

"Yes. I must've sent you half a million emails since Friday."

"Oh," I said. "I wasn't online this weekend."

He raised his eyes to the ceiling, shaking his head like I

was the most hopeless person he'd ever met. "Yeah, I keep forgetting you still live in the Stone Age."

"What did you email me about?"

"Um, duh? You're a you-know-what, and I want to know all about it?"

Ah, that. Giving all the details to Naomi was one thing, but Simon?

"And why'd you have me lie to Naomi about that video?" he asked. "It totally wasn't a fake."

"Yeah, it was," I said. I glanced quickly at the door, just to make sure we were alone . . . and then I told him. About Xavier posing as Vicky and demanding Oliver's ring, then stabbing me in the leg and breaking my finger. Then arriving at the South Star, only to find Xavier on stage, at my gig, pretending to be me.

By the time I was finished, Simon wore the darkest expression I'd ever seen on him. "That asshole. I'm glad he's dead."

I almost said "Me too." But I thought of the pained, broken look on Oliver's face, and said instead, "Look, Simon, I don't want to talk about that stuff anymore."

"Just one thing," he said. "Does that mean the 'sparkle sparkle' song wasn't really one of yours?"

I snorted. "No. Unlike the crap Xavier played, my songs are actually *good*."

"Those songs were good, too," said Simon. "I mean, I'm not saying that makes me like the guy any better. I'm just saying sometimes you have to separate the man from the artist."

"And I'm just saying, *I don't want to talk about it.*"

"Oh," said Simon. "Um. Cool. Yeah . . ." He trailed off, drumming his fingers on his desk.

"We can still talk about normal-people stuff," I said. "Just not . . . you-know-what stuff."

He blinked. "Right. Yeah. So hey, how about that Phillies game?"

"That's, um . . . football?"

Simon shook his head at the ceiling. "Girls. Honestly."

"What about girls?" came Naomi's voice from the doorway. Coffee cup in hand, she claimed her usual seat.

"Margo doesn't know what sport the Phillies play," said Simon, sounding awfully forlorn.

Naomi shot me a look. "Girl, we're going to have a serious talk later. But okay, Lee, did you see that game the other night?"

"Did I ever, dude."

"Third inning, when—"

"I know!" Simon interrupted, actually clapping his hands with glee.

"So awesome!" said Naomi.

"Totally epic," said Simon.

Naomi didn't actually care about sports any more than I did. She did, however, care about being able to participate in any conversation that happened in her general vicinity.

Just one of many reasons why she was popular and I was not.

"By the way, Lee," said Naomi, once the sports-centric hysteria had cooled off a little. "How's the old YouTube account? Any more hacking incidents?"

Simon smiled widely. "Nope. Everything's safe and sound."

That was when I remembered: Naomi knew that Simon knew my secret, but Simon didn't know that I'd told Naomi. I was about to say something, but then——

"Glad to hear it," said Naomi, shooting me a secretive grin. It was the exact opposite of a side-eye——and it was enough to shut me up. If Naomi got a kick out of keeping Simon in the dark, then that's what I would do.

Anything to keep her from giving me that distrustful look again. Or calling me a cheater.

I didn't flicker at school that day. Or on stage at rehearsal that night——which was good, since I ended up spending a *lot* of time on stage. We ran through "Not While I'm Around," my Act Two solo, no less than three times. I was Margo playing Tobias Ragg, singing to Vicky playing Mrs. Lovett, trying to focus on my lyrics and my character's motivation and my blocking, all while concentrating on not shifting into Amber.

By the time Miss Delisio finally moved on to the next scene on her list, I was pretty sure I deserved a Tony Award.

As Dan Quimby-Sato and Callie Zumsky took the stage for

their duet, "Kiss Me," I joined Naomi in the front row, where she was following along with the script.

"Nobody's forgotten their lines yet tonight," I said. "That's got to be a first."

"Don't jinx it," she replied under her breath, rapping her knuckles against the wooden arm of her seat. "Especially since we've got 'Pretty Women' coming up next. Ryan always screws up the lyrics to that one."

I snorted. She grinned and flipped to the next page.

"Hey, speaking of Ryan," I said. Naomi shot me a look, but I kept on going. "You still haven't told me what's going on with you two."

"Nothing's going on," she said shortly. "Just rumors. Ignore the rumors and you'll be fine."

It was more than rumors, and we both knew it. In the space of just a few days, Naomi and Ryan had become the subject of hallway whispers, bad one-liners, and even bathroom graffiti. Plus, I knew what had happened. Ryan had told me. And I'd seen them alone in that room together, right before I'd left the party.

I should never have left the party.

"But if Ryan really did something," I began.

"Then what?" she asked, cutting her eyes at me. "You'd use your super genie magic to travel back in time and undo it?"

"So he *did* do something," I said.

Her face grew pinched, and she heaved an exasperated

sigh. "No. Nothing happened, and there is nothing to tell, and if that ever changes, you'll be the first to know."

Up on the stage, Ryan and Simon's duet began. Naomi and I went quiet for a moment and listened to it. Simon was amazing. Ryan was . . . Ryan.

Leaning over, I said, "I can't time travel, you know."

Naomi just side-eyed me and snorted.

Chapter NINE

There were two Ryan-related facts for which I was end-lessly grateful.

The first: He hadn't called me again since the morning after the party, which made me think maybe I'd managed to intimidate him after all.

The second: I didn't have any classes with him, which meant that I only had to see him at rehearsal.

But he was at *every* rehearsal—filling my head with white noise, never taking his eyes off Naomi. He sat near her as often as he could, touched her arm or her shoulder whenever he talked to her, and grinned this secretive grin whenever she brushed him off and walked away. Which she always did.

As Ryan was quickly learning, even though the love wish had obviously worked, it didn't mean she had to publicly acknowledge its effects.

And then, on Friday, Ryan stopped paying attention to Naomi. No more flirting, no more inventing excuses to touch her, no more anything at all. At first I thought I was imagining it—until our mid-rehearsal break, when I spotted Ryan in a secluded corner of the hallway, talking to a junior ensemble girl named Alison.

They were standing a little too close for casual conversation, and if his body language hadn't betrayed his flirtatious intentions, the wave of wanting that I felt from him certainly did. It broke through the white noise and showed me a single clear, vivid desire. He wanted this girl to like him. To flirt back. And he was getting exactly what he wanted.

When break was over, Ryan led Alison back into the theater by the hand, all the way to the front row—and that was when Naomi spotted them from her stage manager's booth. Her eyes narrowed, and her lips flattened into a thin line.

She stared at them for only a few seconds before looking back at her script. But those few seconds had been enough. Ryan had seen her looking. He'd seen her get angry. And he suddenly looked very, very satisfied.

I was on the road, a block and a half away from my house, when Ryan's call came. It had been so long that it took me completely by surprise, tugging at me with a sudden force that made me jerk the wheel to the side. Somehow I managed to pull over and park before the magic took me: shifting me into Amber, dressing me in cutesy, wispy clothes, and depositing me in Ryan's room.

". . . any second now," Ryan was saying as I appeared. "Hey, there's our girl!"

He wasn't talking to me. He was talking to the person sitting in his desk chair.

The stranger was a man: dreadlocked hair pulled back in a ponytail, skin a shade or two darker than Naomi's, well-dressed in carefully ironed slacks and crisp button-down shirt like he'd just come home from a day at the office. But as he stood up from Ryan's chair and approached me with an eager smile on his face, I amended my first impression. *Boy*, not man. Probably not much older than me, actually.

Still, he looked incredibly out of place in Ryan's teenaged-boy bedroom.

"Um," I said. "Who are you?"

"Right, yeah," said Ryan, stepping closer, like he wanted to remind us both that he was in charge here. "Amber, this is James. He's going to be your next master, after I'm done with you. James, this is Amber, grade-A hottie and one hundred percent real live genie, just like I told you."

He was gesturing at me like he was Vanna White and I was a *Wheel of Fortune* vowel.

"My next master?" I asked. "What do you mean?"

James gave me a friendly smile. "Well, Ryan and I met online, shortly after he found you, and I expressed interest in meeting y—"

"I'm selling him your guitar pick," said Ryan.

I instinctively backed away. Ryan had said *selling* as easily as he might have said *playing video games*—and James was looking at me like he could see the way my insides worked.

"You . . . you can't do that," I said.

James frowned, clearly aware that something was going wrong, but Ryan just shrugged. "Why not?"

I stared at him. "Because I'm a person? Because you don't sell people?"

James's eyes went wide, and he muttered a curse under his breath. "Amber, I'm so sorry. I didn't realize. I just wanted the chance to meet you and see if—"

But Ryan cut him off once again: "Chill out, man. I'm selling your guitar pick, not *you*. Geez."

"She has a point," said James softly. "We should call it off."

Ryan crossed his arms, lifting his chin just enough that he could look down at James. "Too late. We said payment one for an introduction, payment two for the vessel thing. That's the deal."

James glanced fearfully at me, almost like he was worried I was judging him for having agreed to such a deal—which, obviously, I was. It took two people to make a sale, after all. Ryan wasn't the only one at fault here.

"You could just wish for money, you know," I said, trying my best to sound reasonable despite my growing panic.

"Waste of a wish," said Ryan. "Pay up, bro."

"One payment, then," James conceded, reaching into

his back pocket and retrieving his wallet. "But no more."

He started pulling out bills, and suddenly I felt sick.

I stepped into the Between and thought about my bedroom, and within seconds I was there. Then I remembered my car, which was still parked on the side of the road. Cursing under my breath, I jumped again, landing right next to the driver's-side door.

That was when I realized I hadn't shifted back into myself. And I was standing in a major street in a residential neighborhood, where anyone could have driven by or looked out their window and seen me materialize out of nowhere.

To top it off, apparently I'd forgotten to turn off my car before answering Ryan's call. The keys were still in the ignition, the door unlocked, and the engine humming. I slid in, then shifted back into myself before driving home as fast as I could, knowing in my gut that I only had minutes—maybe seconds—before Ryan called me back. Sure enough, as soon as I parked in the driveway and dashed up to my room, the call came. I followed it, letting my magic shift me back into Amber, steeling myself for the worst.

"Thanks a lot," said Ryan, glaring knives at me as I landed on his carpet. James was gone. "You know you just cost me a buttload of money, right?"

"I know it, and I'm glad," I shot back. "Selling me? Seriously? What is wrong with you?"

His face darkened. "I could ask you the same thing. Only

reason I'm selling your vessel to such a low bidder—not *you,* your *vessel*—is that the wish you granted isn't even working."

"The one about Naomi?" I asked, totally taken aback. "Of course it is."

"If it's working," he said, "then how come she treats me like dog crap every time she sees me?"

Biting back a smile, I replied, "Because the wish affected her emotions, not her actions. The emotions are there, but what she does about them is still up to her."

He gave me a long look. "That sucks."

I shrugged.

"Could I use my second wish to make her act different?"

"No!" I said—and then hissed as blinding pain shot through my skull.

"I mean yes, you could." The pain disappeared. "But it's really not a good idea. In fact, maybe you should think about using your second wish to undo what you've already done to her."

He gaped at me for a second, and then burst out laughing. "Why the hell would I do that?"

Very pointedly not hitting him, I said, "Because Naomi has no idea you did this to her. You did it without her consent. And if you really care about Naomi, maybe you should take her feelings into account."

He leaned back on his hands, a suggestive smile spreading across his face. A sense of wanting flared in his mind, with

Naomi right at its center. "Oh, believe me," he said. "I am."

"Not those feelings," I said. "I mean, did she even *like* you before the wish?"

He rolled his eyes. "No, she hated me. But who cares, as long as she likes me now?"

An honest answer. "Me," I said. "I care."

Ryan paused, but only for a moment. "Okay," he said, looking hard at me. "Fine. You care. But the way I understand this genie thing, I make the wishes, you make them come true. Not the other way around. So I don't have to do what you say, right?"

There was a short moment of silence before the headache started creeping back in. "Right," I said.

"Thought so," he said smugly. "Cool. Okay, you can go now."

The dismissal was so sudden, so blunt, that a moment passed before it registered. But as soon as it did, I got right out of there, jumping through the Between and back into my room.

Only once I was safely parked at my desk did I realize: He hadn't mentioned the sale of my vessel. Not after he'd started talking about Naomi, anyway. Did that mean I'd actually gotten through to him? That he'd actually changed his mind about selling me?

Unlikely. If I'd learned anything about Ryan over the past week, it was that he was only out for himself. He wanted

Naomi's affection, so he'd taken it—and if he wanted money for my vessel, he was going to take that, too.

And if Naomi kept snubbing Ryan, who knew what he would do to her? I had to warn her. I had to tell her about the wish.

But the thought of telling her the truth, of watching her trust in me evaporate when she realized that it was me who'd made her fall in love with Ryan?

No. I couldn't do it.

On the other hand, maybe I could tell her about Ryan without giving away my involvement in it. After all, Naomi didn't know that I was a shapeshifter. . . .

Every single day of Naomi's life started with a caffeine fix at Starbucks. Which meant that if I drove three minutes past the Oakvale town border and lurked inside the Starbucks on any given morning, I was bound to run into Naomi sooner or later.

So on Saturday, that was what I did. I wandered in around ten in the morning, ordered a venti latte, and claimed a corner table where I could spy on the door. Or rather, where Amber could spy on the door.

At eleven thirty, Naomi showed up and ordered her usual: a hazelnut cappuccino, medium. I smiled to myself as I set my book down. Despite the preferred Starbucks terminology, Naomi had always been morally opposed to ordering her drinks in anything other than small, medium, and large.

She paid, then waved to one of the baristas before she moved over to the tall counter to wait for her drink. That was when I approached her. "Excuse me," I said, with the biggest, most genuine smile I could muster. "You're Naomi Sloane, right?"

She turned to look at me, and her brow furrowed. I could practically see *Oh crap, do I know this person?* running through her head as she took in Amber's delicate features, her blond hair, and her super-feminine clothes.

"That's me," said Naomi with a tentative smile. "Sorry, I'm horrible at faces. Have we . . . ?"

I laughed, a high and light little Amber-laugh. "We met at a party last week. But you know parties: five zillion people and you can never remember who's who, right? I'm Amber. I'm friends with Ryan."

"Oh, sure, I remember you," she said, though there was still uncertainty lurking beneath her easy tone.

"And I definitely remember *you,*" I said, lowering my voice conspiratorially. "I mean, Ryan's been talking about you like nonstop."

"He has?" he said, her eyes narrowing. "What's he been saying?"

She was suspicious of him, despite the wish's effects. This was good. It might make her more inclined to believe what I was about to tell her. Now I just needed to figure out how to tell it, preferably without sounding insane.

"Oh, you know," I said, shrugging like it was no big deal.

"Just that he's really into you, and you're so pretty and totally the perfect girl. That kind of stuff. Also . . . " I paused, mostly for effect. " . . . that you're really awesome in bed."

"Shh!" she hissed, casting a quick look at the baristas behind the counter. None of them seemed to have heard me.

"Sorry," I said, feigning innocence. "Was that supposed to be a secret?"

A good-looking barista boy delivered Naomi's drink—then, after a quick glance around to make sure nobody important was watching, he leaned over the counter and kissed her. Slightly taken aback, I craned my head around just enough to see his name tag. *Diego.* Naomi's boyfriend. She'd never told me that he worked at Starbucks.

"I'm off at six thirty," said Diego. There was the slightest hint of an accent in his voice. "Meet me then?"

"You bet," she said, somehow managing to make the two words sound incredibly suggestive. She grinned at him until he turned away. Then, swiping her drink off the counter, she grabbed me by the elbow and steered me outside.

"Who the hell are you?" she demanded, eyes fierce as she rounded on me. "You can't just come up to me out of nowhere and expect me to chat with you about my private business. Got that?"

"I'm sorry," I said, widening my eyes and hunching my shoulders like a kicked puppy. "I didn't know that was your boyfriend in there."

"That is *so* not the point," said Naomi. "I don't even know you. You have no right to——"

"I'm sorry, I'm really sorry, I swear!" I held my hands up in surrender.

Naomi sighed and shook her head. "Whatever. No harm done, I guess." She paused, looking back through the window at the counter and the baristas and Diego. "Listen, who else has Ryan been talking to? I know he said something to his stupid bro friends at school, but you don't even go to Jackson with us, right?"

I laughed. "Hell no. I'm in college." I felt my magic make it true. "I have no idea who else he told, but if I know my Ryan, probably everyone and their mom."

She blew out a frustrated sigh. "Great. Just freaking great."

"I know, right?" I said, rolling my eyes with a boys-will-be-boys sort of laugh. "That happened to me once, too. I lost my V-card to this junior. Hot guy, totally fun, great in bed. But then he went around telling people about it—and I mean in detail, too—and that was the end."

My magic made that story true, too.

"Ouch," she said, her face softening in sympathy. "Seriously not cool."

"Seriously," I said. "It was the kind of thing that, you know, made me wonder why I slept with him in the first place. Kinda like you're probably wondering that about Ryan, right?"

"No, I'm not!" she said, throwing her hands up in exasperation. "That's the whole problem. I *didn't* sleep with him! He's spreading all these rumors about me when nothing even happened!"

"Wait. Didn't you sleep over after the party?"

"Yeah, on his *couch*," she said. "I stayed out past curfew, and I didn't want my parents catching me sneaking back in. They caught me twice last month. One more time, and I'm grounded."

This changed everything. On the one hand, it proved that Naomi could absolutely handle herself, wish or no wish. But on the other, it made me hate Ryan even more, and I hadn't even thought that was possible.

"Don't get me wrong," she said, crossing her arms tightly. "I was definitely tempted, and there was definitely some . . . well, some flirting. But I've got a boyfriend, and I wouldn't cheat on him. He knows that, too, but if he finds out Ryan's been spreading that around . . ."

"Why not tell people that Ryan lied?" I asked.

"Please," she said with a bitter little laugh. "I know how rumors work. The more you whine that someone's lying about you, the more people believe the lie is true. Especially if you're a girl. It's the whole 'lady doth protest too much' thing, you know? Better to just let it fizzle out on its own."

"I guess so," I said uncertainly. I'd never really grasped the intricacies of the high school rumor mill. Naomi had always been better than I was at that stuff.

"Plus, I know this sounds incredibly dumb, but . . . I don't want to start a fight with him, because I don't want him to stop liking me." She paused. "Oh my god, I can't believe I just said that out loud. I'm the worst feminist ever."

"No, you're not," I said, but it felt forced. Naomi had never expressed that kind of self-doubt to me, even before our fight.

She grinned, reaching out to give my arm a quick squeeze. "Whatever, I totally am. But listen, I gotta run, okay? It was . . . weirdly cool to meet you."

"You too," I said.

Naomi waved good-bye and headed down the sidewalk, and I watched her go. She'd given me several opportunities to segue into Ryan's wish. I could have said, *Hey, Naomi, speaking of the worst feminists ever, here's something about Ryan that you should know.* But I hadn't. Over and over, I hadn't.

I thought about running after her and telling her now. I even thought about shifting back into myself and confessing my part in the love wish. But mostly, I thought about what she'd just told Amber.

Why would she tell all that stuff to someone she thought was a complete stranger, when she wouldn't even tell her supposed best friend?

Chapter TEN

When my phone rang that afternoon, I wasted half a second imagining it was Naomi, finally ready to confide in me about Ryan and Diego and the girl who'd accosted her at Starbucks. But I didn't recognize the local number that my phone displayed.

I picked up. "Hello?"

"Margo!" said a jovial voice. "Margo, *ma belle. Guten Tag! Buon giorno!* How fares my lady on this fine afternoon? What up, yo?"

"Oliver," I laughed, "please never say 'yo' to me again."

"Sorry. But remember how you said I should get a cell phone? Well, I did, and it's amazing. I even got some apps. There's one where you match up these gem things, and I would have called you sooner except I *can't stop playing.*"

"Ha! Well, since you're obviously busy with your new toy, I won't ask if you want to come meet me—"

"No, it's okay," he said. "They're just games. I can quit whenever I want. You at home?"

"Yup. My room. Come on over."

The line went dead. Almost two hundred years old, and he was enthralled by cell phone games. I was still grinning at the phone in my hand when he appeared just inside my door.

He rubbed his hands together. "Ready to go somewhere awesome? I'm thinking pandas."

"Pandas?" I said. "The zoo?"

"Not the zoo," he said, laughing a little as he held his hand out. "China. We can go panda-hunting. I mean searching. Stalking? Whatever. Pandas!"

"Hmm," I said. "We'll have to do that eventually, for sure, but today is an ice-cream day, not a panda day. I'm having a serious Ben and Jerry's craving."

He nodded. "Vermont, then? I hear they do factory tours."

I grinned. "Actually, I was thinking about the one here in town. No factory tours, but they always give you an extra scoop."

Oliver actually looked sort of disappointed.

"I can't help it. I've been doing math homework, and math homework means going out for ice cream. Mom used to use it as a reward, back in elementary school," I explained, seeing his confused look. "It turned into one of those—you know, those things. With the dog and the food and the bell?"

"A Pavlovian thing?" said Oliver.

"Yeah, that." I glanced back at my notebook and sighed.

"Except I must've spent at least an hour on that last problem, and I still have five more to go. So, no reward just yet. I swear, calculus is the devil."

He sat beside me on the bed, narrowing his eyes thoughtfully. "Have you tried adjusting yourself?"

"Huh?"

A sly grin curled his lips upward. "Repeat after me: Margo is a math genius."

I wasn't sure where this was going, but I repeated anyway.

"Feel it?" he asked, clearly excited.

I shook my head. I hadn't felt anything.

Rolling his eyes, he said, "Okay, say it again, but this time you have to believe that what you're saying is true. Like what I do to make money appear, you know?"

Now I understood. I said it again . . . and this time, something in my mind snapped into place. It was clarity that hadn't been there before—a mental brightening of sorts—but it was so immediate that it felt almost physical.

Oliver must have seen it on my face, because he nudged my books toward me with a grin. "I'll buy you an ice-cream sundae when you're done."

I picked up my pencil. Looked at the next problem. Started writing without even consulting my calculator first.

Seconds later, I was done.

"See?" said Oliver, peering over my shoulder.

"Yeah," I said, completely awed as I looked over the neat,

logical, elegant numbers that had unfolded on the paper before me. I'd never imagined math could be like this. Never.

And then, all at once, I remembered the look on Naomi's face, right after I'd pulled that sixty dollars out of my pocket. *Seems like cheating to me,* she'd said.

"What's up?" said Oliver. "You just went all frowny."

"Nothing," I said quickly. "Just . . . Naomi. Something she said."

"About Ryan?"

Oliver was uncomfortable enough with the idea of Naomi knowing our secret; he didn't need to know that my using magic around her made her antsy.

So I went for a different truth instead. "Yeah. Actually, yeah. Did you know Ryan lied about sleeping with Naomi?"

Oliver's eyes went wide. "Really?"

"Really really. She told me that today. Well, not *me*. She told Amber, who's apparently a much more appealing confidante than I am. But whatever. The point is, he lied."

"Asshole," murmured Oliver.

"Seriously," I said. "And it kind of makes me wonder what else he's lied about. This is the guy who supposedly slept with twenty different girls by the end of sophomore year."

Oliver snorted. "If he goes around telling people that, then he's definitely lying."

"Right?" I said. "And now I'm thinking, did *any* of them actually sleep with him? Was it just a number he picked at random, or did he actually spread rumors about twenty individual girls?"

Oliver's face darkened.

"You could ask him," he said. "Even if he lies, you might hear him wanting you not to know the truth."

"No way." I gave an exaggerated shudder. "Even if I were halfway decent at mind reading, which I'm not, you really think I want to go up to Ryan Weiss and ask what his magic number is? No, I do not."

"Magic number?"

"You know," I said, feeling my face go hot as I made a vague gesture at the bed. "The number of people you've . . . you know."

"Ah. Okay, yeah, good point." He smiled in this adorably embarrassed kind of way, all the while letting his gaze dart around, like he was looking for a good excuse to change the subject. Finally, he zeroed in on my math books. "Calculus! Not the devil anymore, huh?"

I grinned at the non-segue. "Nope. Actually, what are the rules about that? The adjusting thing, I mean. How much could I do, if I wanted to?"

"What do you mean, how much?" he asked.

"Well, for instance, let me try this." Since I didn't want to experiment on my real self again, I let go of the magic in my abdomen, shifting into Amber before I spoke. "Amber is an astronaut with her own personal space shuttle parked in the backyard. There. Did it work?"

But the brain-thing didn't happen that time, so I knew the answer even before Oliver shook his head.

"Okay, so why not? What are the rules, exactly?"

"I'm not sure," he said. "The line seems pretty fuzzy, to be honest. I mean, once I tried making it so I knew Paul McCartney's phone number, but——"

"Paul McCartney?" I interrupted, raising an eyebrow. "Why?"

Oliver's cheeks went pink. "Because."

Realization dawned, and a grin suddenly threatened to tear my face in two. "Oh my god. You totally had a crush on a Beatle, didn't you."

He ducked his head a little. "I mean, me and everyone else in the world. It was the sixties, for heaven's sake."

"My *mom* had a crush on him. Still does, I think. Okay, wow, I'm not gonna think about that. Too weird."

He eyed me warily. "Weird because of the mom thing? Or weird because I'm a guy and so's he?"

"The first one." Then I thought about the second one and added, "Except now I'm thinking about you and Beatles-era Paul McCartney making out, and it's kind of extremely sexy."

Oliver wrinkled his nose. "Don't you objectify me."

"Sorry," I said, taking in the interesting rate at which his cheeks were growing redder. "It's just . . . you seriously like guys, huh?"

"Sometimes." He gave me a big, cheesy smile. "But I don't like anyone as much as I like you."

My chest suddenly felt light and airy, and I grinned like an idiot. "Good answer," I said.

"And feel free to objectify me any time you want," he said. "Point is, the phone number thing didn't work. But when I wanted to be able to eat seventy-three chicken nuggets in a row and not throw up? No problem."

"Seventy-three chicken nuggets? Ew."

He shrugged. "I was an undergrad. There was an eating contest. Sue me."

"Ew."

"Shut up."

"Make me."

So he tackled me. The force of his kiss nearly knocked me over, but his strong arms held me upright. It was only when I started to kiss him back that I realized exactly what was going on.

"Whoa, whoa, whoa," I said, using both hands to push him away.

"What? You okay?"

"It's just, I, ahhh . . ." Thoroughly flustered, I adjusted my shirt, looking everywhere but at him as I collected myself. "I'm Amber. You're kissing Amber. Not me."

He sat back, cocking his head a little. "Amber *is* you."

"But I'm—" I gestured down at myself. "I look different. Do you not find this weird? Because I find this weird."

He looked down at Amber's long, curvy body and wispy clothes and blond hair. Then met my eyes again. "I don't know. I guess I'm just used to it. I've been shifting from body to body practically my whole life, so it's sort of . . . They're just bodies, you know? And bodies are important, but not as important as people."

"Hmmm," I said.

He shrugged. "I mean, you kissed me when I was Ciarán. You didn't seem to think that was weird."

"I know, I know," I said, all the more frustrated because what he'd just said was absolutely true. "I just want to be *me* when I kiss you, that's all. Regular me, not shapeshifter me. The same me that fell in love with you. You know?"

The way his brow furrowed suggested that no, he didn't know. But he still nodded. "You can shift back, if you want."

By the time I did, though, the moment was already gone. I leaned over and kissed him again anyway, but then disentangled myself from him, sitting back on my heels. He just rolled onto his side, propped his head up on one hand, and watched me. His face was still slightly flushed, and I felt a pang of regret at having ruined the moment. All the weirdness here was my fault, not his, yet he seemed strangely okay with it.

"What's *your* magic number?" I asked.

He blinked, startled, and his expression turned decidedly cagey. "Me? Zero. Same as you."

Which didn't make sense in the slightest, until I spotted the loophole in my question. "No. You know what I mean. Not just since you became Oliver. I mean your whole life."

"Ah." He looked down, his finger tracing a pattern on my bedspread. "A lot."

Apprehension crept over me, but I forged straight through it. "How many's a lot? Twenty? A hundred? Five hundred?"

"One of those, probably," he said. And I could tell he wasn't joking. He actually didn't know.

"That many?" I said.

He smiled tentatively. "I've been doing this a long time, Margo. I've had a lot of masters."

"And, what, they *all* wanted to sleep with you?" Not that I had much room to talk. I'd started out as his master, and I wanted to sleep with him, too.

"Not all," he said. "Not even close. But a lot of them, sure. Some wanted me specifically, and some wanted someone else, or sex in general, and I was a warm body that happened to be nearby. Either way, it's my job to make my masters happy, so hey. Not that big a deal, really."

Sleeping with anyone who asked, not because he loved them, but because it was his job? How could something like that not be a big deal?

"Hey," he said, reaching out to touch my hand. "This was before I met you. You know that, right? We're together now. Things are different."

"Okay, let's say we exclude your masters, or anyone you slept with because of a wish. If we do that, then what's your number?"

He gave me a small smile. "Two."

I nodded slowly. "One was Maeve, right?" Maeve had been Oliver's fiancée back in Ireland, when he'd been human.

"Yeah," he said. "We met when we were both pretty young, and . . . well." There was a pause as he pulled himself into a sitting position again. He bit his lip, like he was steeling himself against something. The air in my bedroom seemed to grow sparse, and I wondered if he'd finally say the name out loud this time.

He did.

"Number two was Xavier." It came out like a challenge. Like he was expecting me to judge him for it.

"I thought so," I said.

He blinked. "Oh."

"You told me once that you used to love him," I said, shrugging like it was no big deal, even though it was, at the very least, a medium-sized deal. "It wasn't hard to guess that he loved you back."

"He did, yeah, in his own way." Oliver gave a little laugh, and all at once it was easier to breathe. "You're . . . you're okay with that?"

Okay with Oliver having a past? Sure. Okay with Oliver's past involving some seriously questionable taste in romantic relationships? Well . . .

I chose my response carefully, not wanting to make him

shut down again. "When you were with him, did you already know he was planning to wish you free?"

His eyes grew heavy, and he bowed his head, as if in mourning. "Not at first." A pause. "But eventually. Yeah, I did."

"And you still stayed with him?" I said.

"No," he said. "Well . . . sort of. It was way more complicated than that. I kept trying to break it off, but he'd show up out of nowhere, after nothing but radio silence for months or years or decades, and every time, I'd think this was when he was finally going to kill me. And then, when he *didn't,* I'd be so relieved, so damn *grateful,* that I just let myself fall right back into . . . whatever you want to call it, our *relationship,* and . . . and god, this is depressing! Sorry. Let's talk about puppies or something."

But I wasn't about to let this go so easily. Not when he'd spent more than a week avoiding the subject altogether, and he was finally talking.

"Why did you love him?" I asked, blunt as Naomi.

His face grew suspicious. "Why do you want to know?"

Because knowing about him will teach me about you. Because you loved him before, and you love me now, and I hope hope hope that's all he and I will ever have in common. Because . . .

"I'm curious," I said.

He pursed his lips, and his eyes went wistful, and I realized that, somewhere in there, I'd wanted him to say something like, *Well, you know, it wasn't* really *love, now that I think about it.*

But I knew that wasn't the kind of answer I was going to get.

I braced myself.

Finally, Oliver said, "Neither of us had a home. I think that was the crux of it—or at least the reason why it started. When you don't have a home or a family or a linear, human kind of life . . . well, there's something to be said for finding someone who understands what that feels like. Someone to share that with." He paused, and a dark look flitted across his face. "At least for a little while."

I knew he was thinking about everything that had gone wrong—but all I could think about was the fact that I didn't understand what a homeless, family-less life felt like. I wasn't someone Oliver could share his feeling of rootlessness with.

Reaching over to touch his hand, I said, "Why'd you fall in love with *me?*"

Oliver didn't even miss a beat. "Because you're you."

"Do you think," I said slowly, "that you'd want me to be your number three?"

Something in his expression went taut. "It's been a long time since number two."

"So?" I said.

"So . . . I'm just saying, it's been a while. And I wouldn't be able to read your mind. I can usually—" He cut himself off with a sharp shake of his head.

"So?" I said again.

"So . . ." He gave me a tentative smile. "So yeah. I want

that very much." There was a pause. "That'd make me your number one."

My first. Oliver was going to be my first. He actually looked almost as nervous as I felt, despite the overwhelming number of people he'd been with, and despite the messed-up nature of his number two.

"We'll have to have a plan," I said. "Figure out how to make it special. Later, of course. Right now, you still owe me a giant ice-cream sundae."

"True, I do," he said, pushing himself to his feet. "But while we're on the subject of making things special . . . how do you feel about scented candles and Marvin Gaye?"

It took me a full two seconds to realize he was joking. "Oh, definitely," I said as we headed for the door. "And you have to bring champagne, and I'll get some lacy red underwear. This is gonna be something straight out of a romance novel."

He opened my door for me; then swept his hand out in a grand after-you gesture. "You read romance novels?"

"I went through a phase in junior high. Totally Naomi's fault. Point is, I know how this works. Heaving bosom, throbbing manhood, all that."

"Throbbing? Really? You want me to throb?"

"You throb," I said, heading for the stairs. "I'll heave."

"That's possibly the least sexy phrase I've ever heard in my life."

"Whatever you say, Seventy-three Chicken Nuggets Guy."

Chapter ELEVEN

I drove us into the center of town, where the Ben & Jerry's sat nestled between the McDonald's and a seedy-looking Japanese restaurant. A little bell jingled over the door as we walked in.

"Popular place," said Oliver, glancing around at the small collection of tables, all of which were full.

"Yeah," I said as we joined the line for the counter. "If you see a table open up, pounce."

Just as we received our orders, Oliver spotted a couple leaving a corner table. So we headed over . . . but someone else was aiming for the same table. Someone I'd hoped never to see again.

He saw us, too.

"Did you guys want this one?" asked James, gesturing politely at the table. He was dressed in a T-shirt and faded jeans today, which made him look a little less intimidating than before.

"No," I said flatly. "Come on, Oliver. It's a nice day. Let's take a walk instead."

Oliver looked at me quizzically, but before he could say anything, James said, "Really, it's okay. I'm not here with anyone, and you two are obviously—I mean, I'll just take that stool by the window."

"Thanks," said Oliver, tilting his head slowly as he studied James. "Hey, don't I . . ."

"Oliver, let's *go*," I said, looping my arm through his, trying to tug him toward the door. He didn't move.

Instead, his eyes went wide, glinting green in the fluorescent light. "You're Jamie St. Pierre," he said breathlessly. "What's it been, thirteen years now?"

James looked from Oliver to me, then back again. Something like hope bloomed in his dark eyes. "That's me, yeah. Well, I go by James now, but . . . you're not . . . ? Are you . . . ?"

"Alicia," said Oliver, pointing to himself. "Remember?"

"Remember what?" I asked warily—but neither of them heard me. Mostly because of the sudden onslaught of "It's been so long!" and "You look so different!" and so on as they hugged and thumped each other on the back.

Okay. I was officially confused.

"You have to come sit with us," said Oliver, grinning his face off as they broke apart again. "Let me just find an extra chair."

He ran off, leaving me alone with James, who looked just

as excited as Oliver did. Sticking his hand out to me, he said, "Sorry, hi, I'm James. And you're . . . her girlfriend? *His* girl-friend?" he corrected himself, squinting slightly.

"His," I replied, pointedly not shaking his hand. "And yes. Girlfriend. Name's Margo."

"Well, it's nice to—"

"I also go by Amber," I added.

He sucked in a breath, and one hand flew up to clutch self-consciously at the back of his neck.

"Shoot," he said. "I didn't realize. I'm so sorry about—"

"Here we go," said Oliver, plunking a third chair at the table. Then he noticed the awkward way James was standing, or maybe the way I was glaring. Or maybe the silence. "Um. Everything okay?"

"He tried to buy me," I said flatly.

Oliver looked stunned. "What?"

"Wait, no," James said. "It wasn't like that."

"Then what was it like?" I shot back. A man at the next table twisted around to give me a dirty look, and I pressed my lips shut. It was awfully close quarters for a conversation like this.

"Outside," I ordered.

Oliver nodded. Without waiting for James's opinion, I marched outside and around to the tiny backyard that prac-tically nobody knew existed. I chose one of the two benches and sat down, watching Oliver and James hover uncertainly over me.

"So," I said, jamming my plastic spoon deep into my ice cream, "Ryan calls me a few days ago, and when I show up at his place, this guy's there, saying he'll pay Ryan to give him my vessel."

Oliver took the seat next to me, looking absolutely wounded as he glared up at James. "Is that true?"

"Just let me explain," said James.

"How about if you go away instead?" I said.

I figured Oliver would back me up and tell James to get lost. But instead, he bit his bottom lip, hesitating. Then he gestured to the empty bench facing us. "I'm listening."

James sat, placing his ice cream cup carefully on a wooden slat next to his knee. I gritted my teeth. I didn't want him getting comfortable.

"I was looking for you," he began, nodding at Oliver. "I've actually been looking for you for a couple of years now. Internet, newspapers, magazines, TV. Lots of false leads, lots of dead ends. You know how it goes."

"I do know." Oliver's voice had gone a particular kind of soft. I glanced again at James. He was poised and composed—even cute, albeit in a dreadlocked way that was far more Naomi's type than mine. But was he Oliver's type, too? Did Oliver even *have* a type?

"Get to the point," I said, and shoveled a heaping spoonful of ice cream into my mouth.

James cleared his throat. "Right. I found that kid, Ryan,

on this message board. Aladdin's Cave? Something like that."

"Ali Baba's Cave," said Oliver.

"That's it," said James. "I messaged him and we chatted for a bit. Long enough for me to figure out that he wasn't just some smartass messing around. He'd actually found a real genie. But as soon as I started making noises about meeting his genie, he got all defensive and weird. He actually threatened to block me. Money was the only way I could get him to listen."

"Okay," said Oliver slowly.

"So we made a deal. He'd let me meet his genie, and I'd pay him whatever he wanted. He said it'd be more if I wanted the vessel when he was done with his wishes—but I didn't want more wishes. I swear. I just wanted to find you."

This last was directed at Oliver with such hopefulness, such longing, that I couldn't help myself anymore.

"How well did you guys know each other, exactly?"

"Jamie was my master," Oliver said. "James, I mean."

I rolled my eyes. "I figured that much out myself, Captain Obvious. I mean were you guys *together*."

Oliver burst out laughing. James just shrank into himself, looking absolutely mortified.

"No, no, no," said Oliver, when he could finally speak again.

"I was *seven*," added James.

They exchanged a glance, and suddenly both of them were laughing—and that, finally, was the moment I felt okay about

James being there. Something loosened in my chest, and then I was laughing, too.

James grinned at me, using his thumb to gesture at Oliver. "This one here was basically the big sister I never had. And occasional babysitter. And other things."

"What kind of other things?" I said, completely charmed by the idea of Oliver as an older sibling.

"Other things like how I taught you how to play basketball," said Oliver.

James made a show of looking offended. "You did not. My brother taught me basketball."

Oliver rolled his eyes. "Your brother taught you the *rules* of basketball. I was the one who showed you how to get the actual ball in the actual basket." He grinned at me. "And I used to put on different faces to make him laugh."

"Nothing like this, though," said James, gesturing at Oliver's hoodie-clad, floppy-haired, sixteen-year-old body. "This is a new look for you. You're, like . . . really male. And really white."

"That I am, and that I am," said Oliver with an easy laugh. I thought he might explain that he was *usually* male, that he'd even been male when he was human—but he didn't seem to think it was necessary. "And you must be in college by now, right?"

James's smile faltered a little. "More or less. But back to the point," he said, focusing very suddenly and very intently on me. "Amber—Margo—I'm really sorry about the other day. I thought Ryan would've made it clear that I just wanted to meet you. I didn't think it would go down as bad as it did."

"It's okay," I said automatically—and then realized that I meant it. If all he'd wanted was to get back in touch with Oliver, then I could hardly fault him for that. Oliver was, after all, pretty great. "Let's just blame Ryan and call it a day, yeah?"

James raised an eyebrow. "Yeah. I did get the impression he isn't the nicest guy to have as a master."

"You could say that." Suddenly feeling self-conscious, I folded my arms over my chest. Here they were, with all this shared history, while I was just the new girlfriend with the bad master. "Hey, I could go, if you guys want. Let you catch up for a bit."

"You don't have to do that," said Oliver, reaching for my hand. James saw the gesture, and a small smile crinkled the corners of his eyes. He had nice eyes, I realized. Kind. Far more like Oliver than like Ryan.

"Nah, it's fine," I said, standing up. "Anyway, I still have more work to do. Call me later, okay?"

"Will do," said Oliver. He kissed the back of my hand before he let it go.

But it wasn't Oliver who called me later. It was Ryan. Just as I decided to take a break from homework and scavenge in the fridge for something that could pass as dinner, I felt the familiar tug just below my ribs. Sighing to myself, I shifted and followed the call.

"Are you *supposed* to screw up my wishes?" said Ryan, before I could even get my feet under me. He was sitting imperiously in his desk chair, like a tiny king. A tiny king who was obviously not happy with his single subject.

"Um, no?" I said. "Something got screwed up?"

He leaned forward and rested his elbows on his knees. A little less king than before, a little more lawyer. "Why'd you tell Naomi Sloane to post that thing online?"

"What do you . . . ? I didn't say anything about posting stuff online."

"But you did talk to her," he said. It wasn't a question, so I didn't answer. "Unless there were two Ambers at my party on Wednesday."

I crossed my arms, and still didn't answer.

"So Naomi sends me a text like an hour ago, right," said Ryan, "and it says to check her profile page. She says she's sick of being a bad feminist, and she should have done this days ago. Look."

He gestured to the desk behind him, where his browser was open to Naomi's profile. Right at the top of the page was a status update.

I KNOW RYAN WEISS HAS BEEN SAYING THINGS ABOUT ME. THESE THINGS ARE NOT TRUE. I REPEAT, NOT! TRUE! KNOW

WHAT ELSE IS NOT TRUE? ALL THE THINGS HE SAID ABOUT
CALLIE ZUMSKY BACK IN OCTOBER, AND ALL THE THINGS
HE SAID ABOUT ELLEN MURAMATSU LAST YEAR. ASK THEM
YOURSELVES. BETTER YET, ASK RYAN. LADIES, SPEAK UP IF
THIS HAS HAPPENED TO YOU. AND SPREAD THE WORD. (P.S.
AMBER, IF YOU'RE READING THIS, THANKS FOR THE ADVICE.
SO GLAD YOU FOUND ME AGAIN AFTER THE PARTY! FRIEND
ME IF YOU SEE THIS, K?)

It had only been up for forty-five minutes, but there were
already thirty-four comments. Almost eighty people had
Liked it. Ryan looked livid.

"I had to turn my phone off," he said. "People keep calling
me."

"Poor you," I said—and regretted it immediately. Ryan's
face went taut and dangerous. He stood up slowly. He was
taller than I was. Probably a lot stronger, too. It took every
ounce of courage I had not to back away.

"You screwed it up," he said, his voice gravelly. "You told
her to do this. Okay, so maybe she didn't put out for me, but
she would have eventually. But what now? What am I supposed to do?"

"Um, apologize?" I said.

He snorted. "Yeah, right. She totally ruined my rep. I'm
not apologizing for that."

My hands balled into fists at my sides, but somehow I managed to keep calm. "You forced her to love you, then you

started spreading rumors about her. You really don't think you owe her an apology after that?"

Ryan's expression faltered, and so I continued: "Besides, apologizing might lessen the chances of Naomi's boyfriend coming after you and beating you to a pulp."

"Wait," said Ryan, his voice going hostile again. "Boyfriend? You didn't tell me she had a boyfriend."

"Well, you didn't bother asking," I replied. "I tried to get you to talk your wish out with me before you made it, but you didn't exactly listen."

"Great. Just great." He sank back into his chair, looking defeated. I let out a quiet breath of relief.

"I'm sorry your wish went so badly," I said, not because I actually was, but because maybe expressing sympathy would take the edge off his antagonism.

"How sorry?" he asked, peering at me with thin eyes.

"Um. A little? Very?"

"Do *you* have a boyfriend?"

I tensed, immediately going silent. The last thing I wanted to do was bring Oliver into this. But it was Margo who was with Oliver, and I wasn't Margo right now. I was Amber. "No, I don't."

"Good." Ryan reached into his desk and pulled something out. My vessel.

I realized what he was about to do, right before he did it. "Ryan, no—"

"I wish *you* wanted to sleep with me," he said.

Magic exploded out of me, just like the first time. My skin froze and burned, and my vision went strange—but this time I felt my magic regrouping, turning inward. It reached inside me, sought something, found it, and gave it a little push in a new direction.

And then it was gone, leaving me teetering dizzily on the hardwood floor. Ryan was standing again, his deep brown eyes peering at me with an intensity that made my heart flutter. "Oh," I said, breathless. "Hi."

"You okay?" he asked. "You looked a little weird for a second there."

"I'm fine," I said, smiling shyly at his concern for me. God, he was cute. The stubble on his chin . . . that mop of curly hair . . . even his ratty old football jersey. Totally adorable. "Actually, I'm more than fine," I added softly, leaning in just enough that he couldn't miss the hint.

"Yeah?" he said, his face brightening like a sunrise. "Fine enough for some of this, maybe?"

He reached for me, pulled me close, and kissed me. It was all I could do not to melt right into him as I kissed him back. I pressed myself against him, and he pressed back, and his hands were everywhere, and suddenly I understood why kissing Oliver in this body had felt so strange. Amber's body wasn't meant for Oliver. This body, every molecule of it, had been created to be touched by Ryan. And now that it was happening, it felt completely, utterly, wonderfully right.

Only when one of his hands ventured down past the small of my back, did my brain catch up with what was happening. This wasn't real. Not one ounce of this incredible, electric feeling was real.

I jerked away from him, rubbing frantically at my mouth.

"What? What's wrong?" he said, looking wounded.

I wanted so badly to kiss him again, to beg his forgiveness for making him feel bad. But I couldn't. I wouldn't let myself. "You used a wish on me," I said, backing away and crossing my arms protectively over my chest. "That's low, Ryan. Even for you, that's low."

His jaw dropped, and for a moment he just gaped at me. "Even for . . . ? But I thought it worked! I thought you wanted me! Don't you?"

"Yes." My voice cracked over the word, but it was the truth.

"So relax," he said, grabbing my arm just a little too hard. "Come sit down. We can go slower if you want. No biggie. As long as we, you know, *go*." His sexy smile sent a thrill up my spine, but I would not go with him. I wouldn't, no matter how much I wanted to.

"No," I said firmly, jerking my arm out of his grasp and stepping just out of his reach. "This has gone way too far. I want my vessel back."

I held my hand out, but he just stared at it like it was an unusual species of rodent. "If I'm remembering right," he said, "I'm the master here, not you. Which means you have to do what I say. Look, okay, I made my first wish drunk, and I didn't think it through. That was my bad. But this one? This one's going to work. I can see it on your face, Amber. You want it to work as much as I do. You want *results*."

He'd moved closer to me again, holding me by the elbows as he pressed himself against me, and holy crap was he right. I did want the wish to work. I wanted to fall wholeheartedly into what I felt for Ryan, and never look back.

"Results," I said weakly. "No. No results. Give me my vessel. This isn't fair."

He stepped back, then sat comfortably on the unmade bed, all tousled hair and heavy-lidded eyes and lazy desire. He slid the pick carefully into his back pocket, then leaned back on his hands, grinning up at me. "You want your vessel? Come get it."

"I'd like you to give it to me," I said stiffly.

"Ask nicely."

"*Please* give it to me."

He tilted his head a little. "Ask nicely with your dress off."

I clenched my teeth, refusing to reply. The worst part wasn't even the order itself; the worst part was how badly I wanted to do exactly what he said.

My expression must have given me away, because the next thing I knew, he was leaning toward me, a hungry look on his face. "I can help you with that, if you want."

He reached for my clothes, and I recoiled. I couldn't let

him touch me again. I didn't trust myself not to react the way I'd done the first time.

So I jumped, disappearing from Ryan's bedroom and landing back in the safety of my own. I was shaking. The house was still empty. Huddling on my bed, I fumbled for my phone and called Oliver. He picked up on the third ring.

"*Allô, ma chère,*" came Gwen's bright alto. "Can I call you back in a little while? I'm kinda in the middle of something."

Gripping the phone tighter, I said, "No, I . . . I mean, if you have to, sure, but . . . but there's something . . ."

"Amber?" he said, suddenly deadly serious. "Are you okay?"

Tears pricked at my eyes, and I swiped at them with my free hand. "No," I whispered. "It's Ryan."

Something rustled on Oliver's end, and I heard Gwen again: "Hey, you mind if I cut this short? Got a friend here who needs a shoulder."

But I didn't hear the reply, because that's when I felt it again: the sharp tug below my ribs. Ryan was calling me back, and I couldn't focus long enough to fight it. I dropped my phone onto my bedspread, and the Between swallowed me whole.

"What the hell, man?" said Ryan, throwing his hands up as I stumbled back into his room. "You can't just leave."

My heart sped up, beating a warning through my body, but I refused to let my voice betray how scared I was. "And you can't just keep me here, either."

"Sure I can." He advanced on me, and I backed away until my calves hit the bed. There was nowhere else I could go, unless I wanted to try and sidestep him—unlikely to work in my heels—or crawl onto the bed itself. "See?"

I tried to disappear into the Between again. But as soon as I did, something wrenched inside me, just below my rib cage, holding me firmly in place. That was when I realized he was still holding my vessel. He hadn't let go of the call.

"All I want," said Ryan, "is what I wished for." With that, he backed off again, spreading his arms wide, still holding my vessel. I didn't move.

"No," I said.

"Listen, Amber," he said, ever so reasonably. "I'm not gonna force you, okay? I'm not *that* guy. But I'm your master, and I'm telling you: Grant my goddamn wish."

He smiled—the self-satisfied smile of a guy who was absolutely convinced that magic didn't count as force. I tried to speak, thinking maybe I could reason with him, but my voice was caught somewhere below my throat. It wouldn't budge. I squeezed my eyes shut, dreading—and yearning for—the moment that he decided to just give up on waiting.

But it never came.

"What's going on?" said a new voice. A chillingly familiar voice. Not Oliver, and definitely not Gwen. I opened my eyes to see if I was hallucinating it. I wasn't.

Standing in the middle of the room, one hand pulling

Ryan's head back by his hair, the other wrapped tightly around his throat, was Xavier.

Oh, this was not happening. This was *so* not happening.

"Leggo," Ryan wheezed. "Whothehellareyou?"

"Not relevant," said Xavier. "Ryan Weiss, you are in direct violation of Article 13F of the Unbreakable Treaty. As such, you are bound to relinquish any and all magical artifacts facilitating the binding between you and the wish-granting entity currently in your service." He let Ryan go, shoving him just enough to send him stumbling. I covered my mouth with my hands, wishing I could disappear behind them. Xavier would come for me next. I was sure of it.

Ryan looked at Xavier with wide eyes, rubbing at his throat. "The hell? What are you, some kind of genie police?"

Xavier didn't answer him. He just held his hand out and said, "Amber's vessel, if you please."

Ryan looked over at me, confusion etched in every line of his face. Xavier followed his gaze, his cool stare sliding over me like ice. That was when I saw them. Green eyes. Oliver's eyes. I almost wept with relief.

But Ryan's hand closed tighter around the red pick. "She still owes me one more wish," he said.

"Does she?"

The question was directed more at me than at Ryan, but Ryan still replied, "I just said so, didn't I?"

I didn't disagree. It was true, after all.

"In that case," said Oliver, his Xavier-voice going cold, "you may retain the vessel. You are permitted to use it only for your final wish, which will not be granted by Amber. Another genie will be sent in her place."

Another genie? How was that possible?

Oliver continued: "Do not attempt to contact Amber again, via her vessel or any non-magical means. If you do, retribution will be swift."

He grabbed my hand, and we disappeared into the Between.

Chapter TWELVE

As soon as we landed back in my room, Oliver shed Xavier's image and shifted back into himself. He folded his arms around me, holding me tightly enough that I could feel his warmth, but loosely enough that I could get away if I wanted to. I buried my face in his shirt, shutting my eyes.

"Article 13F?" I said, when I was finally sure I'd be able to speak coherently. "What's that?"

He gave a low laugh. "Something very official-sounding that I just made up," he said. "I'm so sorry I couldn't get there sooner, Margo. What happened?"

I sank to the floor, and Oliver sat down with me. I told him everything; he listened with a tightly set jaw and narrowed eyes.

"You know what the worst part is?" I said, when I was finished. "The wish worked, Oliver. I wanted to just sleep with him and be happy and forget about everything else."

"But you didn't," he said gently.

I shook my head, massaging the place on my arm where

Ryan had grabbed me. "I knew it was fake. But I can still feel it, Oliver, it's . . . it's . . ."

I pressed my thumbs against each of my fingertips in turn, like that would somehow snuff out the magic there. It didn't work, of course. I could still feel myself yearning to go back there, to let him kiss me again, to let him touch me, to let him do whatever he wanted, as long as he kept looking at me like that. . . .

"It's not you," said Oliver firmly, bringing me back to the here and now. "What you're feeling, it's not real—and it's not you. It's only Amber. You just need to shift back into yourself, and you won't feel it anymore. Can you shift?"

I tried. I really did. But shifting took concentration, and my mind kept trying and failing to process what had just happened, and I . . . just . . . couldn't.

Oliver touched my cheek, and I saw his hand come away wet. I hadn't even realized I was crying.

No. I was not allowed to freak out.

I tried to shift again.

I still couldn't do it.

Oliver's arms tightened around me again, and he kissed my hair, and that was all it took: I melted into him, clutching at his clothes, twisting myself around so I could kiss him. His neck. His ear. His lips. They weren't Ryan's, but they were right in front of me, touching me, and I needed so badly to touch and be touched.

Oliver held my face in his hands as he responded to my kisses, and I reached for the zipper of his hoodie. Off it came, over his shoulders and onto the floor. I slipped a hand under his shirt.

But he jerked away. His eyes flew open, and suddenly he was looking at me like he didn't know me at all. "Your hands are hot," he said.

"All of me is hot," I whispered. "Wanna see?"

"Margo, I mean your *hands*." He caught one of mine between both of his. That zing of connection coursed through me, just like before, only stronger. Magnified. Everything I was felt magnified right now. "This isn't you. This is Ryan's wish."

"I know. It's awful. I can still feel it. There's all this energy, and he wanted it to be for him, and I wanted that, too, but I hate him, but not you. I *love* you, and you're here and you saved me and—"

"And I'm not going to sleep with you because of someone else's wish," he said firmly. "I've been a lot of people's second choice, but I won't be yours. We both deserve better than that. You need to get control of yourself."

Control. That one word was all it took to quiet me. Ryan's control of me had followed me out of his bedroom and into my own. Oliver was right. We both deserved better. Taking a deep breath, I closed my eyes. I *forced* myself to shift.

Ryan's wish, which had settled inside me like a rock, finally dislodged itself. I was acutely aware of my lust for him evap-

152

orating, and for that much I was grateful—but the energy of it remained, and now that it had lost its focus, it diffused through my body, traveling up my arms and spreading into my chest, my stomach, my head. I felt nauseated. Raw. Like someone had scrubbed me till I bled, both inside and out.

"I think I'm gonna be sick," I said, drawing my shoulders up and turning away from Oliver, just in case. But I didn't throw up.

The floor creaked, and I felt his hand on my back. "I know," he said. "I know. Just breathe through it."

"You don't know," I murmured, squeezing my eyes shut. "You don't have any idea what this feels like."

"Yes I do," he said gently. "You think this kind of thing has never happened to me?"

"It has?" I said cautiously, turning around to face him.

He gave a wry little smile and handed me a wad of tissues. "Not for a long time. But yes."

"Tell me," I said.

He took a moment to rearrange himself into a more comfortable position. "Well," he began slowly, "it's the power thing, isn't it? Most people won't abuse the kind of power they have over us, but there are always some who try."

"I didn't mean that," I said. "I meant you. Tell me what happened to you."

"Ah." His eyes dropped, and his face closed off a little. It was a moment before he spoke again, his tone low and even.

"Well, I suppose . . . I suppose the worst was when I was still fairly new. I had a master who took her time with her wishes. Close to three years. Her name was Laure, and I was a young man named Jean-Paul, whose image I modeled after her brother. We got on just fine at first, but as she learned more and more about how my magic worked, she began to discover all the little ways she could use it against me.

"She made me her servant, bit by bit, because I was too naïve to know how to fight back, and because she wanted to see how far she could push me. I was her favorite game—her prized possession—but I grew to hate her, and she could tell. It made her angry. She didn't just want a servant; she wanted a willing, even adoring servant.

"By then, she knew that I could shift bodies, and she knew that the changes I made to one body didn't necessarily apply to any of the others. So she made a love wish, similar to Ryan's, but far more complex than I would have liked." He paused, his fingers picking at the sky-blue fibers of my carpet. "She specified that it applied to any body I created, past or present or future, and it would last until the event of either her death or mine."

My eyes widened, and in that moment I was endlessly grateful that Ryan was a run-of-the-mill asshole instead of a *smart* asshole. "What did you do?" I asked.

He met my eyes reluctantly. "I granted the wish, of course. I fell in love, as instructed, and I stayed that way until she died." His lips twisted in a parody of a smile. "Fortunately for me, she died young. Niall saw to that. Xavier, I mean. He was calling himself Xavier by then."

"Xavier killed her?" I said, thinking of switchblades and dark, empty streets.

Oliver nodded, lowering his eyes with an expression I couldn't quite read. "I know there must have been a solution that didn't involve murder, but even then he was far more concerned with freedom than with kindness."

"I mean," I said slowly, "Xavier saved you because you couldn't save yourself. That's what you're saying. Isn't it."

Oliver looked up sharply, confusion knitting his brows. His silence told me everything I needed to know.

He couldn't save himself then, just like I hadn't been able to save myself from Ryan just now. Sure, I could ask him not to call me unless it was about something important, and I could pretend I'd won when I didn't hear from him for an entire week—but that was all it had been. Pretending.

Ryan could even call me back right now, if he wanted to. He could keep me there until he was finished with me. I was lucky that Oliver had managed to intimidate him. *Lucky.*

"So that's the truth of it," I said as numbness crept through my body. "That's what being a genie is about. People can do whatever they want to you, and you just have to sit back and let them."

"Not always," he said with a touch of desperation. "Almost

never. Usually you can talk sense into people. Take what you see in their minds and use it to your advantage, or even use illusions to threaten them, if it comes to that. You'll learn. I'll help you. I promise."

"Threaten them with illusions?" I said. "Screw that. I should have hit him back. I should have kicked him in the nuts, or stabbed him in the—"

"Calm down, okay?" he said, worry clouding his eyes. "If you start attacking everyone who makes a bad wish, that makes you no better than them."

"The point isn't being better than them," I said hotly. "The point is not being assaulted."

"Yeah, I guess . . ."

"You *guess*?" I said. He blanched, but didn't reply, and a new thought crept into my head. One that I didn't like at all. "That woman. Laure. Was it that you *couldn't* save yourself from her, or you *wouldn't*?"

Oliver sucked in a breath, and the question hung motionless between us for what seemed like ages—long enough that I started to get annoyed. If only I were still his master, the binding between us would have forced him to answer me faster than this.

Then I realized what I'd just thought, not to mention what I'd just *said,* and felt like a completely heartless hypocrite.

"Sorry," I said, my voice coming out small as I rubbed my forehead. "It's just, that wish . . ."

But the excuse wouldn't hold up, and I knew it. Maybe I could blame Ryan's wish for the way I'd felt, but not for what I'd done about it. Or not done. Because while I'd tried to run, I definitely hadn't tried very hard.

Was that the sort of person I was now? The sort who gave up and waited for someone else to save her?

"God," I said, and covered my whole face with my hands, as if that would somehow erase everything that had just happened.

"What do you need?" asked Oliver. "Tell me."

What I needed was to undo Ryan's wish. But I knew I couldn't, so all I said was, "I need to get away. Can we go somewhere? Preferably somewhere really, really far from here? And not a concert. I don't think I can do crowds right now."

Oliver thought for a moment, and then a smile brightened his face. "Can I show you something?"

"As long as it's something far away."

"As far away as possible. I promise." He stood up, then extended his hand to help me up, too. "Okay," he said. "Now, in order for this to work, you need to concentrate. Remember what I told you about the Between? How it does whatever you want it to do?" I nodded slowly. "Concentrate on seeing a door."

"Okay."

Oliver gripped my hand tightly, and together we stepped

into the Between. Gray surrounded me. An absence of feeling. Emptiness. It was oddly soothing.

Door, I thought.

Then there was a door. It was plain and white and wooden, just like the one in my bedroom. I reached for the knob.

"No, let me do it," said Oliver, brushing my hand aside. I threw him a questioning look, and he quickly explained: "I want to take you to *my* Between, not yours. Not yet. And that'll only happen if I'm the one who opens the door."

"There are different Betweens?" I asked. "How many?"

"As many as you like," said Oliver. "Or as many as *I* like, since I'm the one opening the door today. Here, just watch." He reached for the knob, turned it, and pulled the door open. On the other side I could see . . . more gray nothingness.

"Go ahead," said Oliver. "Go inside."

So I went. Oliver followed, and I heard the light *snick* of the door shutting behind us. I turned toward him, ready to ask him where he was trying to take me . . . but the words died in my throat as, around me, a world came into being.

Mountains loomed in the distance. That was the first thing I noticed. Rounded peaks blanketed with summer-green trees, stretching lazily toward a clear blue sky. At the mountains' base, the trees thinned out until they gave way to grassy fields: a patchwork quilt of a landscape containing every shade of green I'd ever imagined. A light breeze gave movement to the grass, and something bright glinted just beyond the tree line. A river, maybe, or a lake?

My eyes moved along the peaks and, almost unconsciously, my body followed, turning me in a circle. The mountains ringed us on every side, as if protecting the little patchwork valley from every single living thing except us. It smelled like spring, and it was easily the most beautiful place I'd ever seen.

Eventually I tore my eyes away, long enough to look back at Oliver. It seemed like sacrilege to break the silence, so I settled for a quick, quiet "Wow." Understatement of the century.

Oliver's face broke into a radiant smile. "You like it?" His voice sounded comfortable in the stillness, like he belonged there. Like he was part of the land itself.

"Like it?" I looked out again at the mountains, up at the sky, over at Oliver's eager face. "This is amazing. Where are we?"

"We're still in the Between," he said. "My own Between. This is what I wanted to show you before, the first time I brought you here. This is my real home. Well, more or less."

"Oh," I said softly. "I thought you lived in that empty apartment back in Oakvale."

"Well, I live there, too, at least for now." He shrugged. "It's good to have a home base that's more . . . well, accessible."

"Why?"

"In case a pretty girl offers to drive me home," he said with a grin. "But that's just temporary. This place is permanent. You have one, too. You just have to be the one to open the door. You can make it into anything you want. Create a whole world for yourself, or just a single room, or anything at all. Just by thinking it."

"Really?" I said, more to myself than to him. I thought about trying it out now—creating something out of nothing, just for myself. But I didn't want to leave this place, with its fresh air and its blue, blue sky. I felt safe here.

"Really," he said. "It doesn't always look like this, but today, for you, this seemed about right. It's a little bit Ireland, a little bit upstate New York, a little bit Egypt, and, you know, other places." He waved it off, like it was nothing.

"Egypt?" I echoed, perplexed.

"Oh, did I forget?" He frowned as he looked around. Then he squinted into the distance and, as I watched, a small pyramid appeared just at the edge of the trees. "There," he said. "Egypt."

I laughed, shaking my head. Oliver jumped once on the grass, like he was testing it, and then he flopped down on his back, arms stretched out, palms to the sky. His feet were bare now, and grass brushed his toes.

I bent to untie the laces of my shoes, but Oliver nudged my foot with his. "Just think them off," he said. "You can't change my scenery, but you can still change yourself."

Interesting. *Shoes off,* I thought, and suddenly my feet were nestled in soft, lush grass. Completely delighted, I sat cross-legged beside him, watching him squint into the clear sky. He closed his eyes, breathing deep, then opened them again and looked at me, a smile on his face and a question in his eyes.

"This is perfect," I said, and lay down in the grass beside him.

We watched the clouds together in the warm silence of this nothing-place.

Maybe running away from my human life wasn't such a bad idea after all.

"Oliver?"

"Mm-hmm?"

"Do I have to have another master when Ryan's done with me?"

"No," he said. "If you don't have one, though, you won't be able to have a body."

I thought about that. "But I wouldn't die or anything, right?"

The grass rustled as he shifted onto his side. Propping his head up on one elbow, he looked over at me with worried eyes. "You wouldn't die. But you wouldn't be entirely alive, either. You'd be sort of . . . a living ghost, I guess you could say. You couldn't talk to anyone or touch anything in the real world. Anyone except me, that is."

"So, no master, no body," I said softly. If I was going to give up my human life, that didn't seem like a good way to do it.

"That's how genie magic works, unfortunately," he said, smiling in a weary sort of way that made him look far older than sixteen. "Meanwhile, you should think about who you want to be, next time Ryan calls you."

"Who I want to . . ." For the first time since it happened, I remembered what Oliver had told Ryan: *Another genie will be sent in her place.* "But why?"

"Because the wish he made only applies to Amber. If you don't want to feel the effects of that wish every time you see him, you need to be someone else."

The answer was so obvious that it actually made me laugh. Yet another thing I should have thought of. "That's brilliant," I told him. "Yeah. Someone else. Someone that he won't want to take advantage of, like . . . like someone old enough to be his grandmother, or someone he'd think was ugly, or—"

"Or someone who's a guy," suggested Oliver, an evil glint in his eye.

Apprehension darted through me, and I sat up, looking down at him. "A guy?"

Tucking both hands behind his head, Oliver grinned up at me. "Unless I'm very wrong about Ryan Weiss's sexual preference, and evidence suggests that I'm not, being male would definitely help to get you off his radar. At least in that particular way."

"But what he did was *his* fault, not mine!" I said. "I shouldn't have to turn into a boy to get away from him."

Oliver pursed his lips thoughtfully. "No, you shouldn't.

And in a fair world, you wouldn't. But the world isn't fair, and in this line of work you need to protect yourself however you can. You were willing to be old or unattractive, weren't you?" He shimmered, and suddenly it was Gwen lying in the grass instead of Oliver. "It's not that different. Well, maybe a little different—but at least it's interesting. Enlightening, you might say."

"I don't need enlightenment," I muttered. "I should just shift into a lobster and snap his toes off."

"I'm afraid your shifting options extend to human only," he said, shimmering back into Oliver. "No lobsters. So at least think about it, okay?"

I knew I would. Because even though I was completely weirded out by the idea of turning into a guy, Ryan was about as straight as they came, and being male might keep me a little bit safer.

"There's another thing, too," I said, scooting closer to him. "When I'm sleeping at night, I have to be Amber. And if being Amber means wanting to be with Ryan . . . I mean, god, what if I wake up in the middle of the night and . . . ugh."

"Ah," said Oliver. "Do you want me to stay with you tonight? Just in case?"

The memory of the wish, and the way it had made me act, brought a flush to my face. I plucked idly at the grass, embarrassed at having to ask this of him. "Would you?"

"Spend the night with my gorgeous girlfriend just in case she needs rescuing?" he said. "Gee. Twist my arm."

"You first," I said.

I'd shifted in front of him before, and he in front of me. But now that there was a bed between us, looming large with its suggestion of closeness, the whole affair seemed infinitely more weighted.

"It's really not that big a deal," said Oliver, shifting into Gwen. Loose sweatpants and a V-neck T-shirt masked distinctly feminine curves, but just barely. "Now you."

Closing my eyes, I let go of my magic—but as I shifted into Amber, I thought myself into my own pajamas instead of the lacy, frilly things that Amber always seemed to favor. Being in Amber's body and Margo's clothes felt odd, and the feeling of wanting Ryan was beginning to creep over me again, but at least I was secure in the knowledge that my shirt wasn't see-through.

I darted into the bathroom to scrub my face clean and brush my teeth. I didn't technically need to do either of those things anymore, since I could think myself clean and be done with it, but there was a certain comfort in the bedtime ritual. When I returned, though, there was nothing left to stand between this moment and the moment where I got into bed. With Gwen.

"Would you feel better if I slept on the floor or something?"

asked Oliver, which was more than a little embarrassing. He clearly didn't feel the same amount of discomfort that I did. . . .

If I was the sort of person who became a genie to save her boyfriend from certain death, then I damn well wasn't going to be the sort of person who kicked that same boyfriend out of bed because he happened to be wearing a female body. That would just be pathetic. Forcing myself to relax, I climbed into bed. "No way," I told him, holding the covers up so he could slide inside. "Get your butt in here."

When he lay down beside me, there was that space of breath during which, last time he'd stayed the night, we'd settled naturally into each other's arms. This time, we didn't. I didn't know if I could let Gwen's body hold me the same way Oliver's had.

So we stretched out beside each other, several inches apart and not touching at all. Friend-distance. Like the countless sleepovers I'd had with Naomi—although none of those had ever been so . . . fraught.

"You okay?" he asked, in that so-very-female voice.

"I was just wondering," I said. "Do you want me to call you Gwen when you're, well, Gwen? I mean, when it's just us."

He turned onto his side, and suddenly we were looking at each other again. It was with considerable effort that I kept my focus on his eyes. Not the chest. Not the chest. Just the eyes.

"Well, what do you *want* to call me?"

I thought about that for a moment. "I mean, I still think of you as Oliver. But that's not your . . . your default anymore. And it's not your original name either, so . . ."

"But it's who I was when you first met me. Plus, I like how you say it. Oliver, that is. You say my name like it's really mine. Like you know me."

Even spoken in Gwen's voice, the simplicity of those words was so very Oliver, and the fact that I could recognize him in a foreign voice made me reach out and brush his shoulder with my fingers.

"Oliver it is, then."

Chapter THIRTEEN

Turning into a boy had never exactly been on my bucket list. Sure, I'd been enjoying playing Toby in *Sweeney Todd*, but that was just acting. Being an actual boy would involve having . . . well, certain body parts that only boys had. I did not want to know what that was like.

Or maybe I did.

But the very thought that I *might* want to know embarrassed the hell out of me, even in the privacy of my own head, so I spent most of the next day retreating again and again into the safety of indecision—until late afternoon, when Oliver finally said the magic words: "What if Ryan calls you today?"

Of all the potential solutions we'd come up with, turning into a boy was by far the best one. So I went to the mirror above my vanity, which reflected everything from my hair to my thighs; even with my parents away on their usual Sunday grocery shopping trip, I wasn't about to risk changing out in the hallway, even though the full-length mirror was there.

Oliver stood a few feet behind me. I smiled nervously at his reflection.

"You ready?" he said.

"Ready as I'll ever be," I said. "Any pointers? I mean, I've never turned into anyone except Amber and Margo, so . . ."

He thought for a moment. "It's the same process as turning into your real self. Just picture a different person instead. Be as specific or as vague as you want. Your magic will fill in the rest."

I quirked my lips into a smile. "You mean I can't just turn into you?"

He let out a quick bark of laughter. "If you want . . . although I'd prefer it if you didn't."

"Here goes nothing," I murmured.

I shut my eyes.

Magic washed over me like a tidal wave, settling just below my ribs, like it did every time I shifted into my real self. I clenched my abs, holding it there, but that was the only movement I dared to make.

"Did I do it?" I asked Oliver. My voice came out in a high baritone. A man's voice. "Oh god. Okay. That's weird. That's . . . that's very weird."

"Open your eyes," said Oliver, hushed and excited. "You look fantastic. Really, Margo, great job."

I opened my eyes.

"Oh hell no," I whispered, before I could stop myself.

The mirror showed me exactly what I'd wanted it to: a tall young man with an intimidating build. But I hadn't been prepared for the detail. I could see the contours of muscles in my arms, the thickness of my eyebrows, the sprinkling of stubble across my chin. I was in jeans and a plain white T-shirt. A small reddish birthmark stood out against the tanned skin of my neck.

I leaned slightly closer to the mirror. "My eyes are different," I said. "They're blue."

"Your everything else is different, too," said Oliver. He stood patiently behind me, like a proud teacher, watching closely as I surveyed my handiwork in the mirror.

I shook my head. "I thought they'd stay the same. They did for Amber. Yours always do."

He tilted his head to the side a little, giving me a smile. "My eyes always stay the same because I want them to. It's a personal choice."

I lifted a hand toward my neck, touching the little birthmark. I dropped my arm to my side again.

"I'm afraid to move," I told Oliver, letting a giddy little laugh escape. "Dumb, right?"

"Not at all," he said. "Take your—" But as he said the word *time,* he swung a fist toward me. Instinct took over, and I jumped out of the way with ease. The seal had been broken.

"That was mean," I told Oliver. He just laughed. "Seriously, you're the meanest teacher ever."

"True, perhaps," he said, "but you are a stellar student."

"Yes, I am," I said, stretching my arms over my head, just to see how they moved. "I'm gonna rock at college. Intro to Shapeshifting, here I come."

He raised an eyebrow. "I don't think I've ever heard you talk about college before."

I realized he was right. "Yeah," I said, heading over to my desk, where a small collection of envelopes was piled. "Check this out. I applied to ten places. Six acceptances, two rejections, two waitlists. Awesome, right?"

"Awesome," he said sort of vaguely, flipping through the envelopes. "NYU. Northwestern. Harvard? Seriously? Nice going."

"Yeah, that's one of the rejections," I said with a laugh. "I'll probably pick NYU, but I still have a little while to decide."

He held one of the envelopes, examining it like it was an exotic bug or something. "So . . . you're still going to college."

"Obviously. I didn't apply to all those places just for fun." I paused, taking in his disconcerted expression. He flipped through the envelopes again and didn't meet my eyes. "What, you thought I'd give college up, too?"

"No," he said quickly. "It's just, you know, there's not really much of a point anymore, is there?"

"No point?" I echoed in disbelief. College was the end of

being a kid. The beginning of being an adult. College was the only reason I'd put up with high school for four years.

Oliver shrugged. "Remember how easily you made yourself a calculus whiz? Tomorrow you could write the next Great American Novel, if you wanted."

"And cure cancer the next day?" I said.

"Well, no," he replied with a wry smile. "I've already tried that. But you get what I'm saying, right? College is for learning, and you and me, we don't have to learn things the hard way."

In other words, my magic didn't stop at the ability to cheat at homework. I could cheat at everything, for the rest of my life, if I wanted to.

"Unless we like the hard way," I said.

He shrugged. "Unless that."

I paced in a small circle, just to see how walking felt. Walking became jogging, which became jumping jacks, which became push-ups, which became one-armed push-ups with barely any effort at all. This body liked to move, and it was *good* at it, too: a perfect balance of strength and impulse and control. I felt powerful—physically powerful—for probably the first time in my life.

It felt good.

Ridiculously weird. But good.

And then there was the matter of my jeans. Boy jeans fit differently than girl jeans, of course, because they're made for bodies with no hips to keep them from sliding to the floor. But that wasn't the only thing. There was a new weight there, just below my center—small, compared to the rest of me, but immensely distracting, now that I'd noticed it.

In the mirror, my face went red. I bit my lip, willing myself not to look down. "Another reason to do the college thing?" I said delicately. "I am finding that I have a sudden interest in becoming a gender studies major."

"Oh, that?" Oliver waggled his eyebrows suggestively. "Yeah. That'll take some getting used to."

I laughed. "That's for damn sure. Seriously, I feel like I'm wearing a costume that was made for someone else. How do you do this all the time?"

"Do what?" he said. "Switch?"

"Yeah. Oliver to Gwen, Gwen to Oliver. Male to female. Doesn't it freak you out?"

He considered me for a moment—which was when I realized that he was looking *up* at me. I was actually a few inches taller than he was. All of a sudden, I felt like a skyscraper: disproportionate, unbalanced, and maybe a little too likely to topple over at any moment.

I was Tony Stark, donning the Iron Man suit for the first time.

"Not anymore," he said. "But that's only because I've done it so many times. It can still feel—well, like you said. Like a costume. But there are ways to make it work. Like, you can adjust your personality so you *do* feel comfortable in a male body. Or you can just get used to it."

I could see how the first option could be useful—adjusting myself so that I felt male instead of female. But somehow that was even scarier than the idea of being a girl in a boy's body. The list of things I knew about myself was growing shorter every day, but I still knew for sure that I was female, no matter what body I wore. And I wasn't about to change that.

I would just have to get used to it.

"I think I'll be Tony when I look like this," I said, peering at myself in the mirror again. "And for the record, I hate being taller than you."

"Yeah, the height thing is weird," he said, though he didn't look too bothered by it. Then he tilted his head to the side, narrowing his eyes thoughtfully. "But it could make things interesting."

My stomach did a quiet little somersault. "Interesting how?"

"Although," he said, "if you don't like kissing me when you're Amber, then I probably shouldn't kiss you now, right?"

"No," I said faintly. "No, you probably shouldn't. You *definitely* shouldn't."

"Too bad," he said. "Because you're kinda—"

My door handle jiggled, effectively cutting him off, and I had what felt like a small heart attack before remembering that I'd locked it. Seconds later, there was a knock, followed by my mom's voice: "Margo? Honey? We're home."

Swearing under my breath, I let go of the magic in my abs and let myself shift. Started toward the door, then realized I'd shifted into my default body—into Amber. So I took a deep breath and forced another shift, this time into myself. I took a second to double-check the result in the mirror before opening the door.

"Hi!" I said to my mom, just a little too brightly.

"Hey, honey. Your dad and I were . . ." But she trailed off as her gaze fixed on something behind me. An oddly delighted expression bloomed on her face. "And who is this?"

Sure enough, Oliver was still there, even though I'd assumed he would jump. Panic tugged at my chest, but I shoved it down. "Oh. Right. Mom, this is Oliver Parish. Oliver, this is Mom. I mean mine. My mom. Obviously. Um."

He stepped forward and extended his hand, saving me from whatever my next words might have been. "Pleased to meet you," he said. He sounded nervous. I wondered if he actually was.

"Likewise, Oliver," she said, sing-songing the words into something just shy of suggestive. Somehow I managed not to melt into a puddle of embarrassment. "So, how long have you guys been up here?"

Oliver: "Half an hour or so."

Me, simultaneously: "He just got here."

Mom's smile widened as she looked back and forth between us. "I see," she said, and then paused. Just long enough for me to wonder what, exactly, she saw. Margo the Model Daughter, who would never think of sneaking a boy into her room and keeping him there overnight? Or Margo the Unpredictable Daughter, who had started missing school and disappearing without explanation?

More importantly, was I about to deal with Super-Organized Mom or Lovesick-Puppy Mom?

"Well, this is a pleasant surprise," she said. "It's so nice to see my Margo hanging out with a boy."

So, Lovesick-Puppy Mom. I wanted, just a little bit, to die.

Oliver, though, kept his game face on. "Well, Margo is very nice to hang out with. And I am definitely a boy!"

Usually, I thought.

Mom smiled indulgently at him. "So, are you in the play with Margo?"

He's way more than that with Margo, I thought.

"Nope," he said cheerfully. "But I used to take rehearsal photos for the yearbook, back before I stopped going to Jackson. That's how we met."

Then came the three wishes. And the part where I turned into a genie to save his life. And did I mention we're planning on sleeping together?

"Before you stopped going?" said Mom, looking concerned for the first time since she'd barged in.

"I transferred," Oliver lied.

"To North," I added. Also a lie.

"Oh, that's not far at all," said Mom. "Nice, nice. So what are you kids up to today?"

Me: "Working on play stuff."

Him, simultaneously: "Doing homework."

I shot him a quick look. "Play homework. You know. He's helping me run lines."

That was the moment that Ziggy Stardust chose to join us. Slinking quietly into the room, she bypassed Mom and me entirely, choosing instead to sniff Oliver's shoes.

"Hi, Ziggy," he said, bending over to pet her.

Mom's smile widened, and I knew exactly what she was thinking. He knew our cat's name. Clearly, this wasn't the first time he'd been here.

"Well then," she said, "I'll leave you to your *play homework*." She used quotey fingers. Oh, this was mortifying.

"Actually, I should get going," said Oliver, in a tone that sounded a little too neutral. "Got a call," he added with a meaningful glance my way. "It was nice to meet you, Mrs. McKenna."

"Giordano," corrected Mom with a smile. "I kept my maiden name."

"Right," said Oliver, moving toward the door. "See ya, Margo." And with that, he darted past Mom and into the hallway, and was gone.

Ziggy trotted after him. *Traitorous feline,* I thought.

"He seems nice," said Mom.

"He is," I said. "He's really nice."

"A little on the jumpy side, though."

I raised my eyebrows at her. "I think you scared him."

"Good. Any decent boy should be terrified of his girl-friend's mom." She leaned against the doorframe, raising her eyebrows at me. "So, how long have you two been dating?"

The last word made me pause for a second. Did wish-granting and making out and sharing a bed and occasionally saving each other's lives count as dating? It didn't seem like it should, but I couldn't think of a better word for what Oliver and I had been doing together. Maybe it would feel more like real dating if we went to the movies or something.

"Only a few weeks," I said . . . then thought about that for a second. Had I really known him for such a short amount of time? It felt like half a lifetime.

"You're turning red," said Mom smugly. "I knew some-thing was up with you. I can always tell. Well, you know you can talk to me if you need anything, right? And remember to be safe if you decide you're ready to make love. We've talked about this, right?"

"Uh-huh," I said quickly.

We'd talked about it ad nauseam back in sixth grade, when she'd taken me shopping for my first bra, and again in junior high, when the rest of my *lady changes*—Mom's phrase, not mine——had begun. Nowadays she didn't have much to add, but she did go out of her way, on occasion, to make sure I knew how healthy and responsible her love life was. Her love life with Dad, that is. Since I generally found this even more horrifying than her use of the phrase *make love,* such conversations invariably ended with me sticking my fingers in my ears and fleeing the room.

"Good, good," she said. "Oh, and I should probably meet his parents, shouldn't I . . ."

By now, I could feel exactly how red I was getting. "No parents," I said. Mom gave me a sharp look, and I licked my lips, wishing I hadn't said anything. "I mean, he's . . . um, he's an emancipated teen. Has his own place over on Crawford Circle. It's really cool, actually."

"Really? Interesting. He doesn't seem like the type."

"There isn't a type, Mom," I said.

"Right, of course," she said, shaking her head. "Well, like I said, if you ever need to talk——"

"I'll know who to go to." Not that I would. Ever. Not in a million years.

"Good," she said with a smile. "Then I'll stop embarrassing you. Change of subject: Your dad and I were talking about going out for an early dinner. What do you think: Mexican, Greek, or steakhouse?"

My stomach rumbled at the thought of steak, and I almost said as much——but I couldn't shake the memory of being

Tony, moving around as Tony, feeling that much power contained within my very own body. . . .

"I have too much play stuff to do," I lied. "You guys go without me."

Mom raised her eyebrows, but didn't argue. "Suit yourself."

A few minutes later, their car pulled out of the driveway. I watched from the window until it was completely out of sight. Only then did I shift again.

I examined Tony, taking note once again of all the things I'd noticed before. The discord between how he looked and who I was. The hum of kinetic energy just below the surface of his skin, waiting impatiently for me to put it to use. The way he stood, like someone ready to pick a fight.

Tony was the polar opposite of Amber. Everything about him demanded to be taken seriously . . . which was exactly what I needed.

I'd created Tony just in case Ryan decided to attack me again. But I was not going to let myself be the sort of person who waited around *just in case*. Ryan wasn't going to attack me again.

He wasn't going to get the chance.

A quick inspection of Ryan's house revealed that his parents weren't home, which was good. Less good was the fact that Ryan himself wasn't home either. So I parked myself in his room, turned on his TV and game system, and swapped Rock Band out for Guitar Hero.

Then I thought, *Tony is amazing at Guitar Hero.*

Seven songs later, just as I was about to set a new record on a Red Hot Chili Peppers track, Ryan walked in.

He lunged for me, knocking my hand away from the plastic fret buttons. "Who the hell are you?" he demanded.

I just looked at him. "You messed up my score."

He looked at the screen, where the song was still playing, and then back at me. His neck was starting to turn red.

"*Your* score?" he said at last, the words oozing out from behind clenched teeth. "This is my game. My room. My house."

"Yes, you're right," I said, before he could go any further. "And they're all exactly as Amber described them."

He squinted, and I could see the puzzle pieces clicking into place. "Oh. You're the other genie?"

"I am," I said.

He nodded slowly, setting his shoulders back again, finally somewhat at ease. But only somewhat. Nervousness still lingered in the slight squint of his eyes.

"You, uh, look different. From Amber, I mean. I was expecting someone more . . ."

"Someone more what?" I said amiably. "Attractive? Vulnerable? Someone a little more ready to fall into bed with you?"

He took a step back, his features going hostile again. "Look, man, I don't want any trouble. Why are you even here, any-way? I didn't touch the guitar pick thingy."

"I know you didn't," I said. "But I'm here to grant your third wish."

I took a step forward, closing the space between us. Like Oliver, Ryan had to look up slightly to meet my eyes.

Good.

"Third wish?" he said, forcing his features into a smirk. It looked hollow. "I don't have a third wish. I'll call you when I do."

"No deal, Ryan," I said, smiling at him as I folded my arms. "You're going to make a third wish right now."

Lifting his chin, he fixed me with an arrogant stare. "What's your name?"

"Tony."

"Well, *Tony*," he said, "I don't know if you're new at this or what, but the rules say I'm your master, which means you have to do what I say. And if I say I'm not gonna make a third wish right now, then that's the goddamn truth."

"And if I say no deal," I countered, "I mean exactly that. No deal. Make your wish."

He blinked, clearly thrown—Amber never would've dared to speak to him like this—but he regrouped quickly, a challenge blooming on his face. "What if I don't?" he asked.

"Then I will force a wish out of you," I replied.

I stood perfectly still, watching my words sink in. Watching

Ryan's jaw work as he figured out what to do next. Wondering if getting rid of him would really be as easy as standing in front of him, making my demand, and refusing to back down.

Then he said, "No. You don't get to tell me what to do. Go away and send someone else. Someone who's gonna listen to me."

The next thing I knew, Ryan was pinned against his bedroom wall—and it was my hands that were doing the pinning. I hadn't even made a conscious decision to go after him. I'd just *done it*.

I smiled. "Make your third wish."

"Bro, I told you, I'm not ready," he said. "I don't know what to wish for."

Giving him a pointed once-over, I said, "You could wish for that zit on your chin to go away. Or a better haircut."

Ryan's body tensed against my grip. "Hey, man . . ."

"Or, I don't know, wish for money. Everyone likes money."

"But," he faltered. "But I already *have* money."

I snorted in disgust as I looked around his room. "Then wish it for someone else. I honestly don't care what you wish for, Ryan. As long as you do it now."

"But," he said again, his voice breathy and wobbly, almost like he was about to cry.

"But nothing," I said evenly, pressing him harder against the wall. "Make a wish, or I will force you to."

He looked like he was going to protest again, but then something shifted behind his eyes. Gone was the pathetic and pleading Ryan from a moment ago; in his place was the cunning Ryan of last night.

"I think you're bluffing," he said. "You wouldn't do that. I'm your master."

That was when I punched him in the stomach.

Ryan doubled over, groaning.

Shaking out my hand, I said, "I'm not bluffing."

He looked up at me again, this time with undisguised fear. "But I still don't know what to——"

This time, I aimed for his face. Ryan yelped as my fist made contact. Tony instinctively knew how to pull a punch just enough to hurt him without breaking bones. Ryan would have the mother of all bruises in the very near future, but nothing worse.

As I shook my hand out again, I could feel Tony's body thrumming with tension. With the desire to finish what it had started. But I made myself stay still.

Ryan recovered once again, one hand still on his stomach, the other pressed against his cheek. "Screw you," he spat. "I don't need—*oof.*"

A grunt escaped him as I slammed him against the wall one more time. "I don't care what you need," I said. "I only care that you make your wish. Now, shall I ask you again, or is it time for me to start breaking bones?"

Face squinched up with pain, he tried to pry himself out of my grip.

I didn't let him.

"Okay, okay, hold on," he said. "Just gimme a second. Let me think. God." So I stepped away, letting him have the small illusion of safety that he clearly wanted. He moved his jaw a little, like he wanted to make sure it still worked. Then he eyed me. "Why are you people so keen on getting rid of me, anyway? There was no hurry yesterday."

Calmly as ever, I said, "That was before you tried to rape Amber."

"Rape?" he echoed in disbelief. Then he laughed—actually laughed. "Man, I dunno what she told you, but it was nothing like that. She was a hot little piece, sure, but I wouldn't have *forced* her. The way girls exaggerate. I swear. She's such a liar."

That was it. Tony had served his purpose, and served it well, but I clearly wasn't going to get anywhere by pulling punches. Loosening the muscles of my abdomen, I let myself shift back into my default form—back into Amber.

Amber the Liar.

Lust cascaded through me as I looked at Ryan through Amber's eyes, but I brushed it aside. I would not allow myself to be distracted. Not now.

I watched Ryan's eyes grow wide with fear and recognition,

and I thought firmly to myself, *Amber is even better at fighting than Tony is.*

Then I broke Ryan's nose.

The movement itself was pure instinct, planted there by my adjustment of Amber's fighting skills—but the result unfolded like a slow-motion video, sickening and fascinating. The alien feeling of cartilage giving way under the impact of my fist. The noise Ryan made when the pain registered, halfway between human and wild animal. The *thud* of his head hitting the bedroom wall, with enough force that it bounced back toward me.

I grabbed him in a headlock and wrestled him to the floor. Blood streamed from his nose as he called me every name he could think of. I grabbed the nearest absorbent thing I could find—a brown T-shirt that didn't look at all clean—and held it out to him. "Don't bleed on your rug," I said.

Eyes swimming with tears, he took the shirt and held it to his nose. "Let me at least sit up?" he asked, his voice distorted and raw. "I feel like I'm gonna choke."

I thought about it for a second, then pulled back just enough that he could sit.

"Wish," I ordered.

"Fine," he said, shutting his eyes. A couple stray tears rolled down his cheeks, mingling with the blood that was still smeared there. He reached into his pocket and took out my vessel. "Fine. I wish my nose wasn't broken. Happy now?"

"Happier than I was before," I said, grinning as I sat back, ready for my magic to take the reins.

But it didn't. Not this time. It rose inside me, as potent as ever, but it didn't explode. My skin didn't burn and my vision didn't change. Not yet anyway.

I felt my magic point itself at Ryan, like an arrow notched in a bow, and I felt it mold itself into the shape of his wish. The fixing of the broken nose sat firmly in the center of the wish, immoveable—but I could sense the formlessness that surrounded it.

Do you want to heal the rest of his injuries, too? Clean up the blood?

I registered the questions almost as clearly as if someone had asked them out loud. My magic was asking me to shape it. Just as Oliver had said, I couldn't go against the wording of the wish . . . but the details were up to me.

No, just the nose, I thought. And then: *Go.*

And with that, my magic exploded out of me—not eclipsing me with its power, like before, but carrying me along for the ride. I felt, in excruciating detail, the tendrils of my magic snaking into Ryan's skull, repairing cartilage and bone and blood vessels and flesh—and when I reached out, almost instinctively, to touch his face, the feeling magnified a hundredfold. I could practically *see* the wish at work.

Finally, its job finished, my magic receded into my body,

leaving me breathless and shaking and . . . *complete*. The word came into my head unbidden, and I filed it away for future examination. There was one more thing I had to do here.

"My vessel, please," I said, lifting my chin as I held out my hand, hoping he wouldn't put up a fight about it . . . but also kind of hoping he would, so I'd have an excuse to hit him again.

"Take it," he said, and threw the guitar pick at me. "Take it, and get the hell out of my room."

Which was exactly what I'd planned on doing—except that as soon as I retrieved my vessel from the floor, something started to happen. Something that felt uncomfortably similar to when I'd made my fourth wish: a tingling sensation that spread through my entire body, coating my skin and worming through my veins, *changing* me in a way that I knew I couldn't stop, even if I wanted to.

And when it was over, I felt . . . nothing at all.

It was only when Ryan blinked and looked around his room in surprise that it clicked: I'd disappeared. I'd become just what Oliver had said I would. A ghost, invisible to the human eye.

And I'd stay that way until I bound myself to a new master.

Fortunately, I had a plan for that part, too. Leaving Ryan alone with his bruised face and damaged ego, I jumped into the Between.

Chapter FOURTEEN

N aomi was sitting in front of her giant desktop Mac, typing rapidly, looking down every few seconds to check something in a notebook. I leaned over to see if it was anything interesting, but it was just a paper for her AP History class. Well, at least that explained why she was scowling.

Creeper, I thought to myself. It was time to stop spying and do what I'd come to do.

The next time her gaze moved back to the computer, I reached out, let go of the red guitar pick, and let it fall. It landed squarely in the middle of the notebook, covering part of Jefferson Davis's name.

Naomi saw it. She froze, peering at the pick. "What the . . ."

I couldn't remember if I'd told her what my vessel was, but I'd definitely told her how it worked. All she needed to do was pick it up.

After a quick glance around her room that yielded no clues

as to where the pick had come from, she finally reached for it. There it was. Thumb and forefinger. *Yes.*

The pain came, just as I'd known it would—just as it had on the night I'd gotten myself bound to Ryan—but to my surprise, it wasn't nearly as bad. And not just because I'd been expecting it, either. My magic knew the way this time. It was following a path that already existed, not forging a new one.

In seconds, my magic receded again, leaving the same cool, soothing sensation of mint behind, like a balm. I was solid again. Visible. I could feel it.

I could also feel that I was in yet another new body.

Before I could inspect it, though—

"Ohgod," came Naomi's voice, strangely high-pitched. She clutched her chair with one hand, and the edge of her desk with the other. "Ohgod ohgod. How are you—why—*who*—wait a second." She cast a glance down at the pick in her hand, and I could practically *see* her putting two and two together. She focused on me again. "Who are you?"

"It's me," I said quickly. "Margo, I mean. Um, usually, any-way. Right now, though—"

"You can change how you *look*?" she said, shooting up from her chair, making me take an instinctive step back.

"Um. Yes?" I had an accent. I couldn't tell what it was, but it was definitely there. "Shapeshifting is part of the genie thing, and—"

"And you didn't *tell* me?"

"Um. No . . . ? Hold on," I said, and darted over to her door, on the back of which hung her full-length mirror. I planted myself in front of it and took a look.

And burst out laughing.

"What?" said Naomi, who'd cautiously followed me over to the mirror. There was white noise coming from her head—an unintelligible jumble of wanting—but I ignored it.

"This!" I said, grinning at her as I gestured down at myself. "Look at this!"

Her eyebrows knitted. "I don't get it."

"When I get a new master, my magic gives me a new body," I explained. "It makes me look like someone my master will like and trust and, um, possibly also be attracted to. . . ."

I pointed to the wall above her bed—the only space in her room that she'd decorated with posters and magazine cutouts, instead of the classier fare that dominated the rest of the room. Most of the images were of her two favorite singers: Michael Jackson, who she'd started listening to right after he'd died, and Enrique Iglesias, who she'd been madly in love with ever since she could pronounce the phrase "madly in love."

I was just grateful that my magic hadn't made me look like a teenaged Michael.

I waggled my eyebrows as soon as she looked back at me again. "My name is Enrique," I said, and felt it becoming true. "*Bailamos*, Miss Sloane?"

It was a joke of a question, but I felt that become true, too.

Enrique loved to dance. And like his namesake, he was quite good at it.

Spots of pink erupted in Naomi's cheeks. "Oh god," she said. "Oh . . . my . . . god. Girl, this is wrong in so many ways."

Hysterical laughter spilled out of her, like she couldn't decide whether to be horrified or delighted—but I got the distinct impression that she was leaning toward horrified.

The thing was, I didn't look *exactly* like the picture on her wall. Aside from the fact that I was twenty years younger than the real Enrique, the shape of my face was slightly rounder, and my stature slightly bulkier. Completely intact, though, were the warm skin tone, the deep brown eyes, the pouty lips, the thick hair—all the bits Naomi had regularly waxed poetic about since she was six years old.

She was right. Hilarious though this might be, it was very, very wrong. Especially since I was dealing with someone who didn't trust magic to begin with.

I shifted back into myself. "Better?"

Naomi bit her bottom lip and let out a long *fffff* of a sigh. "Warn me next time you're gonna pull something like that, okay?"

"Definitely," I said. "Sorry. I can't control what body my magic creates when I get a new master, or else I'd've, you know, picked something less . . ."

"Yeah," she said. "I'd freaking hope so."

"Sorry," I said.

"It's cool." She sounded slightly more composed now that I was myself again. "Okay, so we'll get back to the shapeshifting stuff in a second—but first, let me get this straight. You want me to be your master? Like, three wishes, the whole deal?"

I nodded. "The whole deal. Except you're already my master. It happened as soon as you picked up my vessel."

"As soon as I . . ." Naomi narrowed her eyes. "Wait. Why didn't you ask me first?"

I frowned, slightly bemused by the question. "Why, would you have said no?"

But before she could answer, a sharp headache drilled through my skull. Right. Naomi being my master meant I had to start being careful around her questions.

"I mean, I didn't ask because I didn't think I needed to." That was truth enough to make the headache go away—but it wasn't the whole truth. I added, "And because there's one specific wish I need you to make. I did something, and . . . well, you need to fix it."

"What kind of something?" she said, looking at me like she was the mongoose and I was the cobra.

I took a deep breath, then said it as fast as my tongue would allow: "You have to wish to stop being in love with Ryan."

Naomi snorted. "Me? In love with that epic waste of a perfectly good baritone? Are you high or something?"

"No!" I said. "Look, I know you're in love with him, even

192

though you don't want to be. It's why you waited so long to tell everyone Ryan was spreading rumors about you. You didn't want him to stop liking you."

The white noise in her head sharpened—and though I still couldn't read her thoughts, I could guess what she wanted from me. I had to stop skirting the edge of the truth, and just get to the point.

I shifted again—this time into Amber.

Naomi jumped. "Holy—"

"I know."

"I said to *warn me next time*." And then understanding dawned, and she said, "Wait. Starbucks girl."

"Yeah, Amber," I said. "And I know, I should have told you before, but you never wanted to talk about Ryan—not that I blame you, really, because he's basically the worst person ever, but . . ."

"But?" she prompted.

"But he was my master before you were," I said, watching as her dark eyes went wide. "His first wish was for you to fall in love with him. At the party that night. He found my vessel, and I couldn't make him change his mind in time and—"

"Wait, wait, hold on," she said faintly, flapping a hand at me.

"I'm really sorry."

"I said *stop talking*, McKenna. God."

I stopped talking.

For a full minute, Naomi didn't look at me.

I concentrated on the white noise that surrounded her, trying to hear or see or feel something, *anything,* in the jumble. But nothing jumped out. I had no idea what she wanted from me.

Maybe she didn't know either.

Finally, she said, "Did your magic make you into this Amber girl for Ryan? Like it made you into, um, Enrique for me?"

That was when she finally looked at me again. I nodded, and her nose wrinkled in disgust. Since I couldn't have agreed more, I promptly shifted back, again, into my real self.

"But still," she said, far more quietly than before. "That wish. You have to be joking about that wish. That's just not . . ."

"I'm telling the truth," I insisted. "Seriously. If you don't believe me, just ask, point blank. Ask me, 'Margo, did you grant Ryan's wish and make me fall in love with him?' My magic will force me to answer honestly. I swear."

She side-eyed me. "It will?"

I nodded.

She seemed skeptical of this, too—but before I could think of a way to prove it to her, she said, "Okay. Last year, when I auditioned for *Bat Boy,* you said I sounded awesome. Were you lying?"

I sucked in a breath, remembering. Naomi had always claimed to be far more content behind the scenes than on stage, but last spring she'd decided to audition for the cast of the musical, just to see what would happen. It hadn't gone well.

"Um," I said, casting about for a diplomatic response. But the headache was creeping in. "Yeah. I lied."

Naomi raised an eyebrow. "So, how *did* I sound? Like, on a scale of one to awful?"

"Maybe an eight . . . ?"

"I knew it," she said, with a laugh that was genuine enough to set me at ease. "I knew I sucked. I never thought you'd actually say so, though."

I chanced a small smile. "So you believe me about the magic?"

That made her sober up a little. She twisted around so she was facing me directly. "Margo McKenna, did you or did you not grant a wish that made me fall in love with Ryan Weiss?"

"I did," I said.

I'd thought that would settle it, but she didn't stop there. "Margo McKenna, why the ever-loving hell did you not tell me about this wish sooner? Say, for instance, right when it happened?"

That was a harder question.

Rubbing my hands on the knees of my jeans, I said, "Well, you don't like magic. Like, remember that day at the mall when I offered to pay—"

But a lightning bolt of pain shot through my skull, stopping me from saying anything more. And I already knew why. Even if the money-out-of-thin-air had given me a good reason to continue keeping the wish from Naomi, it wasn't the reason I'd first decided not to tell her.

"No, that's not it," I said, and the headache receded just a little, leaving enough of itself behind to serve as a warning.

"Then what?" asked Naomi, looking a little bit scared. Not that I blamed her. The first time I'd seen one of those headaches attack Oliver, it had seriously freaked me out.

I looked up at her through the haze of pain, wondering what I had to say, and how much she would judge me when I said it, and—

And I knew what the answer was.

"I thought you'd be mad at me," I said. "I tried to stop him from making the wish, and I couldn't, so it was a little bit my fault that it happened, and . . . and I thought you'd be mad. That's why I didn't tell you."

The headache was gone. And Naomi was looking at me like I was a complete idiot—which maybe I was. She sighed. "Do I even need to tell you why that's the dumbest reason ever?"

"Heh," I said. "Probably not."

"Good," she said, clapping her hands together in a businesslike manner. "Then we can skip to the part where I tell you that having any kind of feelings at *all* for that giant bag of turds has been driving me *insane,* and thank *god* it was a wish so I can undo it."

I peered at her, trying to see if there was distrust still lurking below the surface of her apparent change of heart. "You sure? I mean, you said the money thing was cheating, and this is way bigger."

She leveled a look at me. "Yeah, but it'll also cancel out what Ryan did to me. Put things back to normal. Won't it? Or is it gonna have some weird side-effect-loophole thing that creates some even bigger problem?"

"No, no, nothing like that," I said. "Just keep the wish simple, and I'll take care of the rest. See, I can shape the wish. Make sure it does what you intended it to do."

She nodded slowly, apparently happy with my explanation. "So, how do we make this happen?"

I grinned. "Easy. Hold my vessel between your thumb and forefinger, just like this . . . and say 'I wish.'"

So she did exactly that, all without side-eyeing me even once. Maybe this was the way to make her trust my magic: by letting her use it for herself.

I stayed over at Naomi's for a few more hours after she made the wish, which, if I do say so myself, went exactly the way it was supposed to. She kept going on and on about the immediacy of the change in how she felt when I granted it, which made me feel a little bit like a superhero.

All in all, not bad for a Sunday evening.

When I jumped back into my still-locked bedroom and

heard my phone buzz, though, I found that there was one thing I hadn't planned for: Oliver.

The text that had just come in said, simply, MARGO? But it was only the most recent of six texts. Plus three missed calls.

I scrolled backward through the messages he'd sent:

9:46 P.M.—MARGO?

9:28 P.M.—CRAP, YOU PROBABLY DON'T HAVE YOUR PHONE W YOU.

8:34 P.M.—JUST LET ME KNOW IF YOU'RE OK . . .

7:19 P.M.—FELT MORE MAGIC. RLY HOPE IT'S JUST A CALL.

6:55 P.M.—MAYBE AM JUST BEING PARANOID, BUT WORRIED BOYFRIEND IS WORRIED! YOU OK?

6:41 P.M.—FELT MAGIC & CAN'T TELL WHAT IT WAS. DID RYAN DO SOMETHING, OR WAS IT JUST A CALL? LET ME KNOW IF YOU NEED MY HELP.

A pang of guilt shot through me as I read; I really should have remembered that he'd be able to feel it when I granted wishes. And given what had happened last night, I could hardly blame him for being paranoid. I started typing out an explanation on my phone, but it was too much. I deleted it all and sent instead:

COME OVER.

He appeared in seconds, all frantic energy and worried eyes that begged to be set at ease. "Are you okay?" he asked immediately.

I answered the best way I could think of: by throwing myself into his arms and drawing him down for a kiss. At first he didn't seem to know how to respond . . . but he relaxed quickly, wrapping his arms around me, holding me tightly, and putting all of his considerable kissing skills to very good use.

When I finally let go of him, he looked sort of stunned. "I'll take that as a yes . . . ?"

I laughed. "Very much yes. Sorry I didn't take my phone with me—but it's fine, Ryan didn't do anything."

"I felt magic, though," he said, his hands clutching tightly at my waist, betraying his lingering worry.

"That," I said proudly, "was Ryan making his third wish. You are looking at a free woman, my friend."

"That's . . . well, I mean, that's awesome, obviously," he said. "But he really made his last wish so soon? Why?"

The sound of Ryan's head hitting the wall. The brightness of the blood that streamed from his broken nose. The resignation in his voice when he'd finally wished himself whole again . . .

The aftershocks of magic were still thrumming through my body. I was alive and immortal and *powerful,* and right in front of me was a boy that I loved, looking at me with tender eyes, like maybe he would have to save me again.

How wrong he was.

"Because," I said, and hooked a finger through his belt loop, anchoring him to me, "I am very persuasive."

His bright eyes went sly, and he leaned down, nearly brushing my lips with his. Nearly. "Are you, now?"

"Yeah." I slid my hand across his shoulder, tucking it between his shirt and his hoodie. "For instance, right now I'm about to persuade you to take this off—"

The hoodie vanished, and my hand froze, suddenly robbed of purpose.

"Oh," I said. "Um."

"Hurray for magic, right?" he said eagerly. "Now the question is, one thing at a time, or all at once?"

"Wait, no," I said. "Neither. No magic."

He tilted his head a little. "But it's faster if I—"

"I don't want fast," I said frantically. "I want . . ."

What *did* I want? Something more natural, that was for sure. Something that sounded less like strip poker and more like two people pushing at each other's boundaries, a little bit at a time, without knowing where they'd want to stop. Or *if* they'd want to stop.

But I didn't know how to say that out loud without sounding completely cheesy, so instead I took hold of his T-shirt and eased it upward, letting my fingers slide across the skin of his chest as I went. Slowly, very slowly. And this time, he seemed to understand. He didn't use magic. Even when I tried to pull the shirt over his head, and it snagged on his nose and made him laugh, he didn't use magic.

I laughed along with him, and it felt so full. So real.

My fingers traced the planes and angles of his face and his neck and his chest, and all the soft places in between—the places that made him breathe a little deeper, made his eyes flutter closed, made it easy for me to push him back onto my little nest of pillows, which he let me do without any protest at all. I leaned over and kissed the little dip right in the center of his chest, letting my lips linger just long enough to feel his heartbeat. I kissed his collarbone. His throat. His lips.

"Margo," he whispered, barely audible. His eyes had gone dark and deep, and he was giving me that look—the one where all of a sudden, I felt like we were the only two people in the entire universe.

This was right.

This was exactly the way I wanted it to be.

I moved my hand down his chest, down his belly, toward the line where skin met fabric again . . . and then his jeans vanished. Suddenly he was lying underneath me in nothing more than a pair of blue striped boxer shorts.

The sight of it felt like a record skipping. My whole body sagged.

"Sorry," he said quickly, his face and neck going pink. "Habit. The let's-use-magic thing, I mean. I . . ."

I climbed off him and perched on the edge of the bed. In seconds, he was back in his jeans and shirt and hoodie. He rubbed self-consciously at his arm.

Habit. He'd done this so many times that he had *habits*.

It shouldn't have mattered. I knew how old he was. I knew he'd been with a lot of people before he'd met me. And I knew that didn't mean he loved me any less.

So why, right now of all times, couldn't I get those other people out of my head?

Giving me a tentative smile, he said, "Do-over?"

Maybe it was because I'd just turned myself into the sort of person who broke other people's noses. Maybe it was the way Naomi had snapped at me when I'd shifted in front of her. Maybe the aftershocks of magic were making me anxious, and none of this was really Oliver's fault at all.

But whatever the reason, the fact remained that the moment was long gone. I shook my head.

He didn't seem surprised.

"Will you still stay over, though?" I asked. "I know I'm not Amber anymore, so that wish won't affect me, but . . ."

"Like you even need to ask," he said, and leaned over to kiss me again. Softly, as though the last few minutes had never even happened. As though we were the same two people we'd always been.

Chapter FIFTEEN

When Naomi arrived in the calculus classroom on Monday, my mind was still replaying images of morning sunlight streaming across Oliver's sleepy face. Which meant it took me slightly longer than it should have to realize that everyone was staring at her. At first, nobody spoke.

Then Eli Simpson said, "Not cool, what you did to Ryan online."

"Hey," I said, and started to rise from my chair. If I could break Ryan's nose, I could damn well deal with Eli, too.

But Naomi held out a hand, stilling me. She tilted her head just so, giving Eli a cool smile. "Oh, no?" she asked. "Why not?"

Eli drew himself up and glared at her. "My buddy doesn't deserve people talking about him like that. He's a good guy. Get me?"

"No, he's not," came another voice—smaller than Naomi's, but firm. Callie Zumsky, who was playing Johanna in

Sweeney Todd, and whose name Naomi had mentioned in her post. "He's not a good guy. That's the whole point."

Kara Kristoff, a senior I didn't know too well, snorted and nodded to herself. But Simon actually spoke up. "Ryan's a dick, dude. About time someone had the balls to say it out loud."

"I'll say it out loud, too," I said. "Guess what? Ryan's a dick."

Naomi shot me a grin. I waggled my eyebrows at her, Oliver-style.

After class, as we walked to second period together, she said, "I did good, huh?"

"You did good," I agreed.

A girl let out a loud fake cough as she passed us—a cough that sounded a lot like "Lying slut." Yet another shouted "Work it, Sloane!" down the stairwell a few minutes later. Lots of people gave her dirty looks or admiring smiles, and plenty of things in between. Naomi ignored them all.

"This," she said, slowing to a stop just outside the French classroom, "is the other reason I didn't say anything sooner."

"What, you knew this would happen?" I asked as a curly-haired freshman boy winked at Naomi, then blushed and ran away.

She sighed, shaking her head like I was the dumbest person alive. "Ryan's popular. I'm popular, too." She wasn't bragging; it was just a statement of fact. "When one popular person basically declares war on another, everyone else is obviously gonna take sides."

"Huh." When she put it like that, it did seem obvious.

"But whatever. I have bigger things to worry about."

"Like your wishes?"

She gave me a look. "No. I can't think about—just, no." She took out her phone and pressed a button. "I meant this."

It was a text from Kristina Sloane. Naomi's sister.

NOW SHE WANTS THE WEDDING DOWN IN GA, SO IT'S EASIER FOR THEIR FAMILY. WHAT ABOUT MY FAMILY? AND ONCE AGAIN, JARED'S NO HELP.

"This engagement just happened, what, two weeks ago?" I asked. "Because that's a lot of planning going on already."

"Tell me about it," said Naomi. "Personally, I think she should back out. Ugh. I'll call her at lunch."

"I'll let you eat *my* lunch," said an oily-looking junior guy, whose name I didn't know.

"That doesn't even mean anything!" Naomi shouted as he passed. Then she turned back to me with murder in her eyes. "This day is so fired."

"I could zap his brain for you," I offered brightly. "Just make a wish."

I was half joking, but Naomi's answering glare was entirely serious. "I'll make a wish when I'm good and ready, McKenna. Don't rush me."

After school, I found a nice surprise: Oliver, waiting for me by my car. When he caught sight of me, he held up a picnic basket. Not a cooler, like my parents used to cart food around on road trips, but an actual double-lidded picnic basket. The kind that would make Yogi Bear drool. There was even a red-and-white checkered cloth peeking out from under one of the lids.

"You're kidding me," I said. "What's in there?"

Grinning wider, he nodded at the basket and said, "One tisket and one tasket. Come with me."

"Where?"

"China! If you're up for it, that is."

"I'm up for it," I said. "Bring on the panda bears. But can we maybe find a more secluded spot to disappear from?"

Oliver looked around and sighed. Students were beginning to swarm the place, laughing and chattering as they headed to their cars.

"Just duck," said Oliver, grabbing my hand. We crouched between my car and the one next to it, and then, without even moving, we were surrounded by gray.

When we stepped out into the real world again, it was pitch-black. I stumbled a little, but Oliver's arms were there, waiting to steady me. Once I righted myself again, I felt around with my foot to make sure it was safe. That was how I realized we were on a staircase. The air was thick and heavy, almost like it was about to rain.

"I, ah, can't exactly see."

"Nope," he said, very close to my ear. "It's almost three in the morning here. Just hold still for a sec. Oh, and could you close your eyes?"

I closed them. Oliver let go of me and moved away, and I heard a weird rustling and a *whoosh* sound, followed shortly by another, and then another. Heat reached my face, and I heard the sharp crackle of flames. A campfire? Maybe there were marshmallows in that picnic basket.

"Okay," he said at last. "Open your eyes."

We were on a stone staircase, lined on either side by short stone walls. At various intervals were torches—old-school, let's-throw-someone-in-a-dungeon-style torches, illuminating the blackness. The steps were horribly uneven, and sagged in the middle like they'd been worn down by trillions of footsteps.

Beyond the torches' light, I could just make out the staircase tapering off into the distance, stretching down before us and then up again, across rolling hills beyond what my vision could reach. Towers dotted the line of stone here and there, and on either side of us the land fell away in gentle slopes. I couldn't see signs of civilization anywhere. No lights. No people. Just Oliver, me, a couple of torches, and a picnic basket, on a stone structure that felt utterly ancient.

It was another moment before it came to me.

"Great Wall of China," I said. "Right?"

"You bet," he said proudly. "No pandas here, I'm afraid, but we can always come back during the day to see those guys. For now, have some impressive architecture instead!"

It really was impressive, despite the lack of pandas.

"And," said Oliver, bending down to open the basket, "I brought snacks. Chinese snacks, since, you know, Great Wall and all. Have at it."

He pulled out the thin checkered blanket, and spread it over the stairs. Then he upended the basket, spilling out a pile of brightly wrapped packages, like a pile of Easter candy. I picked up a small package. "Shrimp-flavored biscuits? Those can't be edible."

"Oh yeah, those are amazing," he said. "Maybe a little bit of an acquired taste, though. Here, try these first. These are my favorites."

He tossed me a long, round canister; I read the label and laughed. "Blueberry potato chips? For real?" I ripped the top off and popped one into my mouth. It was the most confusing thing I'd ever tasted.

"Give me one," said Oliver, snaking his hand into the canister as he sat down beside me. We crunched in silence for a moment.

"I'm pretty sure," I said slowly, after I swallowed, "that chip just gave me an existential crisis."

He side-eyed me. "In a good way, at least?"

"I think so . . . ?"

"Excellent," he said with a grin. "So, listen. I wanted to talk to you about something."

He sounded unusually serious all of a sudden. Swallowing the last bit of Frankenchip, I said, "Something bad?"

"No," he said quickly. "Just . . . something important. It's about James."

James—Oliver's old master. Right. So much had happened this weekend that I'd very nearly forgotten about him. I nodded for Oliver to go on.

"Well, there's a reason he's been looking for me," said Oliver. "He wanted to ask me a favor."

"Oh yeah?" I said, feeling suddenly wary. "What does he want? More wishes, right?"

"In a sense. Although he didn't know it'd require a wish until I told him."

"What are you talking about?"

"Well," said Oliver, looking down at his jeans, and then out into the night, and then finally back at me. "Well, well, well. Here's the thing. The thing is . . . well, James wants to become a genie."

"Wait, what?" I said, absolutely certain I'd misheard him.

"A genie," Oliver said anxiously. "Like us. He wants to be one."

At first, all I could do was stare. It had never occurred to me that *we could make more genies.* That we wouldn't always be the only ones, if we didn't want to be. That the story wasn't over yet, and this—Oliver and me, sitting on the Great Wall of China, eating blueberry potato chips—wasn't a happily ever after.

I was an idiot.

"Um," I said. "What did you tell him?"

Oliver smiled thinly. "I said I had to talk to you first."

That should have made me feel better. I knew that. But how could I have an opinion about something that I hadn't realized was an option until five seconds ago?

I said, "Oh."

"It would be a lot of responsibility," Oliver continued, putting his hand on my knee, rubbing his thumb back and forth. "We'd have to take him under our wings a little. Teach him how to use his magic. How to deal with bad masters. You know."

I did know, because that was what Oliver had done with me—was *still* doing with me—in between kisses and talk of magic numbers and undressing each other, with magic or without. How could he take something he was doing with me, and do the same thing with someone else?

He peered at me. "What are you thinking?"

I was thinking that the past few weeks had seriously changed the way I thought of myself—but through it all, one thing had remained constant: knowing who I was to Oliver, even if I didn't know who I was to myself. I was his girlfriend, his protégé, the person he loved. I was the only living person who really understood him.

If James became a genie, all of that could change.

"I'm not sure yet," I replied.

Oliver nodded and, after a moment, went on: "It could also be fun, probably. Useful, too. I mean, the more of us there are, the more people we'd have to talk to about . . . you know. All the stuff that regular people won't understand."

"Sounds like group therapy," I murmured.

He laughed softly. "Yes and no. You wouldn't *have* to talk to them. The option would just be there if you wanted it."

I didn't want it. I knew that much already. I had people to talk to already: Oliver for all the genie-related stuff, Naomi for all the human stuff. Why would I need anyone else?

"Plus, I liked it when there were more of us," he said, squeezing my knee as he looked out into the darkness. "And now that there isn't someone hunting us down . . ."

"You're welcome for that, by the way," I said, trying for a sassy grin. Only partially succeeding. I wasn't feeling too sassy at the moment.

Oliver squeezed my knee again. "Thank you, awesome girlfriend of mine," he said, his eyes glinting softly in the torchlight. "But you know what I mean, right? It'd be nice. If there were more of us. And if things work out with James, we could even find more people to make fourth wishes. . ."

I paused, taking in his taut, tense body. His serious expression. The way his hand gripped my knee, like a life raft. This clearly meant more to him than he was letting on.

"Seems like you've made up your mind already," I said.

Giving me a smile, he said, "Well. Just because I think we should do it, doesn't mean you have to agree with me. You should take some time and think about it, if you want. And here's his phone number, just in case you want to talk to him yourself."

I took the folded piece of paper and tucked it into my pocket, already breathing a little easier. I didn't have to make a decision right now. I could let the idea sink in enough to think about it rationally. I could make a plan.

But then he said, "It's just that I *can't* do this without you."

Something in his tone, a halting little something, sent up a red flag in my mind. "How do you mean?"

"I mean," he said, "it can't be me who grants him a fourth wish. It would have to be you."

"Me?" I squeaked. "Wait, wait, wait. Why me?"

"Because it's been too long since I granted his first three wishes," said Oliver. "The binding we had when he was my master—it's long gone now. Wore off a few weeks after his third wish, same as it does with every master. And since I've already been bound to him once, I can't be bound to him again. Which means I can't grant him another three wishes— which means I can't grant him a fourth."

"But," I said, shaking my head, "but I can't. I haven't even been a genie for two full weeks yet. I'm only on my second master. If it's me granting the wish, that makes him my responsibility, and I can't teach someone else to use his magic when I can barely use my own . . ."

"You're doing just fine at using your magic!" said Oliver, brightening as he turned his body to face me fully. "Look how far you've come already. You can maintain your own body for an entire school day, with nobody the wiser. You're jumping through the Between like an old pro. You even persuaded Ryan to make a third wish when you didn't want to be bound to him anymore."

"Yeah, by beating him up until he had to heal himself with a wish," I shot back.

And instantly regretted it.

At first, he just went sort of blank, like I'd started speaking gibberish. Then his smile lost its honesty, and he removed his hand from my knee. "You did that?" he asked, his voice just as brittle as his expression.

"Well, okay, that's kind of an exaggeration," I said, trying for a laugh. "All I did was break his nose, but he's fine now, so—"

"You broke his nose?"

"And then I healed it," I said, feeling suddenly defensive. "It's fine. I did what I had to do, and now it's over. The point is—"

"The point is that you *broke* his *nose*." Oliver heaved himself to his feet, looking out over the wall, into the blackness beyond. "That's . . . not like you."

I stood up, too. "Desperate times," I said to his back. "He attacked me, remember?"

"And you got away," he said softly, turning back toward me. The torchlight played oddly over his face, making his eyes look almost hollow. "It was over. He was going to make a third wish. You were going to grant it as Tony. That would've been the end, and you wouldn't have had to turn into . . . *that*."

He shook his head, almost like he regretted what he'd just said.

Almost.

"Turn into what?" I asked icily. "Someone who takes action instead of sitting around and hoping not to get attacked again?"

His eyes narrowed. "Someone who uses violence to get what they want."

"It was one time, Oliver," I said, throwing my hands up in exasperation. "And yeah, okay, next time I'll figure out a better way. A way that'll hopefully involve a lot less blood, because that was seriously gross. But that's exactly my point, see? I'm still figuring this out. I can't start teaching other people what I don't even know myself."

"Well, it'd be *me* teaching him, obviously," said Oliver. "Not you. All you'd have to do is grant his wish."

Something in that *obviously* made me pause. Made me look at him a little more closely. "Wait," I said. "That thing you said before, about the binding. How are you so sure it's gone?"

"Um," he said, looking suddenly guarded. "Well. Because I checked."

There was something he was deliberately not telling me. I had a feeling I knew what it was.

"When you say checked," I said slowly, hoping I was about to be wrong, "do you mean you tried to turn him already?"

"Um," said Oliver again, and licked his lips. "Well."

"You try to turn someone into a genie without even telling me first, and then you turn around and judge *me* for hitting Ryan freaking *Weiss*? Are you kidding me?"

"Hey, hey, I'm not judging you," he said, holding his hands up like stop signs. "I'm just . . . expressing concern. That's all. I'm just afraid of what could happen if you keep going down that road. . . ."

"What the hell's that supposed to mean?" I asked, crossing my arms over my chest.

"Your second wish," he said shortly. "I seem to recall someone hurting you badly enough that you had to use up a wish to heal yourself. I mean, forgive me if I'm jumping to conclusions, but the similarity is kind of—"

"You're afraid I'm turning into Xavier," I said.

Silence. Heavy air hung between us. Oliver swallowed. "Well," he said.

"I'm not him," I said through gritted teeth. "I'm nothing like him. You know that."

"Of course I know that," he said quickly. A little too quickly.

"All I want is control over my own life."

"I *know*."

"And I'm not going to start killing people if I don't get what I want."

He looked sharply at me, his eyes bright and cold. "You mean like you didn't kill Xavier?"

My chest seized up; my jaw literally dropped. "That . . . Oliver, that is way out of line."

"Sorry, no, I know. I just meant that you never would've imagined doing that before——"

"I *saved* your *life*," I said, anger sizzling across my skin, burning my fingertips. I curled my hands into fists. "And I wasn't going to, either. I asked first, remember? You said no. I only did it because you changed your mind. You *told* me I should wish him free, so you are *not* allowed to throw that back in my face."

"I know," he said, holding his hands up as he stepped back from me. "Listen——"

But I did not listen. I'd heard enough already.

"And yeah, okay," I said, "maybe you're fine with flitting around from place to place, breaking into abandoned apartments instead of having a real home, sleeping with every master you have because it's your job to make them happy or whatever——"

"Whoa, wait a second . . ."

"——but I can't do that. My job is to make *me* happy. And if some asshole comes along and tries to change how I think and makes me want stuff that I really, really do *not* want? Then yeah, I'm gonna break his goddamn nose. And if you don't get that, then there is no freaking way I'm granting a fourth wish for that seven-year-old ex-master of yours."

"Wait, what does that have to do with—"

"Everything, Oliver!" I said. "Absolutely everything. Like, this guy James wants to be a genie, but does he actually know what that means? Sure, you get awesome magic that takes you anywhere in the world, and infinite money, and you don't have to go to school, but what's the price for all that? Well, let's see. A body that turns into someone else for every new master, so you actually have to make an effort to be your real self. Friends who find out what you are, and then start looking at you like you're a completely different person, which maybe you are, but you don't know for sure, because you're someone new for everyone you meet. And on top of that, you have a master who can literally do *whatever he wants* to you. So what are you going to teach him? To just sit back and take it, like *you* always do?"

"Always?" Oliver echoed, his face going stony as he stepped toward me, so close that we could have kissed. "Margo, you have no idea what kind of things I've done to get by, so don't you dare talk about my life like you actually know anything. I've been doing this for ten times as long as you've been alive. It's hard, and it's lonely, but I've been making the best of it the only way I know how. James can learn to do the same. And if you're smart, you will, too."

I glared at him. "If I'm smart, in other words, I'll just let myself get assaulted next time."

"Jesus Christ, Margo, that's not what I—" He cut himself off, making a gesture filled with far more anger than meaning. "Fine. If you think that's what I mean, then whatever, keep on thinking that. I just . . . I thought you knew me better than that. That's all."

And with that, he vanished.

I waited in stunned silence, all alone on the Great Wall of China, with my hands shaking and my heart in my throat, for him to come back. He didn't. I pulled out my phone so I could call him and give him a piece of my mind . . . but I had no idea what to say. Shoving my phone back into my pocket, I knelt and began stuffing the sweets back into the picnic basket.

I'd been right to force Ryan into making a third wish.

Hadn't I?

Chapter SIXTEEN

A little while later, there was a knock on my bedroom door. Which was just fine, since I'd been reading the same page of *The Great Gatsby* for what felt like seventeen hours.

"Come in," I said, and Mom's face peered around the door.

"I saw your car in the driveway," she said. "Do you have the night off?"

I glanced at my clock. It was ten minutes to seven—ten minutes till rehearsal started—which meant I should have been back at the school already. When the hell had that much time passed? How had I not noticed?

But I just smiled at her. "No, I'm just running late," I lied, getting up from my desk chair and stretching my arms over my head.

"Aw, too bad," said Mom. "We were about to order Greek food. I thought maybe you'd want some. And Oliver, if he's around."

"Why would Oliver be around?" I asked quickly, trying very

hard not to think of the picnic basket hidden in my closet. Or the anger burning in his eyes, just before he'd disappeared. Or James.

Mom must have seen something in my face, though, because she stepped inside. Just one step. "Margo, honey, are you okay?"

I wasn't. I'd broken someone's nose yesterday—and, hell, I'd *killed* someone else just a couple weeks ago—and the one person who was supposed to understand why, didn't understand at all. Instead he was all gung-ho about creating more genies and teaching them to live like he did. This was the guy I'd stopped being human for?

"Yeah, I'm fine," I said.

"Are you sure?" Mom's eyes were warm and serious, and I knew she was ready to understand whatever I chose to tell her. I felt a surge of affection for her, like I hadn't felt since way before she'd remarried Dad.

I wondered, just for a moment, what would happen if I'd told her about the fourth wish. About what Oliver was, and what I'd become. I could tell her about the fight I'd had with Oliver. I could ask her to tell me who'd been right and who'd been wrong.

But what if she reacted like Naomi had?

"No," I said. "I'm just . . . I don't know, I'm just really tired lately. Actually, could I get in on that Greek food? I think I'm gonna blow off rehearsal."

Mom's eyebrows shot up. "That doesn't sound like you."

I laughed. "No kidding."

"But I'm glad," she said. "I haven't seen much of you lately, and we have plans to talk about!"

My heart sank.

"What kind of plans?" I asked, even though I already knew the answer. These days, when my mom made plans, they only ever concerned one thing.

She beamed at me. "Your father and I are going to Venice! Not until after your play, of course. We wouldn't miss that for the world. And it's only for two weeks, so we'll be back in plenty of time to help you get ready for graduation."

"I don't think graduation is something you have to help me with," I said coolly. "And actually, never mind about the Greek food. I should get to rehearsal. It's too late in the game to just blow it off."

"Oh, honey, are you sure?" said Mom, looking crestfallen.

She was so freaking clueless, it made me want to scream. "Yeah, I'm sure. But we'll talk about Venice tomorrow, okay? And then we can talk about how I'm not going to college. Plans for everyone!"

Mom was speechless for a moment, which was oddly satisfying. "What in the world are you talking about?"

"College. I'm not going." I said this with all the conviction I could muster, even though I hadn't even had enough time to process Oliver's suggestion, let alone make a decision about it. I watched my mom, waiting for her to get mad—almost *wanting* her to get mad.

But she didn't. She just asked, very carefully, "What brought this on?"

I shrugged. "A bunch of stuff."

She peered closely at me, like maybe she could see the real answer somewhere on my face. "What about Oliver?" she said at last. "Is he planning on college?"

So she assumed I'd changed my mind because of Oliver. It was a fair assumption, even though it wasn't true in exactly the way she probably thought.

"No," I said. "He's a sophomore. He's not planning on much of anything just yet."

"Oh, I see," she said. "You want to stay home so you can be close to him."

I almost protested . . . but if I let her keep thinking that, then at least I wouldn't have to come up with a better cover story on my own. I ducked my head a little, trying to look embarrassed that she'd found me out.

But she just looked thoughtful. Finally, she said, "You should defer. That way, if you decide to go next year, you won't have to reapply."

I blinked. That was actually kind of a brilliant idea.

"Huh," I said. "Yeah. Maybe I'll do that."

"Although, you shouldn't stay home the entire time," she added. "You should backpack across Europe. Go on safari.

Something like that. Me, I followed Jack Kerouac's route across the country after I finished high school. Done to death, I know, but I had a lot of fun."

I gaped at her.

"What?" she asked, smiling through her defensive tone. "A lot of people did the Kerouac thing. They still do, I think."

"I just . . . I didn't think you'd be so *okay* with this. With *any* of this," I said, spreading my hands wide.

"Why wouldn't I be?" said Mom with a little laugh. "We've all got to find our own path eventually. Deviate from the norm a little to figure out who we are. I'm glad you're starting to find yours—even if it means putting your future on hold for the sake of a boy with no parents." Her face went soft. "I found my path when I remarried your dad. Hell, I'm finding it every time I take another week off work to go someplace I've never been before."

I took a moment to let that sink in. Despite all the energy I'd put into being annoyed by my parents' vacations, I'd never actually thought about what those vacations meant to her.

"So . . . you're saying I should just do what I want?" I asked warily. "Even if it means not going to college?"

"Even if it means not going to college *yet,*" she said. "I want you to do what makes you happy, but I also don't want you living in my basement when you're forty."

In the end, I was glad I didn't stay home from rehearsal. Not only was it a great distraction from the Mom stuff and the college stuff and the goddamn Oliver stuff—it was also the perfect place to see exactly how seriously everyone was taking Naomi's post.

Which was to say, pretty seriously.

First, there was the hush that fell over the auditorium when Ryan walked in, his face bruised and his chin held high. It only lasted a few seconds, but it was long enough that I knew everyone's minds were on the same thing.

Second, there was the moment he bumped into me as I headed for the stage. He seemed surprised to see me there, but only gave me a cursory "Oh, sorry" before returning his attention to what had distracted him in the first place. I followed his gaze and saw Jill Spalding, another senior in the cast, hips swaying as she walked away.

I went from zero to livid in no time flat, and I literally had to bite my tongue to keep from saying something. But as it turned out, I didn't have to.

"Hey, Ryan," came Simon's voice from a few feet away. "Checking out Jilly? That mean you're gonna start saying you slept with her, too?"

A couple people snickered, including me; Jill turned around, clearly horrified. "Gross," she said. "Stop looking at me."

Ryan turned and stormed away.

Then, of course, there was Miss Delisio. Before she called places, she gathered us and made the speech she always did before the Act Two stumble-through. But in addition to her usual speech material, which was mostly about how we shouldn't worry too much about screwing up, she added a bit about the importance of concentrating on our roles and leaving outside feelings off the stage.

By the end of the speech, Naomi was practically glowing. "Keep outside feelings off the stage?" she whispered to me as I took my place in the wings. "When Weiss's face looks like *that*? Yeah, that'll totally happen. Wonder who hit him, anyway."

I made myself shrug. "Who knows? Maybe nobody. Maybe he ran into a brick wall."

"Nah, that's the kind of bruise a fist makes," said Naomi. "If I ever find out who it is, man . . ."

She headed back toward her booth, shaking her head and smiling.

I thought about running after her and telling her it had been me—especially since I knew she'd approve, even though Oliver didn't. What stopped me, though, was the fact that I'd used magic to hit him. Specifically, to make myself *know* how to hit him. I didn't want to explain that to her, when she'd probably just call it cheating.

I kept quiet and took my place for the top of Act Two.

Chapter *SEVENTEEN*

Oliver didn't call that night—or the next night, either. And on Wednesday, rehearsal was canceled because Miss Delisio had some emergency family thing that she couldn't get out of.

I had to find something else to do. Something that didn't involve staring at my phone and being pissed off at Oliver and hoping hoping hoping he would call.

So I decided it was time to make good on my promise to Vicky. She wanted acting lessons, and I wanted a distraction. Perfect.

We met in the auditorium at seven o'clock, which was exactly the same time a rehearsal would have begun, and started with "The Worst Pies in London," Mrs. Lovett's first and trickiest song. The entire thing was a one-sided conversation between Mrs. Lovett and Sweeney, but since Simon wasn't there, she sang a cappella to a paint-splattered folding chair instead.

After about fifteen seconds of watching from the first row as she moved jerkily through the blocking that Miss Delisio had given her—kneading bits of invisible dough, checking her invisible oven, squashing invisible bugs—I started to remember, with great clarity, why I'd resented Vicky for getting this role. She was wooden and robotic, and she sang her lyrics like she had no idea what any of the words meant. The freaking folding chair was a better actor than she was.

But I kept my mouth firmly shut and let her keep going until finally, somewhere around the lyric about baking cats into pies, she stopped on her own.

"See?" she said, throwing her hands up. "This song is a nightmare. I get why the lines jump around like that, because she's doing so many things at once, but it doesn't feel . . . I dunno . . ."

"Real?" I suggested, getting out of my seat and moving toward the stage.

"I guess so," she said unhappily. "I don't know how to fix it."

I leaned my elbows on the lip of the stage, thinking hard. "Well," I began slowly. "Okay, here's something to start with. What do you *want* in this scene?"

She shifted uneasily. "For people not to fall asleep during my song."

And there it was. The first major problem.

"I don't mean you as in Vicky. I mean you as in Mrs. Lovett. In this scene, you are Mrs. Lovett, not Vicky. It's called *acting*." It was probably a mean thing to say, but to my surprise, Vicky actually laughed. "So what do you, Mrs. Lovett, want in this scene?"

"Ummmm . . ." Her eyes darted around, like something out in the auditorium might give her an answer. "More customers? Better pies?"

I nodded, willing myself to be patient. This was, after all, someone who had never been in a play before. "Sure, that's what you *say* you want. But that's not what you're actually trying to get. Why are you telling Sweeney all this stuff about yourself?"

I held my hands out to Vicky, half hoping to see a lightbulb go on over her head. But she just looked at me blankly.

So I answered for her: "You want someone to talk to. I mean, look at your first lines. You haven't had a customer in forever, so when this guy comes in, you sit him down and tell him your whole life story—"

"Because she wants him on her side," finished Vicky. "She wants a confidant."

"Yes!" I said. "But, not she. You."

"*I* want a confidant," amended Vicky.

"Yes," I said again. "And imagine what that feels like, you know? Not having anyone to talk to for that long."

Vicky wrapped her arms around herself, and I stopped,

realizing just how dumb that sounded. She didn't have to imagine. This was a girl who'd used magic to make people pay attention to her. She mumbled something under her breath.

"What?" I said.

"I said, who would want to talk to her? She's insane."

Problem number two. I let out a long, slow breath. "Maybe she is, and maybe she isn't. But even if she were—if *you* were—would you know it? No. But you would still know what you *want*. You want Sweeney. So that's what you have to play."

She nodded slowly, but still looked hesitant. "She's in love—*I'm* in love with him by the end of the play. Do you think I'm already falling in love with him in this scene? Or at least, you know, interested?"

Her face went beet-red as she asked the question, and I grinned. "You're at *least* interested," I said. "So yeah, play that, too. If you were interested in someone like that, how would you behave around them?"

Vicky froze. "Um. Me me, or Mrs. Lovett me?"

That gave me pause. I'd meant the character, of course, but it was a fair question. And it gave me an idea. "Both, actually," I said. "I mean, how did you act when you started getting interested in Simon?"

I hadn't thought it possible, but her face went even redder. "That's different," she said, sitting down so that we were closer and she could whisper. "I didn't . . . I didn't go after him like Lovett goes after Sweeney. Simon asked *me* out."

I shouldn't ask. I knew I shouldn't. But before I could help it, the question came tumbling out: "Before or after you made that popularity wish?"

Vicky's shoulders hunched up, and she looked away from me. A moment passed—a moment in which I silently cursed my stupid mouth and its stupid, stupid questions—and then she stood up.

"Let's just work on the song, okay?" she said.

"Yeah," I said quickly. "All I meant was . . . find something from your own life that you can use in this scene."

"I know what you meant." She bit her lip, hesitating like she was trying to decide something very important—and then sat down again. "It was after the wish. But Simon knows. He knows what I wished for, and he knows it probably affected him, and he says he doesn't care."

"Really?" I said.

"Yeah," she said with a little smile. "But whether he cares about it or not, I'm still pretty sure that he wouldn't like me at all without that wish. He wouldn't have even noticed me in the first place."

I didn't know what to say to that, especially since she was probably right.

"But whatever," she said, rolling her eyes at herself. "It's not like it's your problem, right? Me and my stupid wish."

"Why didn't you undo it?" I asked. "You had another wish left. You could have just used it to undo the popularity wish, instead of giving it up. I mean, you probably still could. I'm sure Oliver wouldn't mind."

She smiled at me, sort of sadly. "I've thought about it. But the thing is, I really wanted that wish. I wanted people to like me. I just didn't know how much everything would change, or how quickly. But that was *my* fault, you know? I made this totally life-changing wish, and then I got all freaked out when it, well, changed my life." She laughed at herself, in a way that actually made me smile. "So I figured, I can either undo the wish and pretend it never happened . . . or I can deal with the consequences."

"Deal with the consequences?"

"Yes," she said firmly. "People like me all of a sudden? Fine, then, I'll try and be the kind of person that other people like! So there!"

Somewhere in there, my jaw had literally dropped. Seeing me staring, Vicky blushed all over again. "Or, uh, something like that."

I laughed. "No, not 'something like that.' *Exactly* like that. That's . . . awesome. Seriously."

"Um, thanks."

I grinned. "Now, are you going to kick this stupid song's ass, or what?"

She narrowed her eyes, took a breath, and started singing again without even waiting for my cue. It still wasn't great, but that burst of energy gave the song way more life than it'd ever had before. I hopped up onstage and started mimicking Simon's blocking, so she could sing to me instead of the folding chair.

I gave her as many Sweeney-ish reactions and expressions as I could, and this time she actually made it through the whole song. Clearly pleased with herself, she held the last note for a lot longer than she was supposed to, but I still waited for her to finish before I clapped. And then we did it again.

Once Vicky discovered that nothing horrible would happen if she actually sang loudly, gave different inflections to different words, and *acted* her lines instead of reciting them in her usual robotic monotone, she grew increasingly confident. And the whole time, I thought about what she'd just told me.

I'll try and be the kind of person that other people like.

It sounded like the simplest thing in the world, but I could see how hard it was for her. I'd seen it in the terrified look on her face when she'd first taken me aside and asked me for acting lessons—and I saw it again now, in the moments between her lines, when she looked, just for a split second at a time, like she wanted to run and hide and quit the play and live in the woods and never speak to another human being again.

But every single time, she pushed through it and kept on going.

Because that wish had changed her life, and instead of clinging desperately to the way she used to be—which was to say, painfully shy—she was forcing herself to change, too.

I'd always thought of Vicky, when I bothered to think of her at all, as a scared little wisp of a girl. But now, I couldn't help thinking that maybe, in some ways, she was a thousand times braver than me.

Chapter EIGHTEEN

Vicky and I worked together the next night, the night after that, and all through the weekend, before and after rehearsals and sometimes even on breaks. Simon even showed up for moral support from time to time—although his version of moral support primarily consisted of shouting Vicky's name whenever she hit a good note, which always made her blush and forget her lines. Eventually, I had to tell him to keep quiet or get out.

Monday, four days before opening night, was our first rehearsal with the pit orchestra. Mostly comprised of students that George had plucked from the band, the pit was the last addition to the company of the musical. He'd been rehearsing them separately from us until now, and today we were supposed to run through the whole show—or at least as much of the show as we could get through—with the entire pit instead of the piano-only accompaniment we were used to.

"House lights down, go," called Naomi from her stage manager's booth in the wings, just a few feet away from me.

Nothing happened. Naomi adjusted her headset. "I said *go*. Come on, people, get with it. We're already five minutes behind schedule."

The house lights went down.

Simon nudged me. "Got your earplugs?" he said with a grin. I grinned back. Jackson High's band was not renowned for its overflowing supply of talent, so the first rehearsal with the pit was always a screechy, off-key disaster.

"Don't need 'em," I said. "I like to hear them play. It's a huge ego boost."

He nudged me again, his arm lingering against mine a little longer than it probably should have. "Like you need the ego boost," he whispered. "You're always great. Or is that because of your mag—"

"Simon," I hissed, looking around to make sure nobody had heard. "We talked about this."

Repeatedly, in fact. Both he and Vicky were under strict instructions never to bring up the genie thing at school.

"Sorry, sorry, I know," he said. "Point is, these guys are gonna be a bigger disaster than Ryan's Chewie picture."

I gave him a sidelong look. "Than what now?"

Simon stared at me and, after a moment, snickered. "Dude, you haven't seen it?" I shook my head, perplexed. "Okay, but you've seen the blog, right?"

"Simon, what are you talking about?'

"Oh, you're kidding," he said gleefully. "Okay, when you

get home, check your email. I'll send you the link. It's called 'Ryan Slept With Your Mom,' and it's all these captioned pics of, like, people Ryan says he slept with. You know, stuff like Lady Gaga and Dead Elvis and all those Real Housewives. And that was pretty funny and whatever, but then someone put up a pic of Ryan and Chewie—you know, Chewbacca from *Star Wars*—and it exploded."

I stared at him.

"Seriously, dude," he said, "how did you not hear about this? Do you, like, not go online *ever*?"

We started the show a moment later, so I didn't have to answer.

The run-through went just about as poorly as I'd expected; the pit band even threw *Simon* off-key. What surprised me, though, was that despite the general awfulness of the pit, the rhythm remained steady throughout. Whoever George had on percussion actually knew their stuff.

My first real entrance was about halfway through the first act: a song called "Pirelli's Miracle Elixir." I performed it for the small ensemble that had gathered onstage as townspeople, and I was also supposed to break the fourth wall, singing to the audience as though they were part of the show. So when I looked out beyond the edge of the stage, I sneaked a peek at the pit, to see if I could spot the drummer.

It was Gwen.

I almost choked when I saw him. An entire week of not speaking to me, and Oliver had the nerve to show up *here*? In my rehearsal for my musical, in *my school*?

George raised his hand and closed it into a fist, which brought the pit screeching to a halt. I realized that I'd fumbled the last few lines of my song, which was something I'd never done before. My face went hot.

"Hold on, people," said Naomi from her booth. "You okay, McKenna?"

"Yeah, sorry," I mumbled.

"No harm done," said Miss Delisio. "Take it from the top of the second verse."

So we did. I didn't look at Gwen again, and I didn't screw up any more lines.

But when Miss Delisio called for a ten-minute break, I peered around the curtain and into the theater. Gwen was talking to George, who was nodding with a grin on his face. She—or rather, he, as in Oliver—mimed hitting something with a drumstick. George laughed.

Was Oliver bound to my musical director?

"Who's the hottie talking to the Ninja?" came a voice from beside me, making me jump. Simon was peering over my shoulder.

I shrugged, not trusting myself to speak. I was too afraid something like *That's my boyfriend* would come out.

"I'm gonna go say hi," he said, starting out across the stage. Then he reconsidered and turned back to me. "You should come with. It'll look less suspicious if I'm with a girl."

I thought about pointing out that it would be suspicious anyway, but instead I found myself following Simon. And jumping off the stage. And coming face-to-face with Oliver's nose-ringed alter ego.

He smiled when he saw me, a warm expression that I couldn't bring myself to return.

"You," Simon declared, "are an awesome drummer."

"Thanks," replied Oliver, raising Gwen's eyebrows. "And you're an awesome, uh, cannibalistic barber."

Simon glowed.

George gave Oliver a sidelong smile. "Simon Lee, Margo McKenna. Two of our stars. This is Gwendolyn Niall, a friend of mine. Drummer dropped out last week, so she stepped in."

"Niall?" I blurted out, before I could stop myself. Niall was the name Xavier had used when he and Oliver had first met, back when Oliver had been human.

"Yeah," said Oliver. His green eyes hardened almost imperceptibly. "Why?"

"Nothing," I said, narrowing my eyes so he'd know I was lying. "Nothing at all. Yeah, you're a good drummer."

"Yeah, you are," said Simon eagerly. "You're not in Apocalypse Later, right? I mean, duh, of course you're not. I would've seen you at the South Star show. . . ."

Simon babbled on, which gave me the opportunity I needed to duck away from the conversation and head out to the hallway. I made it halfway to the water fountain, then changed my mind and headed for the stairs. Nobody would think to look for me in there. I could breathe—well, for a minute, at least.

Niall? Seriously?

I sat on the bottom step, leaning my head against the wall. I thought he'd come here because he was ready to talk. Ready to apologize for accusing me of turning into Xavier. But he was the one using Xavier's name. Not me.

The door to the stairwell swung open, and I sat up straight to see who it was.

"There you are, McKenna," said Naomi.

I gave her a thin smile. "Break over already?"

"Nah, we've got a few minutes," she said, and came over to sit next to me. "I just saw you run out of there pretty fast, so I thought I'd come check on you. Something wrong?"

"No," I started to say . . . and then hissed as pain shot through my skull. "Yes."

"What is it?" she asked, very delicately, like she was afraid I'd start talking about magic.

"Boyfriend stuff," I said, twisting my fingers together in my lap.

Naomi grinned, an expression that held no small amount of relief. "Ooh. I'm good at boyfriend stuff. Spill."

For a second I wondered how much to tell her—but this was Naomi. We were still best friends even after I'd confessed to my part in Ryan's wish. She could handle this, no problem.

"I think Oliver's still hung up on his ex."

"Ooooooh," she said again, drawing the word out into three syllables. "Who is she? Do you know her?"

"Him," I said. "Another genie. And yeah, I knew him, kinda. Actually, it was the guy who—"

Naomi pulled her head back, her eyes coming alive with interest. "A guy? Really? Parish is into guys?"

"Sometimes," I said, feeling suddenly defensive. "But that isn't the point. The point is—"

"No, hold up just a second," said Naomi. "You can't just drop something like that on me and then not tell me more. How long have you known about this?"

"A while now," I said, exasperated. "But I swear it's not a big deal."

"It's a big deal if he's still into his *ex* who's a *guy*," she said. "Is it like, I dunno, like he broke up with some dude for you, and now you think maybe he'll break up with you and go back to the guy because he was a hundred percent gay the whole time, only he didn't know it till now?"

I stared at her.

"That happened to my cousin," she explained with a shrug. "She's an acting major."

By now the headache was creeping in, and I seriously

wanted to stab Naomi's cousin's gay ex-boyfriend in the eyeball, just for existing.

"No," I said acidly. "That is not what happened."

Apparently oblivious to my tone, she asked, "What's he like in bed? I mean, does he do stuff that he, like, obviously picked up from being with guys?"

"No!" I said, completely mortified. "Naomi, we haven't slept together yet, okay?"

She looked stunned. "Wait. Seriously? You and Parish haven't done it?"

"Seriously, no, we haven't," I said. "We've only been together for a month. That's not a lot of—"

"Let me rephrase," she said. "You turned yourself into an *immortal wish-granting shapeshifter* for this guy, and you haven't even *slept* with him?"

She made a good point. But why didn't she get that she was making it at the worst possible time?

"No, I haven't, so back off about it, okay? I didn't come out here to talk about . . . about stupid sex stuff."

"Oh," she said, going faintly pink. "Right. Sorry. He's hung up on his ex. Talk to me."

But my desire to talk had evaporated with her onslaught of questions. Questions that it would have been a lot easier to ignore if I hadn't been bound to her.

"Never mind," I said, standing up. "We should probably get back to rehearsal."

When our ten-minute break was over, Miss Delisio announced that we wouldn't be tackling the second act tonight, despite her original plan to run the full show. "Naomi and the stage crew, I need you guys to stay. We really have to get that barber's chair working, and I'd like to get those lights fixed before they fall down and kill someone. We're going to get this hammered out tonight, and I don't want the actors getting in the way. Everyone else, you're done for now."

We all looked at one another, dumbfounded. This was the Monday before our Friday opening. The beginning of Hell Week. We'd all planned on staying until at least midnight— or later, if the custodian forgot to kick us out, as he often did.

Then Miss Delisio continued: "But I want every single one of you here tomorrow, Wednesday, and Thursday at four o'clock on the nose. Bring your homework, bring your dinner, and bring as much caffeine as you need. I'm keeping you up all night if I have to. And if your parents have a problem with it, they've got my number and they're welcome to call it. You're dismissed."

That was more like it.

My stuff was backstage in one of the dressing rooms, which meant I had to go through the pit and across the stage to get there. But before I reached the stage, Oliver stopped me. "Can I talk to you for a sec?" He was casual, like he really had just met me for the first time a few minutes ago. But his eyes were dead-serious.

I glared at him. "About what?"

"Well." He winced a little and ran a hand self-consciously through Gwen's streaked hair: a very Oliver-ish gesture, which was downright weird to see on Gwen's body. "Everything, I suppose."

But between the Niall thing and Naomi's interrogation, I was so wired that I couldn't imagine this talk going well. I'd be all defensive, and he'd be all sad, and it would be the Great Wall all over again.

Much as it pained me, I shook my head. "Not now," I said, and went to get my stuff.

Oliver was still there, talking with a few of the other pit players, when I got back. I wondered if he would stop me again. I hoped he wouldn't. I also kind of hoped he would.

But it was Simon who stopped me instead. "Hey, Margo!" he called, when I was halfway across the stage. I turned around; he jogged a few steps to catch up with me. "It's only eight thirty. You wanna come over for a bit? Vicky's coming, too."

"Who else?" I asked.

"Nobody, dude," he said. "Just the three of us. I figure it'd be a nice change from hanging out here all the time. You guys can do acting stuff if you want, or I could show you that blog, or whatever."

"Ah," I said. My eyes moved, of their own accord, to the pit below us. Oliver was watching me.

"Plus," said Simon, "I still need to give you something."

I peered at him. "Yeah, you keep saying that. Why haven't you just brought it to school?"

"Because it's heavy, and I don't believe in carrying heavy things."

"Can't you just tell me what it is?"

He laughed. "Come over and find out."

Part of me wanted to slap Simon upside the head—but another part was intrigued by how secretive he was being. "Sure. I'll follow you in my car."

Chapter *NINETEEN*

Simon's father opened the front door before we reached it. "Home early?" he asked, a hint of an accent coloring his speech. "Do you need dinner?"

"Nope," said Simon. "Dad, this is Margo from school. You know Vicky. Margo, this is my dad. We're just going up to my room for a bit."

"Oh no, you're not," said Mr. Lee, laughter crinkling the skin around his eyes. "You and two girls. You think I'm stupid?"

Simon went pink. "Basement, then," he said.

"Basement with the door open," said Mr. Lee. "Don't think I won't check on you. And your curfew's still at eleven."

"Mine's at ten," said Vicky, raising her hand like she was in class or something. "So don't worry."

Simon shot her a grateful look. I didn't say anything; I was too busy trying not to laugh. With a last fond look at the three of us, Mr. Lee hurried out of sight.

"I only have a curfew on school nights," Simon explained

loftily, like that might somehow make him seem cooler. "Oh, and take off your shoes."

"Why?" I asked. Beside me, Vicky was already taking hers off.

"Some kind of custom-tradition-thing. I dunno."

Simon had a finished basement, complete with a TV, a couple of couches, and even a Ping-Pong table. It wasn't big enough to host cast parties, like Naomi's was, but it was still pretty cool. "Wait here," he said, once Vicky and I had claimed our spots on the couches. "I'll be right back."

As he darted upstairs, I shot Vicky a smile. "You're doing really well," I said. It was true, too. Ever since she'd started practicing her songs with me, she seemed more relaxed onstage, more in character, more . . . *more*. We had less than a week until opening, but I was actually starting to believe she'd be good by then. She had some talent, after all. She'd just never learned how to use it.

"Thanks," she said, lowering her eyes a little. "And thanks for spending so much time on me."

"No big deal," I said, even though it was. I was pretty sure our private rehearsals were the only thing keeping me sane. Without Vicky to focus my attention on, I'd probably have spent the entire week obsessing over everything Oliver had said, and how mad I was at him, and how he should really, really call me.

Not that I wasn't obsessing at all. But still.

Vicky sighed. "I asked Miss Delisio for extra help pretty early on, and she said I was fine already. Same with Naomi."

"Naomi?" I'd almost forgotten that she and Vicky had become friends.

"Yeah, neither of them thought I needed help. The wish got both of them pretty bad." She squirmed uncomfortably in her seat. "That was before I told Naomi the truth, though. She kinda stopped talking to me after she found out she only liked me because of a wish."

I winced. I hadn't told Naomi about Vicky's wish, but I should've figured she'd go and ask Vicky herself. I should've warned Vicky that Naomi wasn't comfortable with magic.

Her eyes flicked toward the stairs, and she added, "Sometimes I wonder if Simon's gonna stop talking to me, too."

I was more than a little surprised to hear her say that so candidly, but before I could reply, Simon came clattering down the stairs. "Margo, check it out," he announced proudly. When I twisted around, there he was, jumping over the last two steps and landing smoothly on the carpet. He was holding a black guitar case.

My guitar case.

"I found it backstage, the day you disappeared," said Simon proudly. "I didn't want to bring it back to school, just in case anyone asked why I had it—and you never seemed to want to come *here,* but at long last, here we are! I figured you've probably been looking for it everywhere, so . . . here it is."

I felt tears prick at my eyes, and for a moment I couldn't speak—but not for the reason Simon probably assumed. The thing was, I *hadn't* been looking everywhere for my guitar. In fact, I hadn't even remembered, until this moment, that it wasn't under my bed, where I always kept it.

Which meant I hadn't played it since before I'd made my fourth wish. I hadn't played it, or written any new songs on it, or just pulled it out and tuned it because I had nothing better to do.

Who *was* I?

I made myself stand up, walk over to him, and take the case. "Thanks for keeping it safe," I said.

"Any time, dude," he said. "But now, we celebrate!"

Simon darted over to the squishy arm chair in the corner of the room, rooted around under the cushion, and produced two large bottles. Holding them aloft, he announced in a stage whisper, "Vodka and bourbon. Pick your poison."

"Ew," I said automatically, fully expecting Vicky to do the same.

But she just laughed and said, "The usual." Simon passed her the vodka bottle, and she uncapped it and took a little swig. She made a face, but seemed to enjoy it.

I pinched my arm with two fingers, just to make sure I wasn't hallucinating. Nope. This was definitely Vicky Willoughbee, drinking vodka and calling it *the usual*.

Simon turned to me. "How about you?"

"Neither," I said. "I don't really drink. Plus I have to drive home. Isn't your dad gonna check on us?"

"Nah," said Simon, settling down beside Vicky. She rested her head on his shoulder. "He figures as long as we're not in my bedroom, and the door's open, we couldn't possibly be doing anything wrong. He always threatens to come down, but he never does."

"Never, ever does," Vicky echoed mournfully.

"Are you gonna put that down?" said Simon, gesturing toward my guitar case. "You look like you're holding it hostage."

Right. I was still standing there like an uptight freak, clutching the case and probably making a horribly judgmental face at them. I made myself smile, set the case down on the floor, and sat on the couch again.

"Much better," said Simon. "Now, here's the thing, dude. Both of us, me and Vicks, we've been keeping our mouths shut about your . . . situation . . ."

"The situation where you're a *genie,*" interrupted Vicky, her eyes already brighter than usual.

Simon shot her an indulgent sort of look. "Yeah. That. But since we're not at school, so nobody can overhear us, and I've been dying to talk about it, since we were both sort of involved in things—"

"Like how I set you up with Oliver," said Vicky proudly.

"And how I was totally there when you made that fourth

wish and disappeared," said Simon. "I even got stabbed!"

Vicky put a hand on his back and looked at him with soft eyes.

"See, I've been thinking about it," Simon continued, "and I was really freaking lucky, dude. He stabbed me, sure, but then you were right there, and not only did you make a wish that totally healed me, but then you freaking *killed* him! You, Margo McKenna, are my hero."

I stared at Simon. There was that word again: *kill*.

"I changed my mind," I said. "Pass the vodka."

Vodka, as I learned a moment later, is one hundred percent gross.

"How do you drink this?" I asked Vicky, feeling my eyes well up as I coughed and sputtered.

"Um, slower, usually," said Simon, wincing. "You're supposed to sip, not gulp it like some meathead show-off. Like, geez, remember Ryan and Eli at homecoming last year?"

"I didn't go to homecoming," I said.

"Oh," said Simon. "Well, whatever. Point is, they were a two-man lesson in Don't Be That Guy. We're trying to achieve buzzed here, not brain-damaged."

"But it tastes like the tenth circle of hell."

Vicky nodded gravely. "It does. You get used to it."

"But why would you *want* to get used to it?" I asked.

They both shrugged.

"So what's it like?" asked Vicky. "Being a genie, I mean."

"Can you turn into other people?" asked Simon.

Vicky went, "Ooh, yeah, can you?"

I nodded, wondering why my head suddenly felt like it contained a helium balloon instead of a skull.

"You should totally show us," said Simon. "Come on, turn into someone!"

"I'd, um, I'd rather not," I said. "It's just, um . . ."

It was just that I felt like he'd asked me to change my clothes in front of him. But that seemed like a stupid thing to say, so instead I took another sip of vodka. A very tiny sip. Still gross.

"But you can appear and disappear, right?" said Simon. "Duh. Obviously you can. I saw you."

"Ooh, are your fingers all tingly?" said Vicky. "Can I feel?"

"Um." I could feel myself shrinking into the couch as they watched me. Simon, who'd kept my guitar safe for me. Vicky, who'd known Oliver longer than I had. They'd spent more than two weeks protecting my secret, and now they were looking at me like I was a monkey at the zoo and they were hoping I'd do a trick.

This, I couldn't help thinking, was exactly the opposite of talking to Naomi. But not in a good way.

"I should go home," I said.

"Noooo," whispered Vicky, leaning dramatically toward me. "You have to tell me about being magical! Have you granted any wishes yet?"

"A few," I said. "Not many. Here, have your vodka back."

With one hand, she grabbed the bottle. With the other, she grabbed my hand. Startled, I jerked away—but not before I felt my magic zinging into her.

"Stop it," I said.

She pouted. "But you're all tingly. Just like Oliver. He used to let me feel."

For some reason, that incensed me even more. "Oliver," I declared, picking up my guitar case, "is not yours to feel."

There was silence. I realized that this pronouncement required clarification.

"What I mean is, he is *mine* to feel."

Simon snickered. Vicky went pink.

"I mean, what I mean is, Oliver is not a zoo monkey. And neither am I."

And since that seemed like a truly excellent parting line, I turned and stomped up the stairs, guitar case in hand. I put on my shoes. I left Simon's house. I went to my car and unlocked it and put my seat belt on . . . and realized that the world was ever so slightly tilty.

Right. I'd had vodka.

What was I supposed to do now? Jump through the Between to my bedroom? Leave my car in Simon's driveway?

Nope, I had a better idea. Sitting up straight, I made an announcement to the empty air around me: "I am officially unaffected by vodka and other such foul-tasting beverages. I do not get drunk. Ever. Including right now."

And then, just like that, I was sober again. It was sort of miraculous . . . until I thought, yet again, of Naomi and the money at the mall.

"This is not cheating," I murmured to the disapproving Naomi-voice in my head. "This is me avoiding a potentially fatal car crash. So shut up."

Then I drove myself home.

Chapter TWENTY

My parents weren't there, which wasn't a surprise. There was a note from Dad on the counter, saying they were out for dinner with friends, and there was lasagna in the fridge if I wanted it. I opted for half a container of coconut sorbet instead, and then went to my room to play my guitar. Maybe that would help me calm down.

For a while, it did. I played through five or six of my favorite Neko Case songs, my fingers remembering all the chords despite being three weeks out of practice, my mind relaxing as I sang lyrics that I knew by heart.

But when I cut away from Neko's songs and started inventing some of my own—soft melodies and elegant words that flowed easily as water, thanks to my first wish—my calm started fraying at the edges again.

My first wish.

What would Naomi say if I told her about *that*?

She'd say I was cheating—and she wouldn't be entirely wrong. Sure, my desire to create music had been genuine, but all the actual talent had come from that wish. From Oliver's magic.

I'd started cheating long before I had magic of my own.

Setting my guitar aside, I dug my phone out of my bag and texted Oliver:

Come over?

Seconds later, he replied:

Still at theater, working on a wish. Tomorrow OK?

My heart sank. Only for a moment, though—because Oliver hadn't just told me why he couldn't come over. He'd also told me exactly where he was.

OK, I sent back. I locked my bedroom door, just in case my parents came home and decided to check on me. Then I stepped into the Between.

When I got to the theater, though, I didn't step back out again. The impulse and the momentum were there—but as soon as I saw my destination in front of me, slightly blurry and separated from me by a thin film of gray, I made myself stop. Maybe Oliver didn't want to see me right now, but that didn't mean *I* couldn't see *him*.

Oliver, still wearing Gwen's image, was sitting on top of George's grand piano. Not in a sexy lounge-singer sort of way, thankfully—his legs were crossed, and in one hand he held a drumstick, which he was tapping rhythmically on the lid of the piano. George was straddling the bench, looking thoughtful. He'd tossed his ubiquitous leather jacket to the floor, and the plain white T-shirt underneath revealed colorful tattoos running down the length of both arms. There was nobody else around.

"Thing is," George was saying, "I'm pretty sure we got more in us. Just not if we stay like this. Something's got to change. Don't know what, though." He rubbed his stubbly chin, looking more relaxed than I'd ever seen him, at least around me or any of my fellow students.

"I have a few ideas," said Oliver, with three quick taps of his drumstick. "It just depends on what would make you the happiest. Or you could just make the wish really general and let things play out on their own. It's your call."

They were quiet for a moment: George thinking hard, Oliver watching George with a keen eye. I wondered what he could see in George's head right now.

George looked up again, giving Oliver a lopsided grin. "Keep it simple, yeah? Success. That's it. Let fate do what she wants."

"Cool," said Oliver, unfolding Gwen's long legs and hopping off the piano. "Then if you're ready, let's go. You just have to hold my ring like I told you to. Thumb and forefinger."

George reached for his jacket. Out of an inside pocket, he pulled something very familiar: Oliver's spirit vessel. The silver ring that had bound him to me, back when we'd first met. The sight of it now, in someone else's hands, sent a sharp pang of longing through me.

Oliver moved toward George and reached for his hands, just like he'd done with me when I'd made my wishes. At the time, he'd explained that the hand-holding wasn't strictly necessary; he just liked to do it that way. And after Ryan's third wish, I was starting to understand why. Everything had become so much brighter when I'd actually touched Ryan's skin.

George started at Oliver's touch—probably at the sudden feeling of magic—but he didn't say anything. I smiled to myself. Somehow I felt better for knowing that George hadn't yet gotten used to how Oliver's hands felt.

"Go ahead," said Oliver, lowering Gwen's voice as he focused intently on George. The moment was warm and deep and intimate, just like the afternoon when I'd made my first wish. I remembered how close Oliver had stood to me. How dark and intense his eyes had been. How powerful his hands had felt, and how the world had seemed to bend toward us. It felt odd to be on the outside of the same scene now.

In a voice more serious than I'd ever heard from him before, George said, "I wish my band and I could finally be successful."

Holding George's hands firmly in place, Oliver let his eyelids flutter closed. He breathed deeply, three times. He was so open, so confident, so at ease—so very much the boy I'd fallen in love with.

Finally, Oliver said, "There." He looked completely worn out. And completely content.

I felt, strangely, like I'd just been cheated on.

George looked down at the ring, then back up at Oliver. "What'd you do?"

"Granted your wish," said Oliver simply, punctuating his reply with a breathy little laugh. "I changed a few things here and there, put a few other things in motion, and then . . . well, it's like you said. We let fate do as she will."

"Hm. Right on." George tucked Oliver's vessel back into his jacket pocket. "So we just . . . see how it plays out, huh?"

"That's about the shape of it," said Oliver.

"Well, thanks," said George. "This wish stuff is . . . yeah. It's cool of you."

Oliver shrugged, obviously flattered. "Just doing my job," he said.

"Right on," said George again. "Well, gotta be getting home. You need a ride?"

"Nah," said Oliver, hopping back up onto the lid of the piano. "I'm gonna stick around here for a bit. You can lock up if you want, though."

George looked about as bemused by this as I felt, but he didn't question Oliver. He just gathered his stuff and left, locking the auditorium doors behind him.

Oliver, meanwhile, stretched out on the piano, fingers laced together to pillow his head, eyes closed, knees bent over the side so his shins bumped against the instrument's beat-up wood. He looked peaceful. Maybe even more so than when we'd gone to his Between together and watched the clouds go by.

Nothing but a single thought and a single step separated me, in the Between, from Oliver in the real world. It would be so easy to talk now, when he was so happy and I'd had some time to cool down—except, if I appeared in the auditorium with him, he would know I'd been spying.

No, I had to go home. I'd talk to him tomorrow.

But before I could tear myself away, he opened his eyes again and shifted from Gwen back into himself. "Margo?" he said softly to the ceiling. "I know you're still there."

My heart leaped into my throat. How had he caught me?

"I thought I was hiding," I said meekly, as I stepped out into the real world and breathed for the first time in a solid ten minutes. Maybe longer. It felt good.

He turned his head just enough to meet my eyes. "You were. Well, mostly you were. But even when you hide, your magic is visible. That glowy aura thing," he added with a vague little wave of his hand. He still hadn't gotten up from the piano.

"Oh," I said, inching slowly closer to him. "I still can't see *your* glowy aura thing, you know."

"Give it time," he said easily. "Time's all it'll take. And that, as it happens, is something we've got plenty of." Settling back onto his hand-pillow, he smiled at me. "So what'd you think?"

I sat down on the piano bench, which put me at eye level with him. "About what?" I asked.

"George's wish. Me, granting it. I don't know. I assume you came here looking for something, so . . . did you find it?"

A solid assumption, and an excellent question, although I had no idea how to answer it. What I did know, though, was that this Oliver was very different from the one I'd fought with on the Great Wall of China. That Oliver was all nerves and tension and judgment. This one looked like he'd just had a two-hour massage followed by a soak in a Jacuzzi.

I wondered if that was because of the wish.

"I'm not sure. You look really happy, though."

He grinned at me, eyes alive with mischief. "That was the first wish I've granted in almost three weeks, Margo. Three weeks! So yeah, you could say I'm pretty happy. Hey, come up here."

He rapped a hand once on the lid of the piano, then held it out to me, like he was somehow going to help me up from his prone position. I eyed the old, scratched wood on which he lay. "It could break," I said. "Come down here instead."

Oliver didn't argue—nor did he hesitate. He simply vanished, only to reappear beside me a split second later. Before I knew it, he was backing me up against the piano, his body flush against mine. He kissed my nose. "You smell good," he said, and leaned down to press his face into my neck, kissing me there, too.

"Someone could come in," I whispered, laughing a little as his hair tickled my chin.

"Psshh," was his only reply. He kissed me everywhere he could reach, finally settling on my lips, where I could kiss him back. Which I did, for quite a long time.

"You reeeeally like granting wishes, don't you," I said with a laugh, when we finally came up for air.

"Oh, Margo," he said, letting my name rumble low in his chest. His face looked like the face of someone who'd say yes if you suggested jumping off the top of Mount Everest just to see what would happen. "Margo, Margo. Give it time. You'll understand soon, too."

"Understand what?" I said.

"That the wish is everything!" he said. "You get to give someone what they want, and in exchange you get to feel like *this*. I mean, all the rest—the traveling, the food, the shape-shifting—that's all fine and fun. But in the end, the wish . . . is . . . everything."

He let go of me then, punctuating the last word by throwing his arms up in a V, like he was opening himself up to the ceiling, or maybe the whole room. Maybe the whole world.

"It does feel pretty good," I agreed. "I didn't think so at first, but once my magic started slowing down enough to let me shape it, then . . . yeah."

"That wasn't your magic," he said, his voice hushed with excitement. "That was you. You're catching up with your instincts. See? You shape it until it becomes as much yours as your master's, and then, when you finally let it explode, it's just . . ." He shook his head, like he couldn't find the word to describe it.

"Awesome," I suggested.

"*You're* awesome," he said. "And I'm sorry I said all those things to you on the Great Wall. I really am. You're nothing like him, Margo. You're so much kinder, not to mention so much prettier, and . . ."

And he was angling for another kiss, only now he'd brought up Xavier, which was about as much of a turn-on as a pile of roadkill. I put a hand on his chest, holding him away.

"You named yourself after him," I said. "Gwendolyn Niall."

He blinked, startled. "Doesn't mean anything," he said. "It's just a name."

"Obviously it means something, or you wouldn't have done it," I said. "And, well, the way you talk about him . . ."

He sighed, running a hand through his hair and taking a step away from me. Good thing, too, because the lip of the piano lid was starting to dig into my back.

"It's just a way of saying good-bye," he said at last. "He was in my life for a long time, and . . . I'm not still in love with him or anything, if that's what you're worried about."

A laugh slipped out, somewhat against my will. "I wasn't worried about that," I said. "Well, not a *lot* worried, anyway."

Oliver cupped my face with both hands. "You don't need to be worried at all," he said softly, and gave me a long, deep sort of look. "We should go somewhere. Hide in a fancy hotel in Paris for a week, or find some band and follow them around on tour, or—"

"I have school tomorrow," I said. "And rehearsal. It's Hell Week."

"I know," he said with a sigh, snaking his arms around me again, resting his hands against the small of my back. "I just . . . sometimes . . . I still wish you'd run away with me. I really do."

"You know I can't," I said.

"You could," he said. "If you really wanted to, you could."

Hiding away in foreign hotels. Following bands around. Were those the kinds of things he'd done with Xavier, back when they were together? Had they just done whatever they wanted in between wishes, without worrying what anyone else thought, because neither of them had a home to go back to?

"Wait," I said. "Is that why you want me to give James a fourth wish? So you can have someone to travel with when I can't go with you?"

"No," he said quickly . . . then bit his lip and ducked his head a little. "Well, it's not *only* that."

I was about to ask what else, when I realized I already knew. He'd told me, back on the Great Wall, even though he probably hadn't meant for it to come out that way. *It's hard, and it's lonely, but I've been making the best of it the only way I know how.*

He was lonely. Not for Xavier in particular, as I'd feared,

but for someone, anyone, to share his rootless life with. And it couldn't be me—at least, not while I still had my own name and my own family and my human life to come home to.

My human life, where I lied to everyone around me, and the few people who knew the truth treated me like I was either a circus animal or a con artist, and . . .

"You know what?" I found myself saying. "Yes. Let's run away."

"What? Wait. Really?"

"Yeah! Why not, right?" I said. "After graduation. It's only a month and a half away—and you're right, I don't need college after that. And if I ever decide that I do, then hey, I'll go back in another hundred years or whatever."

Oliver took a step back, like he wanted a wider shot of me. Like he wanted to make sure it was all of me saying this to him. "You're . . . you're sure. You're *really* sure?"

"Yes," I said, absolutely meaning it. Then I paused. "Mostly yes. You just have to promise me one thing."

"What's that?"

"Next time someone attacks me and I break their nose— which I will, make no mistake about that—you are not allowed to judge me." I grinned. "In fact, you are not allowed to say a single thing about it, unless it's to congratulate me on a nose well-broken."

"I've actually been thinking a lot about that, you know," he said. "And you're right. You did what you had to do."

"I . . . really?"

"Which isn't to say that I would've done the same thing in your place," he said, sort of heavily. "You deal with things differently than I do. I have to respect that. Besides, he deserved a hell of a lot worse, given what he did to you with that wish."

I paused. "Does that mean you promise?"

"Yes. I promise." A sly grin crept across his face, making his eyes shine. "So, after graduation, huh? You really want that diploma?"

I couldn't tell whether he was angling for me to admit that yes, I did—or for me to change my mind and say we should just leave now. But either way, it made me think. High school diplomas were only useful for getting jobs—and my job, whether I wanted it or not, was granting wishes. The only qualification I needed for that was having magic.

Which I already did.

"After the play," I said, my blood thrumming with the excitement of a plan set in motion. An impulsive plan, but a plan nonetheless. "We've got opening night on Friday, then closing night on Saturday. And after that . . ."

I spread my arms wide, shifting first into Tony, then into Amber, and then finally into Enrique—the body that my magic wanted me to be.

"After that, it's just you and me," said Oliver. "Where do you want to go?"

Just you and me. Which meant no James. No fourth wishes.

We didn't need anyone else, not when we had each other.

"Anywhere," I said, my fingertips tingling with anticipation. "Everywhere."

"Everywhere," he murmured, eyes sparkling with barely contained glee. And then, before I could say anything else, he swooped in and kissed me again. With tongue. While I was still Enrique.

Why the hell not? I thought, and kissed him back.

Chapter TWENTY-ONE

*F*our more days, I thought over and over as I parked my car the next morning. *Four more days,* as I slid into my seat in the empty calc classroom. Four more days of school, two performances of *Sweeney Todd,* and then I'd be done forever—or at least for as long as I wanted to be.

Four.

More.

Days.

"Dude," said Simon, taking the seat next to me and dumping his stuff on the floor. "Are we cool? You left pretty fast last night."

My brain was so full of the countdown that at first, I had no idea what he was talking about. Then, of course, it clicked.

"Yeah," I said. "I dunno. You guys were just all, 'Let's make grabby hands at Margo!' and I was like, 'Personal space, personal space!' Plus, there was vodka."

"Vodka, man," said Simon, nodding sagely. "That stuff can

seriously alter your chemistry. Sorry about the grabby hands, though."

"No problem," I lied. "That was mostly Vicky, anyway."

He winced. "Yeah, she's . . . she's been wanting to talk to you about that for a long time. Plus, as you said: vodka."

"It's fine. Really."

Seemingly satisfied, Simon whipped out his phone and pressed a few buttons. "So, I never did get around to showing you that blog. Here, check it out."

He put it on my desk and let me scroll through the pictures. They were slightly distorted on the small screen, but I still got the gist of it. It was exactly as Simon had described: a series of poorly Photoshopped pictures of Ryan Weiss with various people and animals. There was even one of him with a Care Bear. Its caption said "Bones-a-Lot Bear." That was the one that finally made me laugh.

"Right?" said Simon. "Here, look at the next one. It's John and Yoko doing their bed-in, with Ryan in the middle. Effing hilarious."

I was still laughing when the classroom door banged open and Naomi burst in. "Please tell me," she said breathlessly, "that you guys saw the art wing."

The art wing was where the senior lockers were, but I hadn't gone to my locker yet today. I shook my head; so did Simon.

"Why?" I asked, slightly afraid of what the answer might be.

Rolling her eyes, Naomi sat on one of the desks and propped her feet on its chair. "Okay, you saw that Ryan blog, right?"

The question was directed at me, which meant I had to answer. "Yeah. Just now."

"The John and Yoko one is the best," added Simon.

Satisfied, Naomi nodded. "Well, someone printed out a bunch of pictures and blew them up, and . . ." She spread her hands expressively.

Simon raised an eyebrow. "And suddenly Bones-a-Lot Bear is all over the art wing?"

Naomi laughed. "I don't know who did it, but if I ever find out, I'll . . . I dunno, I'll buy them a freaking yacht or something."

I didn't get to see the art wing collage before the powers that be took it down, but as with any brilliantly controversial piece of art, people kept talking about it long after it was gone. Restlessness pervaded the classrooms; teachers had trouble keeping their classes quiet. By third period, when the loudspeaker crackled and the voice of Mrs. Esberg, our principal, piped into the chemistry room, I knew what was coming.

And I was right. Fourth period was canceled. Instead, the entire student body was to report to the gymnasium for an assembly. Such a thing hadn't happened since my freshman year, when some junior had been caught selling pot on campus, so everyone was pretty excited about it.

All I could think, though, was how ridiculous this was. I was surrounded by a tidal wave of students heading, lemming-like, for the gym, yelling to each other about how awesome it was to have a free period, when in reality all they were about to get was some cobbled-together lecture about respecting your peers. A lecture that would change the lives of exactly no one—a lecture that I definitely didn't need, especially not with only four school days left before me.

Well. Three and a half, by now.

So when my phone buzzed in my pocket, I didn't even hesitate before ducking out of the tidal wave and into the first empty classroom I saw. A classroom with sombreros on the walls and a piñata hanging in the corner. Freshman Spanish, it looked like.

The text was from a number that wasn't in my phone—but before I could read the message itself, I heard someone clear their throat. I looked over, fully expecting a teacher to have followed me in. But it was Naomi. And she looked far less ecstatic than she had before first period.

"Hey," she said, shutting the door behind her.

"Hey," I replied.

She cocked her head, giving me a smile that looked practiced. "I didn't want to say anything in front of Lee earlier, but . . . we're okay right?"

"Yeah," I replied automatically—and winced as pain shot through my skull. I quickly amended, "I guess so."

"I know you were in a bad mood last night, and I should've been more sensitive——"

"It wasn't a bad mood, Naomi," I said. "It was you. Asking questions about Oliver."

"Um," she said. "You're my best friend. He's your new boyfriend. Asking questions is what you *do* when your best friend has a new boyfriend."

Half sitting on the edge of the teacher's desk, I crossed my arms and gave her a look. "Not when the best friend in question is a genie, and you *know* her magic forces her to answer every question you ask. Even when she doesn't want to."

Naomi's face fell. "Oh, that. Crap. Sorry, I totally forgot about the question thing. You should've said something."

"I shouldn't have had to," I murmured. "Plus, you didn't exactly give me the chance."

"Yeah, I may have been a little . . . um, overenthusiastic? But listen, I actually have been thinking about what you said. And I think this is one of those times where maybe you should just ask Parish directly if he's still into this other guy. If he's at all worth your time, he'll give you a straight answer."

"Already did."

"Oh," she said, eyebrows shooting up in surprise. "And?"

"And he's not. I mean, it's more complicated than that, but he's not."

"Well, good!" she said. "Anyway, that's part one. Part two is that if you're still worried, you track down the other guy and ask him if he's still into Parish. That way you know if there's a chance that he might show up someday and try to steal your man."

"Good plan," I said with a tight smile. "Except the other guy's dead."

"Wait, what?" she said, looking absolutely horrified. "How? Why didn't you say so?"

"Because, yet again, you didn't give me the chance. And the how is because I wished him free. He's the one who was trying to kill Oliver. And stop it with the questions, okay?"

"Sorry, sorry!" she said. "But . . . seriously, that guy? The one who stabbed you?"

I nodded. "Like I said. It's complicated."

She pursed her lips and let out a low whistle. "Damn. Sounds like that boy of yours has some issues."

And with that, I was officially done discussing Oliver with Naomi.

"Shouldn't you be getting to the gym?" I asked.

"Shouldn't you?" she countered.

"*Questions,*" I sighed. "Yes, I should. I'll be there in a sec."

"Oka-ay," she said in that sing-songy way where she clearly didn't believe me at all. But she didn't ask whether or not I was lying. Instead, she just said, "See you in a few."

Once she was gone, I pulled out my phone to check out that text. The number had a New Jersey area code, but not the same one as mine. The message read: HELLO. DO U HAVE TIME 2 TALK SOON?

I frowned at the message. WHO IS THIS? I replied.

Mere minutes later, another text came in: SORRY! IT'S JAMES. ALICIA/OLIVER GAVE ME UR DIGITS.

Ah-ha. So, not a friend of mine at all. I thought about ignoring the message altogether, but that would just be mean. If I was going to deny him a fourth wish, the least I could do was tell him in person.

The bell rang, signaling the start of what would have been fourth period, if not for the assembly. Since it was safe to assume the assembly would take up the entire period, that gave me a solid forty-five minutes of nobody—except maybe Naomi—noticing I was gone.

Me: YOU FREE NOW?

James: YES! U STILL IN OAKVALE? I CAN B THERE IN 30 MINS.

Me: TELL ME WHERE YOU ARE, AND I CAN BE THERE IN 3 SECONDS.

The place was called Bettina's Café, and it was right in the middle of Newark, on a street that boasted things like fried chicken places, bright red signs offering to cash checks or buy gold, and a handful of empty lots. I'd been to Newark once before—somewhat inevitable if you lived in northern New Jersey, since it was as close to a big city as you could get without actually venturing into Manhattan—but that had been for a production of *Godspell* at the New Jersey Performing Arts Center.

Bettina's was in a very, very different part of town.

Although the word *café* was in the name, it actually looked more like a deli, except with tablecloths and chairs. There was a sandwich counter along one wall, behind which were two coffeepots and two fridges, one full of soda and the other full of beer. A bored-looking girl with pink-streaked hair was doing something on her phone behind the counter. There were no customers besides me.

The girl raised an eyebrow at me when I walked in, as if daring me to order something. But it wasn't until James walked in, just a moment later, that she put down her phone.

"Hey there," said James, giving me a megawatt smile. "Thanks for coming."

"No problem," I said. "It's . . . a cute place."

He rolled his eyes with a little laugh. "Please. It's a dump." Streaked Hair looked like she was about to argue, but then James continued: "I should know. I worked here all through high school."

"Oh, that's why you look familiar," said Streaked Hair. "Jason, right?"

"James," he said. "Close enough."

She shrugged. "You guys want something?"

"That grilled chicken salad looks good," said James, pointing at the handwritten menu on the chalkboard wall. Then he turned to me. "Get whatever you want. My treat."

"Chicken salad for me, too," I said. "And a Coke. But I'm paying."

He shook his head and reached for his wallet. "No you're not. This is a huge favor I'm asking you, so paying's the least I can do. Two grilled chicken salads, a Coke, and a water," he said to Streaked Hair. As she sauntered over to the other end of the counter, where the salad bowls were, James glanced at me again. "Alicia *did* tell you about the, um, favor. Right? Oliver, I mean?"

I nodded.

Excitement flashed through James's dark eyes. "And?" he asked.

I looked pointedly over at Streaked Hair, who was dumping iceberg lettuce into a mixing bowl. "And let's wait till we get our salads, okay?"

Something in my voice must have given away my intentions, because his shoulders sagged and his excitement melted away. But in its place grew a look of pure determination. "Sure," he said. "Go grab that table in the far corner. I'll bring the food over."

A few minutes later, James came over with our order. "One wilted-lettuce salad for you, and a Coke. Oh, I forgot a straw. Do you want a straw?"

"I'm good," I said, before he could dash off again. "Thanks."

He settled himself across the table from me, and I took a moment to study him. A serious expression on an otherwise very young face. Clever eyes and a friendly smile.

How was I supposed to let this guy down easy?

I should have planned a speech.

James speared a small piece of chicken and ate it quickly, sighing when he was done. "Hell of a morning," he said. "Pardon my French. But man, I'm starving."

"Classes?" I asked. I vaguely remembered him mentioning college.

"Nah," he said with a laugh. "Work. I'm a manager at the CVS a few blocks down."

"Oh," I said, giving him a smile. "Yeah, I'm not going to college either."

"No, no, I *am* in college," he said. "Just not full-time, because hey, I still gotta pay my rent. At this rate I probably won't get a degree till I'm thirty, but . . . well, maybe that won't matter so much anymore, right?"

He shoveled a forkful of iceberg lettuce and shredded carrots into his mouth, his expression suddenly shrewd. I knew he was talking about the wish—about becoming a genie—but all I could think about was how this guy couldn't afford to be a full-time college student, while I literally had unlimited money at my disposal, and I'd just let him buy me lunch.

I was such an insensitive jerk.

"So," he continued, before I could figure out what to say, "how much did Oliver tell you?"

"Just that you want a fourth wish," I replied. "And it'd have to be me who grants it, not him."

"And you don't want to." There was no bitterness in his voice, and no judgment. Just a statement of fact. "But just so we're clear, all I wanted was to become a genie. I didn't know it would take four more wishes to do it. I really wasn't after more wishes, I swear."

He seemed very keen on my understanding the distinction, so I nodded. "I believe you. It's just . . . I mean, why would you *want* to be a genie? It's not easy, you know, being bound to people. Having to do whatever they tell you. Answering all their stupid questions," I added, thinking of Naomi.

"I bet it's not," he said. "But easy's not what I'm after."

"You're not?" I'd figured his difficult financial situation was a pretty good reason to turn into an immortal being who could create money at will. "Then what?"

Taking a swig from his water bottle, James smiled at me again. "I grew up here, in downtown Newark. Did Oliver tell you that?"

. I shook my head. What with Ryan's attack, my counterattack, and the Great Wall fight, after which we hadn't spoken for an entire week, he hadn't had the chance to tell me much of anything.

"Well, I did," he said, nodding to himself as he looked at

the café walls that surrounded us. "Kind of a typical story, if you're from around here. Mom who worked two jobs to support us. Dad who didn't do much of anything except swear at anyone who got between him and his rum. Older brother who fell in with a bad crowd, only got out when they sent him to rehab, and then moved across the country to get away from us. You know. Not bad enough that they sent me to foster care, but not good enough that I graduated without a few bruises along the way."

"Bruises?" I said, remembering what I'd done to Ryan. "Like . . . like from your dad?"

"Nah, nothing like that. He was a lazy-ass good-for-nothing, but he never got violent. Got my ribs broken a few times at school, though. Teenagers. You know."

"Yeah," I said, even though school fights were something I saw far more often on TV than in person.

"Anyway," he said, "so I'm seven years old. It hasn't even been a month since Charlie started sneaking out at night. That's my brother, by the way. Charlie. And one day I find this silver ring in my backpack, and . . . Well, you know the deal."

"I know it well," I said with a smile.

"Alicia was . . . sorry, I mean Oliver," he said, cutting himself off with a wince.

"You can call him Alicia," I said. "I don't mind."

Which wasn't entirely true, of course. But I wanted to hear his story, not waste time discussing Oliver's name.

"Well," said James, "Alicia appeared out of nowhere, looking like the girl next door. Big earrings, big hair, big smile.
Definitely the kind of girl Charlie would have gone for. But
she was there just for me, not for him. She said so, and then
she proved it, over and over again."

"Because the wishes were yours, not Charlie's," I said.

James raised an eyebrow. "Well, that too, obviously.
But it was more than that. She was a big sister, the way
Charlie never tried to be a big brother. She taught me hand
games and card games, and we played basketball till I was
good enough to play with the fourth-grade twins down the
street. . . ."

He trailed off with a wistful smile. I said, "Sounds nice."

Which *was* entirely true.

"Yeah," he said. "She must've stuck around for three, four
months. And it would've been longer, except I didn't know
that making a third wish meant she'd have to leave."

"What did you wish for?" I asked.

Leaning an elbow on the table, he rested his forehead in his
palm, squinting like the memory actually pained him. "Oh,
stupid stuff. I mean, I was seven. Nobody's gonna make smart
wishes when they're seven. Like, I knew we were poor, so
I wished for my mom to have a million dollars. Great wish,
until you realize there's nothing in there to keep your dad
from finding the million and drinking most of it away. Give
me that wish again, man, and I'd wish for a steady source of

income. The bigger, the better. But what seven-year-old even knows the word *income,* right?"

He had a point. "Well, at least you didn't wish for a pony. Apparently some people actually do that."

He laughed, gesturing at me with his fork. "I bet they do. Yeah, I just bet they do." A pause, as he thought about this some more and shook his head. "But like I said, the wishes were . . . well, they were fine, but they were beside the point. They didn't last. Money gets spent eventually. Friendship with the cool kids fades away. What lasted wasn't the wishes. It was Alicia herself. Having a big sister. Someone I could look up to, whose number one priority was me. You know?"

I nodded—not because I'd ever had a big sister, but because I knew exactly how it felt to be the sole object of Oliver's attention. It felt very, very good.

"I never forgot that," he said. "Not even for a second. And I've spent the past thirteen years wondering, well, what if I could be that for other people?"

"That's why you want to become a genie?" I asked faintly, trying to keep from sinking down into my seat. "To help people?"

I'd made a fourth wish so I could be with Oliver. So we wouldn't have to break up because our lives were too different, like he and his human fiancée had done a zillion years ago. Suddenly, that felt like the stupidest reason ever—and I did not like feeling stupid.

"Yep," said James. His eyes glinted mischievously at me as he speared the last forkful of salad in his bowl. "So, have I convinced you yet?"

"Um," I said, somewhat thrown. Yet again, he'd cut right to the point. "Well, I mean, what about your human life? Your family? Your job? They're harder to juggle than you'd think, believe me."

"I do believe you," he said seriously. "Let's see. Family. Dad passed away six years ago. Mom's living with my aunt in Toronto, and we only talk once a month or so, if that. And Charlie's in some hippie commune in California. No wife, no girlfriend, no kids—me, that is, not Charlie. He's probably had at least twenty girlfriends so far this week. And my job is a job that a monkey could do. See? I wouldn't be giving up much."

Giving up. So he was planning on leaving his human life behind. He knew what he was getting into—better than I'd known, at least.

"What about that degree you want?" I said, not caring that I was starting to sound desperate. "What are you in school for, anyway?"

"Social work," he said with a wry smile, and didn't elaborate. Not that he needed to.

"Of course," I muttered, which only made him grin again. He clearly thought he had me right where he wanted me.

No way. I'd made my plan already. I was going to perform

in *Sweeney Todd*—the last high school landmark that I actually cared about—and then I was going to run away with Oliver, grant wishes for strangers when I had to, and spend the rest of my life traveling to interesting places and turning into interesting people. This James guy was *not* going to step in and ruin it.

Sitting up a little straighter, I asked, "What was your third wish?"

"Hm?" he said.

"You said you wished for a million dollars, and to be friends with somebody. What else?"

"Oh. It's dumb." He gave me a squinty smile. "D'you remember that band Legend Thirty-Five?"

I shook my head. The name didn't even sound remotely familiar.

"Well, that's okay," he said. "Nobody does. They were this European dance group, and they were huge for about five minutes or so, back when I was a kid. I was completely obsessed with them. But they were from Belgium or Austria or . . . somewhere . . . and they never did shows in the States."

"Wait, you wished for a *concert*?"

"I did," he said, shaking his head at the memory. "I made the wish, and a week later there they were, playing a show in New York. And I had four front row tickets."

"How was it?" I asked, almost despite myself.

Leaning forward, like he was about to confide the world's biggest secret, he said, "It was the best. Thing. Ever."

He thought Oliver was awesome, he wanted to devote his life to helping other people, *and* he liked music.

I hated him.

"Look, James," I said, folding my hands on the edge of the table.

"Call me Jamie," he said with a shrug. "Honestly, I keep trying to make 'James' stick, but I think it's too late. I went by Jamie for too long."

And he had an endearingly little-boyish name. Ugh.

"Jamie," I said. "Okay. Here's the deal. I get where you're coming from——I really do——but your timing's a little, um, not-awesome. Did Oliver tell you *why* it'd have to be me who grants your fourth wish? Like, as opposed to any other genie in the world?"

He furrowed his eyebrows. No, apparently not.

"Well," I said, "it's because Oliver and I are the only two genies left. And this is only as of three weeks ago. There was this guy who was killing off every genie he could find. He's gone now, but Oliver and me . . . well, we're the only ones who survived. And we're both still kind of . . . I mean, it was just really recent, you know?"

A skewed version of the truth, and by no means the *entire* truth——but it wasn't exactly a lie.

Jamie nodded. "How long will it be until it's *not* too recent?" His voice was soft, like he already knew the answer.

I just shrugged, not quite meeting his eyes.

"Well," he said, standing up abruptly, collecting his empty salad bowl and water bottle. "I guess that's it, then. It was nice to get to know you a little bit, Margo. Thank you again for coming all the way here to meet me."

His tone had gone from friendly to formal faster than I could blink. It wasn't a real thank-you. It was a speech well-practiced by someone who was just a little too good at taking disappointment in stride.

"Wait," I found myself saying as he walked away.

Turning back toward me, he said, "Yes?"

"You can still have three wishes, if you want," I said. "It's not the same as becoming one of us, but . . . it's better than nothing, right?"

I'd thought it a generous offer a few seconds ago—but hearing the words come out of my mouth, watching his reaction to them, I realized that it wasn't much at all. He'd asked for a real, live pony, and I'd offered him a tiny plastic toy in its place.

Still, Jamie tilted his head to the side, mulling it over. "Better than nothing," he said, more to himself than to me. "But what's to stop me from making a fourth wish after I've made my third?"

My stomach churned. I hadn't thought of that.

Lifting my chin a little, I said, "Before I give you my vessel, you're going to promise me that you won't. That'll be enough to stop you."

"A promise?" he asked, arching an eyebrow at me. "That's all?"

"Do I need to take more precautions than that?" I asked.

Jamie's jaw worked, but after a moment he shook his head. "No, you don't. And I'll take those three wishes."

"Good," I said, feeling slightly less guilty. "I'm gonna tell my current master to make all her wishes by Saturday. You can have my vessel then. But start planning now, okay?"

"I've been planning for thirteen years," he said with a smile. "Never thought I'd get a do-over, but I always planned for one, just in case."

"Cool," I said. "Well . . . I guess I'll call you on Saturday, then."

"Saturday," he agreed, and left me alone at the table with a half-eaten salad, seven minutes until the next bell rang, and a nagging sense that maybe I wasn't as nice a person as I'd always imagined myself to be.

Chapter TWENTY-TWO

Since it would hardly be fair to give Naomi a wish-making deadline with no advance notice, I made a point of getting to rehearsal a little bit early, so I could pull her aside and give her the news.

Of course, early didn't mean much during Hell Week; since we only had an hour between the end of school and the beginning of rehearsal, most people tended not to bother going home in between. Which meant that by the time I showed up, the auditorium was crowded with people camped out in the aisles, their belongings strewn over seats and stuffed under the stage.

In the middle of it all, though, was a crowd of people, right by the pit—all gathered around Naomi and Ryan, who were facing each other down like a couple of cowboys at high noon. I edged toward the crowd until I could hear what was going on.

"Come on," Ryan was saying, a calculatedly innocent look on his face. "Why would I even do something like that?"

"Gosh golly, let me think," said Naomi, her voice thick with disdain. "Could it be because you're pissed off at me for telling everyone the truth about you?"

Ryan spread his hands wide, shaking his head. "You're the one who's pissed here, not me. How would I even have done that, anyway?"

"How should I know?" she said. "I don't know how hacking works. But it can't be hard, if you did it."

Hacking? What the hell was going on? I'd gone back to my house for maybe twenty minutes tops, just long enough to make a couple sandwiches, but apparently that had been enough time for Ryan to ruin Naomi's life yet again.

"I didn't do anything," he said calmly. "Look, it's not my fault you like spreading rumors about people. Turns out I was just your first victim. So, the way I see it, either all of it's true—everything you said about me, *and* everything you said about everyone else—or none of it's true. Which is it?"

Naomi narrowed her eyes. "Listen, you worthless son of a—"

"What the hell, Naomi?" came a new voice. MaLinda Jones, the senior who played Pirelli, was storming toward us with murder in her eyes; the crowd parted to let her through. "Paying for grades? Are you serious? What have I ever done to you?"

Putting a defensive hand up between herself and MaLinda,

Naomi shook her head. "It wasn't me, I swear. Ryan hacked into—"

"Again with the accusations!" interrupted Ryan, rolling his eyes. "I told you, I didn't do anything."

"Shut up, Ryan," said Naomi. "Look, MaLinda, I swear I didn't post anything about you. But everyone knows you'd never do that, so—"

"Yeah, everyone except my father," she said. "You tagged me in that post, and it showed up on my wall, and he saw it. I'm grounded for two whole weeks after the show closes."

The horrified look on Naomi's face pretty much said it all. I couldn't decide which was worse: Ryan making a public post about MaLinda paying for grades—because obviously it had been Ryan—or MaLinda's dad actually believing it.

"It wasn't her," I said, fighting the urge to cringe as everyone looked over at me. "Naomi wouldn't do that."

"Shut up, Mrs. Robinson," said MaLinda, curling her hands into fists. I stepped back, completely confused.

Ryan smirked, and Naomi's eyes went wide—but before either of them could reply, Miss Delisio appeared, placing a hand on MaLinda's shoulder. "If you two are going to start pulling each other's hair, take it outside, all right?"

MaLinda seemed to shrink into herself. "But Naomi—"

"I don't care," said Miss Delisio. "What happens outside this theater, stays outside this theater. This is Hell Week, people, which means you eat, sleep, and breathe *Sweeney Todd*. Nothing else. This rehearsal starts in ten minutes, which does not mean that in ten minutes you start putting your stuff away and getting your costumes on. It means that in ten minutes, I want each and every one of you in your places for the top of Act One."

She strode away, leaving a trail of silence in her wake.

Naomi was the first one to speak: "What are you guys all looking at? You heard her. Places in ten."

The small crowd dispersed, Ryan and MaLinda included. But I lingered behind. As Naomi turned toward her stage manager's notebook, which sat open on the stage, I tapped her on the shoulder.

She whirled around. "What do you want?" But her face softened almost immediately as she saw it was me. "Oh. Sorry. Listen, thanks for sticking up for me. God. Did you *see* those things he posted from my account?"

"No," I said.

Naomi took out her phone, which already displayed what she wanted to show me: her profile, full of status updates all posted within the past half hour.

There was one about Callie Zumsky having gotten a boob job last year. Another one about Dan Quimby-Sato only being good at cross-country because he was on steroids. Another one about Simon selling weed out of his locker. And then, of course, the one about MaLinda Jones paying her biology teacher for an A on her midterm—along with a pointed innuendo about her currency of choice.

"There's one about you, too," she said, using her thumb to scroll down.

SUPER-DUPER CONGRATS TO MARGO MCKENNA. I WOULDN'T HAVE PUT MONEY ON YOU GETTING IT ON WITH A SOPHOMORE, BUT WAY TO THINK OUTSIDE THE BOX! ABOUT TIME YOU LOST THE V-CARD, MRS. ROBINSON!

As I rolled my eyes, extremely relieved that Ryan hadn't come up with something worse to say about me, Naomi said, "See? It's the stupidest stuff. I don't get how anyone believes it was really me. And what does that Mrs. Robinson thing even mean, anyway?"

"Oh, it's from this movie where a college kid has an affair with someone his mom's age, and there's this great Simon and Garfunkel song . . ." But Naomi was staring at me, her raised eyebrow telling me plainly that she couldn't care less. "Never mind," I said. "You're right. There's obviously no way this was you."

"But there's also no way to prove it," she said. "I was hoping if I left them up long enough . . . well, I don't know what I was hoping. I should probably just delete them and hope this blows over."

It wasn't a lot to hope for. I thought about suggesting that she make another wish to end the feud once and for all—but she'd already wasted one wish on Ryan. It would be stupid to waste another, especially over something as petty as this.

"You could get back at him," I said.

"He'd just get back at me worse," she replied. "There's no point in escalating this even more."

Which was a valid point. But there had to be something she could do. I made a mental note to think more about this later. For now, though, I had more pressing things to discuss.

"Listen, can we talk for a sec?" I said, and lowered my voice enough that she'd catch my meaning. "Somewhere private?"

She led me over to the corner of the pit behind the piano, which was private enough, since George hadn't arrived yet. "What's up? Is this about—oh, sorry. No more direct questions."

"No worries," I said. "And no, it's not him. It's about your wishes. Do you think you could make them, like . . . soon? Like before Saturday?"

She frowned. "Why Saturday?"

I had to answer, of course—but should I tell her about Jamie, whose dreams I'd crushed just hours ago, or about my plan to run away with Oliver?

Jamie would be easier to explain . . . but I'd have to tell her sooner or later that I was leaving.

Might as well be sooner, I thought, just as the headache started to creep in.

"Because Saturday's my last day in Oakvale," I said. "I'm leaving after closing night."

"Leaving," she echoed blankly, and then narrowed her eyes. "To go where?"

"Wherever I want." Then I realized this didn't mean much without context, so I added, "With Oliver. We're running away together."

She studied me for a second, like she was trying to figure out whether or not I was kidding. I tried to look as dead-serious as I possibly could.

"As in . . . like, *running away* running away?"

I nodded.

"As in leaving me behind?"

I blinked in surprise. It wasn't about leaving her; surely she could understand that. But before I could think of a way to explain, my magic forced the truth out of me: "Yeah. And stop it with the freaking questions already."

"I think you dropping a bombshell like that means I can ask anything I want," said Naomi, her voice growing rougher around the edges. "What brought this on, anyway?"

"Everything," I said.

"Five minutes, people!" called Miss Delisio from the stage.

"I should get my costume on," I said, and started away from Naomi—but she caught me by the arm.

"Oh no you don't," she said. Then she called over to our director: "Hey, Miss D.? McKenna's not feeling too great. I'm gonna take her to the ladies' in case she barfs. We won't be long."

"But I'm not—"

"Yes you are," she said. She pulled me up the aisle, out of the auditorium, and down the hall, finally letting go of me just outside the girls' room.

Rubbing the spot where she'd gripped my arm, I scowled at her. "You didn't have to do that. We could've just talked later."

"McKenna, we've got Hell Week, school, and more Hell Week between now and the day you're apparently leaving. There is no 'later.' What happened?"

I slumped against the brick wall. The truth was, now that I'd made the decision to leave, it felt inevitable—a choice that had been lingering just below the surface of my life, just waiting for me to notice it. But I had a feeling that would sound stupid if I said it out loud, so I went for the easier explanation instead.

"Oliver happened," I said. "You know that ex of his? The one who wanted to kill every genie in the world, and then off himself, too?"

"The homicidal maniac," she said. "Yeah, you've mentioned him once or twice."

"Well . . . he's gone now. And for the first time in his entire life—well, most of his life—Oliver's not running from anything. Being a genie doesn't automatically translate to having a target on his back. So he figures, hey, time to make more genies!"

Naomi looked completely disgusted. "As in, he wants to have *kids* with you? Hello, McKenna. You're eighteen. I know he's from the Middle Ages or whatever, but women aren't baby factories anymore."

"No, no, no!" I said with a laugh. "Not kids. As in, he wants to grant fourth wishes for more people."

"Ohhhh," she said, pressing a hand to her chest in relief. "That's way better. Geez. For a second I thought I'd have to track Parish down and kick his ass for you."

"No ass-kicking necessary," I said. "He just wants friends."

"Well, that makes sense. Cool." Then she paused, taking in the look on my face. "Wait. Not cool?"

"Cool in theory," I said. "But in reality . . . I mean, he already found this one guy. Or, I guess, the guy found him. Whatever. Point is, this guy wants to be a genie *specifically* so he can give up his human life and go around granting wishes all the time, just like Oliver does. So Oliver's all like, 'Woo, yay, finally someone who can live like I do and understand all my weary-traveler problems and not have to worry about being on time for school the next day!' And, like . . . where do I fit into that? You know?"

"You're his girlfriend," said Naomi, like that ought to explain everything.

"Sure, for now," I said. "But what if he keeps granting

fourth wishes for really interesting people, and they all leave their human lives behind, and he gets so caught up in them that he forgets about me?"

Naomi stared at me. "You sound like a crazy person. You know that, right?"

I leaned my head back against the wall, closing my eyes with a sigh. "I know," I said. "I'm not explaining it right, is all."

"Then try again," she insisted.

Keeping my eyes closed, I said softly, "When I made my fourth wish, I didn't know what I was getting into. I do now. And the truth of it is, I can't have both. I can't be fully human when I'm always bound to a master, always afraid my master will call me to make a wish, and always wondering if one of those wishes will be like what Ryan did to you. And I can't be a hundred percent genie when I'm doing all these human things, like being in the play and checking in with my mom and—"

"Hanging out with me," Naomi said.

I was so thankful that that hadn't been a question. I didn't think either of us would have liked the answer.

"So, that leaves two options," I said. "Change back into a human being, or give up the human stuff and just . . . be a genie."

"Is it even possible to change back?" asked Naomi.

"I don't think so," I said. "So, only one option, I guess. Hence the running-away plan."

"Would you change back, if you could?"

I hadn't even considered that before, but I found that I already knew the answer. "No, I'm pretty sure I wouldn't."

"McKenna," she said slowly, leaning one hand against the wall so our faces were inches apart, "did I ever tell you about last Christmas break?"

"Yeah," I said. "Gift cards from your parents, another reindeer sweater from your aunt . . ."

"Not that part," she said. "I'm talking about the part where Diego and I went to New Mexico."

I racked my memory, but came up blank. Weird. Surely she would've told me about something as cool as that. "No . . . ?"

"Well, we did," said Naomi. "I paid for his plane ticket. We'd been going out for, what, two weeks? Three? I'm not sure. But we were so freaking head-over-heels for each other, it was ridiculous. I'm talking full-frontal honeymoon phase."

"That I do remember," I said with a smile. There'd been full weeks when Naomi had refused to talk about anything except what kind of coffee Diego liked, or how proud she was that he'd gotten straight A's in all of that semester's classes, or the way his shirts showed off his arms. It was completely adorable, and completely infuriating.

"But he was in college," she said. "He had all these college friends who were dating college girls, and he felt really weird about dating a high-schooler, even if he was totally crazy about me. And for me, opposite side of the same coin. I'd feel weird bringing him to high school stuff, because it would make me feel too young for him. So we decided to go to New Mexico. Neither of us had ever been there before, and it didn't have any memories for us, or any traces of who we'd been before we met each other. We'd be able to start from scratch."

"You mean you were planning on staying?"

"You bet," she said. "And we were there for four whole days before we both realized what a stupid-ass idea it was. We had no money. No way to get good jobs. Nowhere to live. We'd even left our cars behind."

"It's not the same for me," I said.

"It's *exactly* the same," said Naomi. "You're riding high on this honeymoon-phase feeling of, like, being so in love with someone that nothing else matters. But it *all* matters. Who you are now, sure, but also who you used to be, and the people around you, and the things you do, and all those weird little things you still have hanging on your wall from when you were a kid, and . . . all of it. All of it matters. You can't just throw it away like it's nothing."

Her eyes were unusually bright and, with no small measure of shock, I realized that she was seconds away from crying. Naomi did not cry.

"Why didn't you ever tell me about New Mexico?" I asked softly.

She gave a single snort of laughter. "Because, McKenna, you are the sensible one. And I figured if I told you, you'd look at me exactly the way I'm looking at you now. Like you are a crazy lovesick beeyatch who should probably be in a padded cell."

"I don't think you're crazy," I said.

"I'm not saying I'm crazy," she said. "I'm saying *you're* crazy. I'm saying you should give it some time. You've only been with Parish for, what, twelve seconds?"

"About a month," I said.

"Same thing."

"It's *not* the same thing," I said again. "None of it's the same, Naomi. You don't understand——"

"But I'm trying to!" she said.

"But you can't!" I said. "You don't have all these weird magical powers, and you're not going to live forever, and you don't have to grant wishes for people. Okay? You don't know what it's like, so you can't understand."

A long silence stretched between us, and she pushed herself off from the wall. "Fine. We should get back to rehearsal."

She turned and stalked back toward the auditorium, with me hot on her heels. "Will you make your two wishes by Saturday?" I asked.

For a second I thought she wasn't going to answer at all. But then she said, "What if I wished for you to stay in Oakvale?"

"Then I'd have to stay," I replied, even as a fear pricked at my skin. "But . . . you wouldn't do that, right? It's my life. You wouldn't."

Resting her hand on the handle of the theater door, she gave me a long look. Then she shook her head and disappeared into the darkened auditorium. A long, long moment passed before I followed.

As I darted down the aisle and headed for the dressing rooms backstage, it occurred to me that this conversation would have been so much easier if Naomi were a genie. If she really *could* understand how different it was from being human.

Then I realized how Oliver-ish that thought had been, and I dismissed it. I didn't need her to understand. I just needed her to make her wishes and let me go.

Chapter TWENTY-THREE

Naomi barely spoke to me for the rest of Hell Week. This wasn't saying much, since everyone in the company was so busy, we barely had the time—let alone the energy—to do anything except for, in Miss Delisio's words, eating, sleeping, and breathing *Sweeney Todd*.

Hell Week was the one time of year where we drama club students got the kind of treatment usually reserved for kids who played varsity sports. Undone homework was forgiven. Tests and papers were postponed. And since it was only late April, most teachers even put off final exam reviews until after the show was over.

My parents, who were just as used to this routine as my teachers were, made a point of keeping leftovers in the fridge, microwave-ready in case I wanted a midnight snack when I got home—which I always did. And then, after I'd eaten and finished whatever homework I hadn't managed to do during rehearsal, I would curl up in Oliver's arms and sleep like a rock until morning.

By Friday, coffee was basically the only thing keeping me awake. I was a total zombie.

But once classes ended, I made my way up to the theater—and everything changed. The whole place was alive with opening-night jitters and sudden onslaughts of stage fright and people running around doing last-minute prop things and costume things and freaking-out things.

The adrenaline was infectious, and more potent than a triple shot of espresso, and suddenly I was wide-awake. I wasn't a person counting down the hours until she could leave her hometown for good. I was a person about to step into a spotlight and do what she loved most: sing for an audience.

One costume change, two break-a-leg speeches, and three hours later, we were ready. *I* was ready. Sure, I wasn't playing the part I'd wanted to play when all this had started—that was Vicky's job now—but I was going to get out there and be the best damn Tobias Ragg anyone had ever seen.

"House lights, go," said Naomi, standing next to me in her booth. I tried to catch her eye and grin, but she wasn't paying attention to me. "Curtain, go."

The curtain rose. The orchestra swelled. The entire cast, me included, stepped into the glaring stage lights. Two thousand people, an entire sold-out house, watched us. And we began to sing.

It wasn't spectacular; this was still a high school show, after all. But everyone was in the right place at the right time, nobody forgot any lines, and our harmonies sounded pretty damn awesome. Simon was amazing, which surprised nobody. Even Vicky was good, which made me proud. Ryan was entirely too convincing as the villainous Judge Turpin. And I was pretty pleased with my own performance, too.

Okay, fine. I was freaking great.

The audience was full of people we knew, so it goes without saying that the standing ovation started with the very first ensemble bow. Ensemble, then bit parts, then leads, ending with Vicky and Simon. We held hands and took our final bow. The audience roared. Gwen, sitting in the pit below me, gave me two thumbs-up and grinned like a loon. When we gestured toward George and the pit in order to let the audience applaud them, too, I blew Gwen a kiss. I didn't even care if anyone noticed.

After the show, there was a thick crowd of relatives and friends and teachers and such, but I still found my parents easily. My dad loomed over most of the crowd, and my mom, from whom I'd inherited my lack of height, was literally bouncing on her toes as she tried to peer over other people to spot me. I waved and wove through the crowd toward them.

"Margo, honey, you were amazing," said Mom, crushing me into a hug.

"So good," said Dad, considerably less gushy but visibly proud. "So good."

"Your best role yet," said Mom, without missing a beat.

Dad handed me a bouquet of gorgeous pink and yellow roses.

When Mom finally loosened her grip, she gave me a secretive little smile. "Don't look now, but your boyfriend's here."

Obviously, I looked. Oliver was only a few layers of people away, leaning against one of the brick walls. He waggled his fingers at me. I waggled mine back.

"We didn't spot him at the show," Mom continued, in probably the worst stage whisper the world had ever heard. "We thought he'd be up front with us, but he probably came with his own friends."

"Seems like a nice kid, though," added Dad, glancing Oliver's way.

I laughed. "You haven't even met him."

Dad spared a moment to look thoughtful, then shrugged. "I like the look of him."

Oliver was still watching us, the very picture of infinite patience. But it was a patience I didn't share. I gestured toward him and looked back at my parents. "Mind if I . . . ?"

Mom grinned. "Don't let me stop you."

Handing the bouquet off to Mom, I wove through the crowd again—but just before I reached Oliver, I realized that I wasn't the only one trying to get to him. And it wasn't me who got there first.

It was Naomi.

"Hey there, Parish," she said. "Haven't seen you around in a while."

Looking mildly bemused by the edge of accusation in her tone, Oliver replied, "Well, that's because I haven't *been* around in a while." That was when he spotted me, hovering just behind Naomi. His entire face went bright and sunny, and he enveloped me in a huge bear hug. "You're amazing—no, beyond amazing. Stunningly, indescribably, sexily, wonderfully, transcendently awesome. Except more so."

"So are you," I said, leaning up for a quick kiss.

I could practically hear Naomi rolling her eyes. "Okay, kids, break it up," she said. "We have to talk."

My heartbeat quickened as I pulled away from Oliver. "Here?" I asked. "Now?"

"Here and now," she said firmly. "Unless you'd rather I talk to them instead."

At first I didn't know who she meant—but then I saw that she was pointing across the room. Right at my parents, both of whom were watching us with a clueless sort of fondness.

"You would *not* do that," I whispered.

But before Naomi could answer, Oliver put a hand on my shoulder and said, "What's up, Naomi?"

Naomi glared at him. "What's up is that you somehow convinced my bestie to abandon her whole life and run away with you."

Oliver cast a worried look at me, then back at Naomi. "What are you accusing me of, exactly? Margo made her own decision."

"Sure," she said, "after you threatened to replace her with new genies who're more okay with leaving their lives behind."

"Not so loud," I said.

But Naomi wasn't done. "Wait. I'm sorry. Did I say 'convinced' before? I meant 'blackmailed.' Because I think we both know that McKenna's not stupid enough to do something like that on her own."

I wasn't sure whether to be insulted—because it *was* my own decision, dammit—or touched that she'd tried so hard to find a way not to blame me.

"I never threatened . . ." Oliver trailed off, looking at me with an uncertainty that hadn't been there a second ago. "Margo, what's going on?"

"He didn't blackmail me," I said. "I just want to leave."

Ignoring me completely, Naomi said, "You know what's going on. You've got another guy lined up to turn himself into a genie and take McKenna's place."

Oliver blinked, completely confused. "Who—wait, you mean James?"

But before either of us could answer, another voice reached my ears: "Margo!"

All three of us looked toward the source of the voice, just in time to see Vicky barreling toward us. She threw herself at me, almost knocking me over with the force of her hug.

"Thank you," she said, fixing me with a firm, no-nonsense sort of look. "Seriously, thank you times a million for going over all those songs with me. I would've completely sucked if we hadn't . . ." She trailed off with a frown. "Wait, I *didn't* suck, right?"

I laughed. "No, you definitely didn't suck. You were awesome."

Beaming, she turned to Oliver. "And you!"

"Me?" he said, bewildered by her enthusiasm—which was understandable. Vicky and Oliver hadn't parted ways on the best of terms; her stint as his master had ended with her getting pissed off about her second wish and leaving his vessel for me to find.

"Yeah, you. You said the . . . you know . . . it would work out if I just gave it a chance. You were right. You were so, so right."

She hugged him with the same iron grip as she'd used on me. Oliver grinned and hugged her back.

Naomi, however, hung back, watching Vicky and Oliver's hugfest with a critical eye. After a moment, she turned back to me. "Either he's really good at pretending not to be a manipulative bastard," she said, "or this whole running-away thing actually *was* your idea."

"You really think I'd run away with a guy who'd do that?" I asked.

"I don't know what to think," she said.

"Think about your wishes," I said. "Saturday's tomorrow, you know."

"I know." She bit her lip, looking a lot more uneasy than she had a moment ago. "I actually do have a second wish."

"You do?" I asked. She nodded. "Good. Let's get this done."

I made a call-you-later gesture at Oliver, who was still chatting with Vicky. He gave me a somewhat worried look in return, but nodded. Naomi and I headed back toward the greenroom, in which a few people were still milling around— and then the wings of the theater, which were entirely empty.

"So what's the wish?" I asked.

Naomi held out her phone, and I took it. The screen displayed an email from her sister, Kristina.

THE LATEST? HIS MOM'S SAYING SHE WON'T PAY FOR HER HALF IF WE DON'T GET A CATHOLIC PRIEST. I MEAN, FOR SERIOUS? I'M NOT CATHOLIC! AND JARED KEEPS SAYING SHE'S RIGHT! WTF? I HATE THIS WOMAN. HAAAAAATE.

"Ugh," I said. "His mom sounds like the worst."

"She is," said Naomi darkly, shoving her phone into her back pocket. "But what I've been realizing is that the mom isn't the real problem. She's not the one Kris is marrying. She *is* marrying Jared, and he's a stupid little mama's boy who won't even stand up for the woman he supposedly loves. First the dress, then the location, now this. Jared's got to go. And that's what my second wish is gonna be."

"It is?" I said, sort of dumbfounded. For someone who got so nervous at the mere mention of magic, Naomi had decided on an awfully big wish. "So, wait . . . what do you mean by 'go'? Like, do you want him physically gone? Should I send him away to live in Brazil or something?"

"No, I just want them broken up. Quickly and permanently."

Quickly, as in before the wedding. Permanently, so Naomi wouldn't have to deal with this again if they hooked up five years down the road. I could do that.

"Okay," I said. "Bring it on. Remember how to make the wish?"

"Duh," said Naomi, and held up her thumb and fore-finger, which were already holding my vessel. She looked nervous. Well, the Naomi version of nervous, which was still nine times more confident than most people. "Okay. Margo McKenna, I wish Kristina and her stupid fiancé would just break up for good."

My magic swelled within me, and I could feel it molding itself into the wish's shape, the same way it had done with Naomi's first wish, and with Ryan's last. It targeted Kristina and Jared, two people whose images sat suddenly vivid in my mind's eye, even though I'd never met Jared in my life. It planted a breakup between them, like a bomb. And then it asked me if I wanted to add details.

But I didn't. My magic had healed Ryan exactly as much as I'd wanted him healed, and it had granted Naomi's first wish perfectly. I trusted it to make this one work just as well.

Go, I thought, and let the explosion happen.

When it was done, Naomi was looking at me with an expression halfway between amusement and sheer fascination—and I was so woozy that I actually had to sit down. That had been a big wish. The biggest one I'd granted so far, without a doubt.

"Did it work?" asked Naomi.

I nodded. "No more Jared, and no more crazy mother-in-law-to-be."

"Sweet," she said . . . and then eyed me again. And the chair I was sitting in. "You okay?"

"I will be in a sec," I said as the wooziness gave way to the pleasant feeling of magical aftershocks coursing through my veins.

"Good," she said. "Because you really shouldn't sit there."

"Why?" I said, half a second before I saw the answer. I was sitting in Sweeney's barbershop chair—the most important, and most disgusting, prop in the entire musical.

I shot up and gave myself a quick once-over. Sure enough, a blotch of stage blood had stained my elbow orangey-red.

"Ew," said Naomi appreciatively.

I'm clean, I thought. The stage blood vanished.

Naomi recoiled, just a little bit. Now that the stage blood was gone, she actually looked far more grossed out. Looking from my elbow to my face and back again, she said, "Well. Okay, then. Diner time? Oh, wait, hold on."

Her phone had started playing one of her many individually selected ringtones: a Michael Jackson song whose name I didn't know.

"Kris?" she said, looking smugly at me as she brought the phone to her ear. "What's up?"

A shrill voice blared through the speakers, loud enough for me to understand that there was yelling going on, but not loud enough that I could hear the words. Naomi's face grew pinched as she listened. "What did—hold on—no, honey, slow down—read me exactly what he said."

She pressed a button, and suddenly Kristina's voice rang loud and clear through the empty theater wings: "—st what I told you before. 'I don't think this is working. We have to break up.' Eleven words! *Eleven*! Over *text message*!"

"Oh my god," I breathed, unsure whether to be horrified on Kristina's behalf, or insanely proud that the breakup had happened so quickly, and all thanks to me.

"Wait," said Kristina. "Is someone else there? Am I on speakerphone?"

"No, no, no!" said Naomi, glaring at me as she clicked the speakerphone feature off.

"Sorry," I mouthed. She glared harder.

"Text, though?" Naomi continued. "Okay, how soon can I come down to Baltimore and bash this guy's head in?"

She started to pace, and I hung back, somewhat surprised by her reaction. Not the violence of it—that was pure Naomi—but the way she clearly wanted to direct some of that violence at me. Pace, pace, glare. Pace, pace, glare.

I didn't get it. She'd wanted them broken up, hadn't she?

The phone call alternated between threats of stabbing and soothing assurances that everything would be all right. Then, finally, she hung up. And rounded on me.

"Are you kidding me, McKenna?" she said. "I wanted them to break up so my big sister could finally be *happy,* and you had him break it off over *text* with *no explanation*? What the hell?"

"Whoa, whoa," I said, holding my hands up and taking a few steps back. My leg bumped against the seat of the barber-shop chair. "You just said they should break up. You didn't say how."

But even so, guilt began to curdle inside me. My magic had asked me for input on the wish's details—which meant I could have shaped it into any kind of breakup Naomi wanted, if only I'd thought to ask her first.

"I didn't say how, so you picked the worst possible way?" she seethed.

"I didn't pick anything," I said. "My magic did."

"I thought you could shape your magic," she said, narrowing her eyes at me.

I nodded, feeling my face go red with shame. That was exactly what I'd said. "I'm sorry. I'm just really new at this. Oliver can read people's minds so he knows what they really want, but I can't do that yet, and . . ."

I trailed off, biting my lip and waiting for her to yell again.

But she didn't. She just sighed and rubbed her forehead with her knuckles. "No, I know. Sorry, I just thought it'd be . . . well . . . but whatever, it's fine. You did your best. At least there won't be a wedding now."

She turned back toward the greenroom and started typing on her phone, effectively ending the conversation.

"Are you going to the diner with everyone else?" I asked, hoping that maybe I could offer her a ride. Anything, as long as we had more time to talk—more time for me to make sure our friendship was still salvageable.

"Maybe later," she said. "For now, I have to find a quiet corner and talk Kris off the ledge. And you know Kris. That might take a while."

She shot a last halfhearted smile back at me, and then left.

Chapter TWENTY-FOUR

After the opening night of any given show, everyone went to Tom's Diner. It was loud, and it was fun, and it had been a Jackson High Drama Club tradition for as long as anyone could remember.

Which was why, when I went back out to the lobby and told my parents I was heading to Tom's and probably sleeping over at Naomi's, they believed me without question. In truth, I actually didn't know yet where I was going. All I knew was that I needed to go somewhere to think.

I followed the line of cars out of the parking lot, but turned left when everyone else turned right. I thought about stowing my car somewhere safe and jumping across the world—back to the Great Wall, maybe, or into the middle of the Australian Outback or something. But instead, I just drove aimlessly, taking comfort in the familiar gritty smoothness of the road, and in my stereo, blasting all the worst dance-pop songs I could find.

Only once I was almost there did I realize where I'd been

headed: the empty second-floor apartment that Oliver had temporarily claimed as his home.

I parked the car and jumped inside.

I hadn't been to Oliver's apartment in quite a while—not since the night he'd told me that he wasn't really a sixteen-year-old boy who happened to be a genie, but rather an immortal shapeshifter who was pushing two hundred. Every detail was burned into my memory. The saggy couch. The threadbare carpet and the cheap folding chair and the shoeless shoe rack. Just enough odds and ends to give the whole thing an air not just of emptiness, but of abandonment.

I wasn't sure why I'd come here, exactly, but now that I'd arrived, it felt right. I sent Oliver a quick text, telling him where I was, and waited for a few seconds for him to appear. But he didn't.

Figuring he was busy and he'd show up when he was ready, I looked around for a place to go that was less depressing than the living room. And found one pretty quickly, behind a closed door next to the kitchen. Oliver's bedroom.

It was just as barren as the living room, with only a mattress on the floor and, beside it, the kind of wooden nightstand that couldn't seem to decide whether or not it secretly wanted to be a filing cabinet.

Some strange impulse drove me toward the mattress, where I stretched myself out on top of the covers and arranged my head on the pillow. The mattress was comfortable enough, and the pillow was incredibly fluffy. Somehow, that made me feel a lot better about the lack of a bed frame.

It also made me feel like a spoiled brat for owning what was probably the most comfortable queen-sized bed in the history of the world. Although, these days, Oliver was spending practically every night with me—so at least I was a spoiled brat who knew how to share her toys.

The nightstand held a lamp, which didn't actually work, and a small pile of books. I peered closer, wondering what sort of books Oliver liked to read—but they all had titles that didn't sound Oliver-ish at all. *Anna and the French Kiss. The Boyfriend List. Vampire Crush.* They looked like books that someone my age—most likely a girl—might read. Maybe they'd been left by the previous tenant.

So I ignored the books and moved on to the drawers. The top one was empty, but there were actually a few things in the bottom one. Including two cameras: one pocket-sized and digital, one complicated and fancy-looking.

Found you, Oliver, I thought, smiling as I touched the bigger camera.

Even though I kind of wanted to take it out and fiddle with it, I didn't dare. It looked expensive, and I didn't want to risk breaking it. But I did move it to the side, because there was something underneath it that looked very intriguing indeed: a large, bulky manila envelope. Unsealed.

Unsealed and unlabeled, which meant there was nothing

telling me that I shouldn't look inside. Well, nothing except a deeply ingrained knowledge that it wasn't cool to snoop through other people's stuff—but it wasn't like Oliver had never gone through *my* stuff. So I opened the envelope and let the contents slide onto the dark blue bedspread.

Pictures.

A whole pile of pictures was inside, some of places, some of people. None of them were familiar, and none of them were labeled.

Oliver had told me once that he took pictures because he wanted to remember all the lives he'd led, all the masters he'd been bound to, all the people he'd been. But these pictures seemed like they were all from the same era—the late eighties or early nineties, if the hair and clothes were any indication. I sifted through them, smiling to myself, wondering who they all were, and how Oliver had felt about them, and how they had treated him, and a million other things.

I was examining a picture of a bright-eyed, mischievous-looking man lounging in a wicker chair, a martini glass in one hand and a cigar in the other, when I heard the soft sound of footsteps behind me. Standing up, I turned to face Oliver.

"Find anything interesting?" he asked, looking sort of amused.

"Only your deepest, darkest secrets," I said, holding up the picture of Cigar Guy. "Who was this? He looks like he'd have some fun wishes up his sleeve."

Oliver spared half a second to glance at the picture, then let out a snort of laughter. "That was me," he said. "So, more granting than making, where wishes were concerned. Don't tell me you don't recognize me."

Despite his teasing tone, I peered more closely at the picture. Cigar Guy looked nothing at all like Oliver, of course. His hair was short and graying at the temples, and he was thick around the middle where Oliver was slim. But now that I was looking for it, I could see the similarity around the eyes—bright green and shining with mirth.

Still, the rest was kind of weird.

"You look like you're my dad's age," I said, handing him the picture as unease began prickling at the back of my mind. What if I ended up with a master who wanted me to be that old? I had no idea how to be any older than eighteen.

"Probably so," he replied, heading for the nightstand. He stood over the open drawer for a second, like he was trying to figure out what I'd seen, but in the end he set the Cigar Guy picture down atop the pile of books. I'd almost forgotten about the books.

"Oh, right, and you're apparently a fan of vampire romances?" I teased.

"Actually, the vampire one was particularly good," he said with a raised eyebrow. "Those are a couple of Vicky's favorites. I got them when she first became my master so I could, you know, have stuff to talk about with her."

"Ah."

"Anyway," he said, "sorry I took so long—but are you gonna tell me why Naomi thought I was *blackmailing* you?"

"Oh, geez," I said, sinking down onto the mattress. "She's just mad that I'm leaving, and she's looking for someone to blame. I'll talk her down. It'll be fine."

That, at least, was enough to get him to push the pictures aside and sit down next to me—but he still looked worried.

"Okay," he said. "But you told her about James?"

"Jamie," I corrected him with a small smile. "He said he tried to make James stick, but everyone still calls him Jamie anyway."

Oliver's eyebrows shot up in surprise. "You've talked to him?"

I shrugged. "Well, I figured if I wasn't gonna give him a fourth wish, I could at least tell him so to his face. You know? He didn't seem too happy about it, but . . ."

"Wait," said Oliver, eyes narrowing. "You're not giving him a fourth wish?"

"Um, no?" I said with a laugh. "Obviously? I'm running away with you instead."

For a second he just stared at me, uncomprehending. Then he blew out a quiet breath. "Oh," he said. "Margo."

"Oh Margo *what*?" I said, suddenly on edge. What else had I done wrong? "We talked about this. I said I'd run away and travel around with you, and we wouldn't have to turn anyone else . . ."

But I trailed off, trying to remember. Had either of us actually said out loud that we wouldn't grant any more fourth wishes? I could have sworn that we had, or at least that it had been understood, but now, seeing the look on Oliver's face, the way he was slowly shaking his head . . .

I bit my lip. There was silence. And then the creak of the mattress springs as Oliver shifted his weight.

"Margo," he said softly, taking one of my hands in his. "The thing with Jamie . . . I mean . . . you didn't think I was trying to replace you or something . . . did you?"

"Well, obviously not *replace* me," I said with a roll of my eyes.

He paused. "No? Then what?"

His face reflected the hurt I heard in his voice—and the combination was enough to make me stop and think. About Jamie. Replacing me.

Oliver and Jamie, traveling around whenever they wanted to; Oliver and Jamie, spending that week in Paris or that month following a band; Oliver and Jamie, finding dark corners of exciting cities and pressing close to each other, lips touching and—

And where the hell had *that* thought come from? Oliver had told me, point blank, that I was the only one he wanted, even though he'd been with so, so many people before me.

But despite all that, maybe part of me really did think he was trying to replace me.

My breath was coming faster, and Oliver was squeezing my hand, and the room was just too barren and small. I pushed myself to my feet, rubbing my hands over my face as I tried to clear my head enough to think straight.

"Is that the only reason you decided to leave?" he asked after a moment.

When I turned to face him, I saw that he'd stood up, too—and that he was hovering a safe distance away from me, like he wasn't sure getting too close would be a good idea.

"No," I said. "Not only that."

"What else?"

"Well," I said, and licked my lips as I tried to remember. The Jamie thing had been the final straw, but it certainly hadn't been the first. "Well. I mean, I broke Ryan's nose, *and* I lost my guitar for three weeks and didn't even realize it. You know?"

Oliver just looked confused.

I explained, "As in, I suck at being a genie, *and* I'm losing touch with the stuff that made me human. I keep trying to be both, but I'm not really either. You know?"

"Jack of all trades, master of none," Oliver murmured. "I do know."

"*Master* of none?" I said, giving him a sidelong grin. "Har-har."

"What do you—? Oh," he said, smiling sheepishly. "Unintentional, I promise. I never pun on purpose."

"Uh-huh," I said, happy that the mood had been lightened

a little, pun or no pun. "But yeah, that's exactly it. I'm doing two things I'm no good at. I'm not human enough for Naomi, and not genie enough for you. So I'd rather just pick one thing and be awesome at it."

"Not genie enough for . . . ?" Eyes widening, he crossed the space between us, and took me by the shoulders. "Margo, listen to me. Whatever you are will always be enough for me. *More* than enough. Even if you got yourself transformed into, like, a three-headed giraffe, I'd still be crazy in love with you."

"Um, 'three-headed giraffe'? You'd also be just plain crazy," I said as something ballooned in my chest. Something like laughter, or tears, or some combination of both.

He gave a theatrical wince and let go of my shoulders. "Okay, maybe that's a bit much. But you get what I mean, right? There's no right way to be a genie. There's my way, which doesn't involve punching people in the face—but there's also your way, which apparently does. And that's fine! Sometimes people just really need to get punched in the face."

A wild giggle escaped me. Ryan was definitely one of those people.

"My way also involves leaving your hometown and never looking back," said Oliver, his bright gaze holding mine like a magnet. "Well, at least after the engagement ended. But your way doesn't have to be the same. It can, but it doesn't have to. It just depends on what you want."

I took a step back, giving myself more space to think. What did I want? To run off with Oliver and start fresh? To stay in Oakvale and keep living two half lives instead of one full one? Both had their perks; both had their drawbacks. I didn't know which one I wanted. I didn't know anything at all.

Except, weirdly, the one thing that insisted on sticking in my head.

"A three-headed giraffe," I said, and my shoulders started shaking with laughter.

At first Oliver just blinked owlishly at me—and then he was laughing, too. And then, before I knew it, he was kissing me. Soft, at first, but then harder. More insistent. More like he wanted this to lead to something more than kissing, and so did I, and—

I reached up and pulled his hoodie off his shoulders. He shrugged out of it, and let me reach for the hem of his T-shirt, all without breaking the kiss. There was no magic. There was just us.

This, I realized, was what I wanted. Not a plan for tomorrow. Not an easy decision about whether to stay or leave. Just me and Oliver and—

"Not here," he said, nearly breathless as he broke the kiss.

"No?" I said, my fingers pressing into the smooth, bare skin of his back. "Why not?"

"It's not mine. This place. It doesn't belong to either of us." He took a moment to breathe, looking at the bed, the nightstand, the emptiness of the space around us. "Your room?"

I shook my head. Somehow that didn't feel right either.

He thought for a moment, then took my hand. "Jump," he said, mischief glinting in his eyes.

I did.

"Picture a door," he said, his voice ringing hollow in the emptiness of the Between.

I did. He was going to take me to his Between again, with its rolling hills and its mountains in the distance and its peaceful solitude. I liked that plan.

But then he said, "You open it this time, not me. That way, you can make it whatever you want. Your choice."

At first I balked at the idea. I didn't want another choice to make. But on the other hand . . . this was a choice that wouldn't affect anyone except Oliver and me. It wouldn't be permanent, and I could change it on a whim, just like Oliver had done with his own Between. So really, it wouldn't be a choice at all. It would be more like . . . well . . . art.

I closed my eyes and let an image swim into my mind. I arranged and rearranged it until I could picture exactly what I wanted to see. Then I opened the door. And when we went inside . . .

"Ohhh," said Oliver. It was more a breath than a word. I looked over at him and smiled; the look on his face reminded me of how I'd felt the first time he'd brought me to *his* Between.

Which was appropriate, since his Between had actually

inspired mine. I hadn't forgotten lying with him on thick green grass, so soft and lush and clean that you almost didn't believe there was dirt underneath it. We were standing on the same grass now—except instead of patchwork hills and open sky around and above us, we were surrounded by skyscraper-tall trees. A whole forest of them, enclosing our little clearing in dark green and the smell of pine.

And it was nighttime. There was a full moon above us, bathing Oliver in soft, clean light.

"You like?" I asked . . . even though what I was thinking was, *You are ridiculously attractive without a shirt on.*

"I do," he whispered, tearing his gaze away from the moon and focusing on me instead. Moving toward me. Taking me by the hips and pressing me against him.

"Let me take this off you," Oliver murmured, tugging at my shirt. I nodded, breathless, and he lifted it over my head, tossing it off to the side.

He ran one finger down my throat, across my collarbone, down my arm, across my stomach, until his hand skimmed my jeans and nerves made me jump. I couldn't help it: I laughed.

He just smiled. "Are you okay?"

"Yeah. Very, very okay."

Then his hands were reaching for my back—and before I even realized what he was doing, I felt the elastic of my bra go slack. I went still, painfully aware that even the slightest movement would expose more of me than anyone had ever seen before, at least in this context. Going shirtless was one thing; I'd been in enough backstage dressing rooms that I'd long since stopped caring. But going braless meant something entirely different.

At my sudden intake of breath, Oliver pulled away, eyes wide, like he was afraid he'd done something wrong. "We don't have to . . ."

"No, we don't," I said. "But I want to."

I shrugged out of my bra and let him look at me. And he did, his gaze dark and soft as velvet. His hand followed where his eyes led, fingers tracing experimental paths along newly exposed skin. I sighed, shuddering under his touch, and he just . . . kept . . . touching. . . .

We undressed each other slowly, so slowly—and when neither of us was wearing anything at all, I spent one long moment just holding him close, relishing the miraculous fact of his skin against mine, the way his stomach moved in and out as he breathed, the way his—

I looked down.

And felt my face go bright red.

And looked up again.

"Hi," said Oliver, his voice light with laughter. *Laughter.* When I was over here and my clothes were over there and *things* were about to happen. I'd always assumed this sort of situation called for serious faces and whispered promises of eternal love.

I liked the laughter better.

"Come here," he said, pulling me down with him onto the grass. Me on top, him underneath, his breath moving us up and down in a steady rhythm that managed to soothe me and drive me crazy at the same time.

Here was a thing I hadn't realized about Oliver until just now: Clothes or no clothes, he was utterly at home in his own body. He made the whole lying-naked-in-the-grass thing seem downright elegant, in a way I suspected most sixteen-year-old boys couldn't pull off.

Not that I'd ever seen a real live naked sixteen-year-old boy before.

Not that he was actually sixteen, either. And I knew he'd invented this body himself, and he only looked this way because he wanted to, but still . . .

"You're staring," he teased as he ran his fingers down my back.

"Uh, obviously," I said. "Have you seen you?"

"Speak for yourself, Margo," he said, and leaned up to kiss me. "Amber. Enrique." Kiss. "Tony." Kiss . . . and a small, wicked smile. "Master."

The word ignited something inside me. Something wild and huge, whose shape I couldn't begin to define.

"I'm not your master anymore," I said.

"You mean you don't have my ring anymore," he said, voice rumbling low from his chest into mine. "That's different. As far as I'm concerned, you're my master for as long as you want to be."

Then, in a flash, he rolled me over and trapped me against the soft green grass. Every part of his body touched every part of mine. Every inch of me was awake. Oliver was silhouetted in moonlight, and I was holding my breath.

Did he really see all those people in me, all at once? Amber, flirty and feminine. Enrique, handsome and graceful. Tony, bold and strong. *Master,* even if I no longer held his ring.

And Margo. Whatever that meant.

His eyes were dark with desire—the same desire I felt—and I let myself pretend he could see all those things and more.

"Ciarán-Gwen-Alicia-Oliver," I whispered, pretending I could see all of him, too.

"What do you wish of me?" he asked.

I looked at him. He looked at me. We were a live wire. An explosion waiting to happen.

I said, "Everything."

And then he was kissing me again, and I was kissing him back, and it was exactly the way it was supposed to be. No magic numbers, no jealousy. No decisions about going or staying or Jamie. Nothing but the two of us, together, in a place where nobody had ever been before. A place where, just maybe, nobody would ever be again.

Chapter TWENTY-FIVE

Waking up in the Between was definitely one of the weirder experiences I'd had in my life. First, there was the prickly-soft sensation of grass against my cheek. Second, there was the fact that it was still dark. I felt incredibly rested, but the sun wasn't up yet. That didn't make sense.

But as soon as the thought occurred to me, sunlight hit me all at once, like someone turning on high beams in the middle of the night. I looked up, squinting as my eyes adjusted. Had the sun appeared overhead just because I'd thought it should be there?

Okay, then.

"Tnnggggup?" murmured Oliver, all messy-haired and sleepy-eyed and, yup, still not wearing anything. He hadn't shifted back into Gwen during the night—and come to think of it, I hadn't shifted into Enrique, either. Maybe that was because of the Between, too.

I grinned and thought myself back into my clothes. "Sorry, what'd you say?"

"I said, is it time to get up?" Pajama pants appeared on Oliver's lower half as he blinked himself awake.

"I have no idea what time it is," I said. I also didn't really care. "But I'm up anyway."

"Mmkay," he said, and let his eyelids flutter closed again.

Stop shining right in my eyes, I thought at the sun. It obliged immediately, hiding itself behind the treetops instead of beaming down from directly overhead. That was better.

As Oliver's breath evened out beside me, I stared up at the cloudless blue sky.

Tell me whether to stay or leave, I thought at the Between.

It didn't tell me anything at all.

"Margo, honey, is that you?" called my mom.

"No, it's Johnny Depp," I called back, ducking out of the late-morning sunlight and into the cool darkness of my house. I set my shoes neatly in the rack and followed the sound of my mom's voice into the living room.

Mom was in her bathrobe, watching a rerun of some old black-and-white sitcom and clutching what looked suspiciously like a mimosa in her hand. She looked happy.

"Where's Dad?" I asked.

"Hitting the mall before the crowds show up," she replied. "One of his office buddies convinced him that he'll need water shoes for Venice. I said that was a stupid idea, because if you're going to touch that water, you'd be better off with a vaccine than shoes. But did he listen? No, he did not."

"So you just let him go?" I asked, sitting beside her on the couch.

"There's no letting him," she said, giving me a little smile as she sipped her drink. "He wanted to go, so he went. He'll waste money on shoes he won't need, and I'll get to watch him walk around Venice looking like an idiot tourist with water shoes."

The mental image was pretty funny, I had to admit.

Less funny was the reminder that they were, once again, leaving me here. Or they thought they were, anyway. Little did they know, I could go to Venice anytime I wanted to. Right now, even.

Little did they know, I might not be here when they got back.

"When's your flight, again?" I asked.

"Tomorrow night," she said, reaching over to smooth my hair. "Want to come to the airport and see us off?"

A sour feeling rose in my chest. Not because going to the airport was just about the worst thing I could imagine doing, but because she wasn't asking for my company. She was asking for a ride.

"Too much homework," I lied, and headed upstairs.

While I still hadn't finalized a staying-or-leaving plan, today's schedule still held two things that I had to do either way. One was the play, of course. The other was keeping my promise to Jamie.

So as soon as I reached my room, calling Jamie was the first thing I did.

He picked up on the second ring. "Hello?"

"Jamie? It's Margo—um, Oliver's—I mean, Alicia's friend?"

A short laugh crackled down the line. "I know who you are."

"Right, yeah, of course," I said. "Well, today's the day. Want to make some wishes?"

"Really?" He sounded genuinely surprised.

"Well, yeah," I said. "I promised, didn't I?"

"I suppose you did," he said. There was a pause. "Well! My lunch break's just about over, and I'm back to work until seven. How about after that?"

Working on a Saturday. Eesh.

"Well, my call's at six," I said.

"Your what?"

"Sorry. Call time. I'm in a musical, and I have to be at the theater at six."

"A musical?" he said, sounding absolutely delighted. "Which one?"

"*Sweeney Todd*," I said. "Ever seen it?"

"Saw the movie. Good stuff. Are you playing whatserface? Helen Something?"

"Helena Bonham Carter," I said, gripping the phone tighter, like that would keep my old Vicky-centric resentment from leaking out. Helena Bonham Carter had played Mrs. Lovett in the *Sweeney* movie. "And no, I'm playing the weird kid that works for her. Toby."

"Still. Cool."

"Yeah. But I should be free by, say, eleven?"

We agreed to meet at Ben & Jerry's, even though I suspected it would be closed by then. Saturday night or not, Oakvale was a pretty small town.

As soon as I hung up with Jamie, I texted Naomi: NEED MY VESSEL BACK TONIGHT. PLEASE THINK ABOUT MAKING YOUR THIRD WISH, OK? I WON'T SCREW IT UP THIS TIME. PROMISE.

She didn't reply.

"I come bearing a peace offering," I said, when I finally managed to corner Naomi at the theater. "Won't make up for last night, but it might help with certain . . . goings-on."

I gestured over to MaLinda, who was sitting in the front row reading a book—and who had made a point of not speaking to Naomi ever since the hacking incident.

Lowering her voice, Naomi said, "I don't want to talk about wishes."

"This isn't about wishes," I said, even though that was definitely on my agenda, too. Handing her a black folder, I said, "It's about Ryan."

Looking understandably suspicious, she took the folder and opened it. "What the hell is 'The Cave Openeth'? What does this have to do with . . . ohhhh. TenaciousRW—that's him?"

"That's him," I said proudly. "These, my friend, are print-outs of a role-playing game that Ryan plays. None of that fancy-schmancy World of Warcraft stuff. All old-school message board posts—which means all printable."

"Ooh," said Naomi, her eyes skimming the first page. "So he's . . . a werehyena? Seriously, that's his character?"

I laughed. "That's one of them. There are three more. He's also a fisherman's ghost, a zombie snake, and a harem girl."

"Oh, you're kidding," said Naomi gleefully, shuffling through the papers until she got to the last set of posts. "Oh my god. Ohhhh my god. *Amina dances right near the prince. She tries to get his attention with her double D's and the way she's wearing almost nothing. She's sweaty from dancing, but that makes her smell better, not worse.* Oh my god oh my god oh my god."

"I know, right?" I said.

"This is so gross!" she said. "And so amazing!"

I grinned. "And I'm willing to bet he'll do just about any-thing to keep you from, say, scanning these and emailing them to every single person at school."

She turned to me with wide eyes. "Evil genius," she breathed. "I love you."

"Then my work here is done."

I started to head back toward the dressing rooms—but

Naomi grabbed me by the wrist. When I turned around again, her face was dead-serious.

"Don't go," she said.

"Go?" I repeated. Then, "Oh."

She said, "You're too good at this."

Forcing a smile, I replied, "What, helping you smite your enemies?"

"No," she said. "Well . . . yes. That too. But I mean *this*. Living your regular life. Being human. You're *good* at it."

In other words, I was absolute crap at being a genie.

"Plus," she added, "I'd miss you."

"I'd miss you, too," I told her, absolutely truthfully. "But I don't know. I'm not sure what I should do."

She tilted her head, eyeing me keenly. "Oh? I thought you already made up your mind."

"I did. But now . . . I'm just not sure."

"Hmm," was all she said.

"Either way, I promised someone else three wishes tonight. That friend of Oliver's. Can you make your third one before then?"

Her shoulders slumped, and her grip on me lost its intensity. "I told you, McKenna. I'll make another wish when I'm good and ready."

Somehow, I got through the entire show without once getting distracted by what might happen afterward. Would Naomi

make her last wish? Could I grant Jamie's three wishes without screwing them up? Would I stay, or would I leave——or
would I keep putting off the choice, letting it linger forever in
the back of my mind, slowly driving me crazy?

Instead, I thought about being Toby, and about making my
entrances on time, and about the words I had to sing and say.
And about not accidentally shifting into Enrique.

But then, way too soon, the show was over and it was time
to take our bows: the last curtain call of my high school acting
career.

I knew my parents didn't have tickets for closing night, but
I went out to the hallway anyway, just to see if any of my
teachers had shown up. But the first familiar face I saw wasn't
a teacher at all.

It was Jamie.

"What are you doing here?" I said, maybe a little bit more
harshly than I'd intended. "We're not supposed to meet for
another half an hour."

"I wanted to see the show," he said with a shrug and a smile.
"You were good, by the way."

"Oh," I said, more than a little confused. Jamie coming
to the show hadn't been part of the plan. "Well . . . thanks.
Um. I haven't exactly gotten my vessel back from my current
master yet, so . . ."

"No worries," he said. "Take your time."

But I didn't want to take my time. Not now that Jamie was

here and, presumably, ready to make his wishes. If I waited around with him until Naomi showed up, there was too big a chance that the conversation might turn toward the fourth wish that I was refusing him.

I searched the squealing, hugging crowd of actors and tech kids and musicians and parents and friends and teachers. Naomi was nowhere in sight. So I made my way through the throng and back into the theater, where the crowd was thinner. No Naomi there either. I checked backstage, in the greenroom and all the dressing rooms. Still no Naomi.

Since I was already backstage, I changed quickly and grabbed my stuff so I wouldn't have to come back again. But when I picked up my phone, I saw a text sitting there, from just five minutes ago. It was from Naomi.

MEET ME IN THE BAND ROOM. I HAVE A THIRD WISH.

Quiet relief swept through me. At least Naomi wasn't going to put up a fight about the wish anymore. And the band room was an excellent choice for a private location—one floor down from the theater, and far enough out of the way that there wouldn't be much chance of anyone interrupting us.

When I got back to the hallway, I spotted Jamie right where I'd left him. In my absence, Oliver had found him.

"But she said I could have the first wishes anyway," Jamie was explaining as I reached them.

Ah, right. I hadn't told Oliver that part.

"Well, that's something," said Oliver. "Hey, Margo."

"Hey," I said, and then lowered my voice. Not that it mattered in a crowd like this. "Naomi's waiting for me downstairs. She's ready to make a third wish. Jamie, I figure you can just come with me so she can pass my vessel straight to you, and I won't have to disappear in between. Cool?"

He nodded. Oliver, beside him, seemed unsure about whether or not he was invited, too. So I grabbed his hand and we all headed downstairs to the band room. I flipped on the light. And stopped short.

"Um," I said. "I see you brought an entourage."

They all turned to face me when I spoke: Naomi, Simon, and Vicky, who looked like she wanted to hide behind Simon, or possibly run for her life.

"As did you." Naomi nodded at Oliver and Jamie, who lingered beside me, looking just about as confused as I felt.

"Right," I said. "Naomi, this is Jamie. He's the one who's getting my vessel after you make your last wish. I just figured it'd be easier if—"

"I'm not making a wish, McKenna," said Naomi, hooking her thumbs through her belt loops and leveling a Stage Manager Glare at me. "This is an intervention."

"A . . . sorry, what?" I said, frozen stiff and completely mystified. That was a word for addicts and therapists and bad reality TV. Not for me.

"You heard me," said Naomi, and cleared her throat. "Margo

McKenna, one month ago you never would have dreamed of doing what you're thinking of doing now—which is to say, abandoning your entire human life, including your family and your friends, including *me,* and running away with a two-hundred-year-old guy that you basically just met."

Oliver stepped forward. "Naomi, I don't think this is—"

"Quiet, Parish," she snapped. "You've done enough already." Turning back to me, she continued her speech: "Lee, Willoughbee, and I are here today to present you with a list of reasons why you should stay here, and not run away like some boneheaded moron who doesn't care about her friends."

Simon said, "Number one, obviously, is that running away would make you a boneheaded moron. And we are pretty sure that's something you don't want to be."

"Number two," said Naomi. "As I said before—"

"Stop it," I said, my voice coming out soft and shaky. Although, all things considered, I was proud that it had come out at all. "I told you, I haven't made up my mind yet. And I won't be able to if you don't give me any room to think, and now really isn't a good time . . ."

I said the last part with a pointed look at Jamie, who'd pressed himself against the wall, looking very much like the Token Normal Kid who'd accidentally landed right in the middle of the crazy neighbor's family drama. Which, in a way, he was.

"Okay, screw the list," said Naomi, taking a few strides toward me and holding up her palm. My red guitar pick sat right in the middle. "Here's what's up. I talked to these two about how that genie magic of yours actually works, and you know what I found out? Two things. First, you can't force me to make a wish. Second, until all my wishes are done, unless I give your vessel back to you, you're still bound to me. Which means that whenever I do this"—she picked up the vessel with her thumb and forefinger, and the faint feeling of a call hooked into my chest, anchoring me to the room—"you have to come running. And as you know from the wish I used on my sister and her ex-fiancé, I am not above saving people from their own stupidity, even if I have to use magic to do it. You see what I'm getting at?"

I saw it very clearly. Naomi was going to hold me in Oak-vale the same way Ryan had held me in his room that night. The beginnings of panic nipped at me, turning my skin cold.

"You're wrong," I said, my voice strangely steady. "I can force you to make a wish. Same way I forced Ryan."

For the first time, her determined look faded into some-thing bordering confusion. "What do you mean?"

I narrowed my eyes at her. "I mean his last wish healed his broken nose, but not the rest of the bruises I gave him."

Vicky took a furtive step backward. Simon looked kind of impressed.

"That was *you*?" said Naomi.

"That was me," I said. "So you'd better start rethinking those threats of yours."

Turning and skirting around Oliver, I fled the band room. The sound of raised voices followed me, but I didn't listen closely enough to make out words.

I finally stopped running when I rounded the corner that led to the library. Slumping against the wall, I hid my face in my hands.

But only a moment later, footsteps echoed down the hallway, growing steadily louder. I braced myself. The trouble with making a dramatic exit was that someone usually took it upon themselves to follow you—and you never got to pick who it was.

My money was on Oliver.

But seconds later, Jamie rounded the corner, stopping short when he spotted me. "Hey," he said.

"Where's Oliver?" I asked, right before I realized that was probably rude. "Also, hey."

Jamie jerked a thumb in the general direction of the band room. "Giving your friend a very stern talking-to. Explaining exactly why keeping you here against your will wouldn't work out in anyone's favor."

I snorted, rubbing at my eyes with my fingertips. "Awesome," I said dully.

"Listen," he said, his voice low and serious, "I just want to apologize. I didn't know all this was going on—you know, that you hadn't . . . well . . . figured all this stuff out."

"Well, now you know," I said irritably. "Doesn't change anything. You still think I'm a selfish jerk for not giving you a fourth wish."

And you're right, I added silently. I was selfish enough to try and keep Oliver for myself; I was selfish enough to threaten violence against Naomi, just to keep her off my back; I was selfish enough to keep stringing everyone along as I tried and failed, and tried and failed again, to figure out what path my life should follow.

"No, I don't," said Jamie.

I peered suspiciously at him. "You don't?"

"Not anymore," he replied, leaning his head against the wall. I wondered if his dreads made a good pillow. "When you said you were in *Sweeney Todd* tonight, I figured I'd find some community theater thing. Not a high school show." He raised a pointed eyebrow. "I didn't know you were in high school."

"Well, I am. So what?"

He raised an eyebrow. "No, I mean—you're not some four-thousand-year-old genie *pretending* to be a teenager. You actually *are* a teenager." He paused, giving me room to contradict him. I didn't. "Which means you're brand-new at this. Aren't you."

It wasn't a question, but I nodded anyway. "I've only been a genie for three weeks. Well, three weeks and a few days."

Closing his eyes wearily, Jamie let out a long sigh. "No wonder you're so set on defending your turf. You've only just earned it."

I'd never thought of it like that.

I studied Jamie, with his nice face and muscular arms and cool hair. Even with the dreads, he seemed so . . . adult. Only two years older than me, and he was adult enough to know what he wanted out of life. To know how getting it would change him. To have a backup plan in case it didn't work out.

He was adult enough to know exactly who he was, and who he wanted to be.

Whereas I'd never planned on being anything other than human. Why would I? Yet here I was, trying to live my life at the same pace as always, without ever taking the time to regroup, to think, to figure things out at my own pace.

To make a new plan for how I was going to live.

I needed to give myself that time.

"Hey, Jamie?" I said.

He looked over at me. "Yeah?"

"Do you still want that fourth wish?"

Chapter TWENTY-SIX

"**H**ere's what's going to happen."

The sound of my voice stopped everyone in their tracks, and four heads turned to look at Jamie and me: Naomi, who looked inches away from killing Oliver with her bare hands; Oliver, whose blatant annoyance turned to worry when he saw me; and Simon and Vicky, who'd backed themselves into a corner, a safe distance away from the real action.

"Margo, are you—"

"I'm fine," I said curtly, and Oliver snapped his mouth shut. "I'm fine, and I have a plan."

"In other breaking news, the sky is blue," murmured Simon. I ignored him; so did everyone else.

"And the plan is . . . I'm staying here, at least for now." I felt weirdly like a TV announcer in front of a studio audience. So I stopped trying to talk to everyone at once, and focused only on Oliver. "I have to," I told him. "I mean, I *want* to. Because the thing is, Naomi's right. I have a whole life here, and I'm not ready to give it up yet."

She shot a smug look at Oliver, who didn't look particularly surprised.

"But I also can't do this double-life thing anymore," I continued. "I can't walk around pretending to be normal when I'm constantly making an effort to look like myself, constantly wondering if my master's going to call me, and all that."

Oliver's brow furrowed. He knew as well as I did that there was no way around the having-a-master thing. Not if I wanted to walk around in a visible human body.

"So, step one. Naomi, you're either going to make a third wish, or give my vessel to Jamie without making one." I put a hand on Jamie's shoulder—an awkward move, since he was approximately five times my height. "If you don't make a third wish now, you can still have one somewhere down the line." I hesitated, realizing I was uncertain about whether this was possible, and glanced at Oliver. "Right?"

He nodded.

"Step two. Jamie is going to make three wishes. I am going to grant them." I took a deep breath. "Step three. Jamie is going to make a fourth wish, and I'll grant that one, too."

"Wait, are you sure?" said Oliver, darting toward me, only to stop himself a few feet away. He gestured awkwardly at Jamie. "You're—you guys . . . you talked about this?"

Jamie and I exchanged a look. He shrugged. We hadn't talked about it at length—but then, we hadn't really needed to.

"I'm sure," I said. "And lastly, step four. Jamie, after you make your fourth wish, you're going to give my vessel to Oliver."

"What?" shouted Naomi. Oliver just went still.

And then, slowly, he nodded. Smiled. "You want me to be your master without making wishes."

"Not right away, at least," I said. "That's how it works, right? If I'm bound to somebody, I stay bound to them until they give up my vessel, or all three wishes are made. Whichever comes first. Which means as long as Oliver doesn't make any wishes, he can be my master for as long as he wants."

"For as long as *you* want," he said.

"Well, yeah," I said. "And you have to promise not to call me with it, either."

"I promise," he said firmly. "I will use a phone, like a normal person."

"That doesn't fix anything, though," said Naomi. "You're not running away with the guy, but you're letting him be your *master*? How is that better?"

I gave her a cool stare. "First of all: *questions*. Second of all, yes I am. Third of all, it's better because, for one thing, Oliver wouldn't keep me anywhere against my will. Which is more than I can say for you."

Her face went ashen, and she faltered for a second. "I wouldn't have actually done that. I . . . I just wanted you to stay."

"And I just wanted *you* to be okay with the fact that I'm different than I used to be," I said. "But you aren't. Every time I talk about magic, you give me that, you know, that *look*."

As if on cue, she side-eyed me. I pointed. "That one. That's the look. And yeah, okay, I know it's weird to hang out with someone who's basically not even the same species as you anymore, but if we're still gonna be friends, you're gonna have to deal with it."

"I . . ." But she didn't finish. I didn't know if it was the ultimatum or the word *species,* but she suddenly looked like she needed a moment to compose herself.

Meanwhile, Oliver stepped in. "All right. If this is what you want, then I'll do it. Are we back to the running-away-after-graduation plan, then?"

"I don't know," I said. "Maybe . . . but I don't know. Probably not. Because I literally have *the rest of eternity* to run away and be a full-time genie, but I've only got one shot at living my regular human life—and that's right now. And I don't know how long I'll want to keep living it. I might be sick of it by graduation, or I might stick around until I'm twenty-five. Or forty-five. I seriously just don't know. But I'm sending that first tuition check to NYU, just in case." I paused. "Is that okay?"

"Tomorrow or forty-five years, NYU or no NYU—it's all okay," said Oliver, his voice low. Then his lips quirked up into a sly little smile. "Although I still wish you'd run away with me right now."

"As long as you don't wish that out loud while you're my master," I said, which made him laugh. "All right, guys. Let's do this."

In the end, Naomi decided not to make a third wish. Half because she'd been so set on keeping me here that she hadn't spared the time to think of one—and half because Vicky reminded her that she'd given up Oliver's vessel after two wishes, too.

"Although," said Vicky, turning back to Oliver, "does that mean if I ever want a third wish, I can still have one?"

"Just say the word," said Oliver, looking immensely gratified that she'd asked.

So Naomi passed my vessel to Jamie—and as soon as he held it between his thumb and forefinger, pain ignited. The familiar, needle-sharp pain of my magic creating a new default body.

I'd forgotten about this part. Well, not forgotten exactly— but I'd been so focused on thinking in big-picture terms that I hadn't really zoomed in on the details. Specifically, the part where I'd have to transform into someone new—someone I'd never been before—in front of an audience.

At first I tried to stall it, thinking maybe I could run out of the room just long enough to do this on my own. But my magic would have none of it. The transformation was already over.

My magic receded, my skin tingled, and I was someone new again. A girl this time—that much I could tell right away. And I was taller than usual. Almost as tall as Tony had been. But beyond that, I had no idea what I looked like. Which was especially weird since everyone else in the room could see me.

Spreading my arms wide, I gave Jamie a stage-worthy smile. "So, am I your dream girl?"

"You're," he said, blinking fast all of a sudden. His voice sounded like it was coming from awfully far away. "I mean, it's been a long time, so I could be wrong, but—well, you look an awful lot like—"

"Me," Oliver supplied, stepping toward me as unrestrained glee brightened his face. "Me as Alicia. Right?"

Jamie nodded, looking sort of amazed and also sort of mortified.

"Hel-*lo*, Alicia," said Simon. Vicky laughed and elbowed him.

"Want to see?" asked Naomi, pulling a compact out of her pocket and offering it to me. Since I doubted there was a better mirror in the band room, I took it and examined my new face. Or Oliver's old one. Whatever.

I definitely had big hair, just like Jamie had said in the café, and big features to go with it. I looked like the sort of person who broke up other people's fistfights. My nose and eyes were exactly the right shape, and my skin exactly the right shade of brown, to hint that Jamie and I might just be related.

I considered asking Jamie if he'd had a crush on Alicia, or if this was just the image in his mind's eye whenever he thought about what a genie ought to look like—but I decided against it.

"Nice," I said, and then shifted immediately back into my real self, which made Jamie relax a little. Giving the compact back to Naomi, I said, "Ready to make some wishes, Jamie?"

He was.

I made him talk them through with me before officially wishing, just so I wouldn't screw them up, like I had with Naomi's. There was one about lifelong health for his mom, his aunt, and his brother. There was one about funding for the extracurricular arts programs at his former high school. And one about finding true love—not for himself, but for his painfully introverted best friend.

All annoyingly unselfish wishes, just like I'd suspected they'd be.

He was going to make a seriously awesome genie.

When I'd granted all three, right in a row, the aftershocks of my magic left me shaking so hard that I could barely stand up. Oliver, who didn't seem at all surprised by this, toed a music stand out of the way and steered me over to sit in one of the plastic band chairs. I collapsed gratefully, breathing hard.

"God, I'm sorry," said Jamie, hovering over me like a nervous bee. "Should I have gone slower?"

"Nah, you did fine," I said. "I'll be good in three . . . two . . . one . . . Except, wait." I turned to Oliver. "How do I . . . I mean, should I do anything different than the other ones? For the fourth wish, I mean?"

"Nope," he said, sitting down beside me. "Same as the others. Slow it down and shape it if you want; otherwise, just let it happen." Giving my knee a squeeze, he asked, "Do you want us to leave?"

The question wasn't directed at me. I looked up; Jamie was still standing there, visibly steeling himself for what was about to happen. I was willing to bet he hadn't counted on making a fourth wish in front of an audience of strangers.

"Yeah, I can kick these guys out, if you want," I added, standing again, albeit somewhat shakily. "All we need is you and me."

Jamie hesitated for a moment, but then shook his head. "I'm cool if you are."

"I'm cool," I said, finding with some measure of surprise that I actually meant it—and not just in regards to having an audience. I was cool with the whole thing.

The thought of Jamie being in my life, and in Oliver's, had settled well in the short while since I'd promised him a fourth wish. Sure, maybe a small part of me was still mildly terrified that he and Oliver would fall madly in love and abandon me entirely—but it was only a small part. Easily ignored.

Besides, whether I liked it or not, Oliver had been lonely too long, and he needed someone like Jamie in his life. Someone good. Someone selfless and kind. Someone who wished for things like funding for the arts in high schools, for heaven's sake.

Who knew? Maybe someday I'd also be that sort of person. But for now, all I wanted to be was myself, whoever and whatever that might be.

Jamie held my vessel between his fingers, and I touched my hands to his, the way Oliver did when he granted wishes.

His fourth wish, just as elegantly stated as the first three, was for his aunt to have enough money to buy a house and send his little cousin to college, with enough left over to finance a comfortable life.

A surge of power. Hot and cold burning my skin. A lightning-bolt-photo-negative change in my vision, burning through my lids even after I closed my eyes. I could feel it as my magic fulfilled Jamie's wish. It placed money in his aunt's accounts, where there hadn't been any money before. And then it created records proving, to anyone who cared to look, that it had been there all along.

But instead of receding back into me when the wish was over, my magic held on to the connection, keeping me tied to

Jamie. He clutched my hands tighter, and I opened my eyes again.

"What . . . what's . . ."

But he couldn't seem to finish. So I held his hands, held his gaze, and told him what Oliver had told me when I'd made my own fourth wish:

"Just remember to breathe."

Squeezing his eyes closed, Jamie did as I'd instructed. I kept hold of his hands. I couldn't feel, or see, what my magic was doing to him—but I remembered very clearly what becoming a genie had felt like for me. I remembered the pins-and-needles sensation of magic awakening inside me for the first time, and I remembered the sense of being encased in a bubble of light, with everything outside muted and muffled.

I remembered falling out of my own body. I wondered if that was what it felt like for Jamie.

My magic snapped, and the connection between us was broken. Jamie's eyes flew open. Holding his hands suddenly felt like holding almost-solid air.

I let go.

"Where'd he go?" Naomi asked softly, almost reverently. Jamie looked over at her, confused.

"He's right here," I said. "You just can't see him. Oliver and I can, though."

Jamie looked like he was on the verge of panic, but Oliver stepped up and slung an arm around his shoulders. "Don't worry. I'll explain everything. Just calm down. I promise you're fine."

"Uh-huh," said Jamie. "Sure. Okay."

"Breathe," I reminded him one more time. "And Oliver, if you're planning on taking him to the Between right away, do yourself a favor and tell him what the Between *is* first, okay?"

"Between?" Jamie echoed faintly. "Between what?"

"Between everything," said Oliver, all bright and excited, just like he'd been with me. "Margo, you want to come with?"

It was tempting, the thought of hanging out with them and watching Jamie learn to use his magic, just like I'd done only a few weeks ago. Maybe even teaching him a few things myself. But I shook my head.

"You may recall," I said, "that we just played the closing performance of the last show of my senior year in high school. It's cast party time."

"Crap," murmured Naomi, taking her phone out and tapping on the screen. "Forgot to tell them I'd be late. . . ."

The cast party of the musical was always at Naomi's giant house, mostly because she had a huge finished basement, complete with a fancy karaoke machine. Apparently she'd been so caught up in planning Operation Intervention, she'd accidentally left her parents in charge of hosting.

Oh well.

"You're sure about being human, then?" said Oliver. "Living your old life, all that?"

I nodded. "For as long as I can."

"Speaking of which," said Jamie, who seemed slightly more composed than a moment ago. He held out my vessel. Oliver took it. Held it between his thumb and forefinger. And for the second time in less than ten minutes, I felt the pain of transformation racking my body.

When it was done, Oliver was wearing the smuggest grin I'd ever seen.

"What?" I asked, suddenly nervous. "What do I look like?"

He tilted his head to the side, peering at me like a sculptor inspecting his work. "Like my dream girl," he said.

Naomi and her compact had left, so I was stuck with looking down, trying to find a clue to what everyone but me could already see.

Then I spotted it, right there on my arm. A constellation of freckles, shaped like the Big Dipper.

I was me.

"Gag me," muttered Simon.

"Aw," said Vicky.

But I didn't pay them any attention; I was too busy kissing Oliver with everything I had. With the confidence of a good decision made for the right reasons, with the bursting energy of four wishes granted back-to-back, with more love than I'd ever thought I could feel for one single person.

And with more tongue than was probably advisable, considering there were people watching us.

"Call me later," I said, when I could finally bring myself to pull away.

"Always," said Oliver.

That was when Naomi came rushing back in. "Paging Willoughbee, Lee, and McKenna," she said. "Every single other member of the *Sweeney Todd* company is partying at my house without me, and I am determined to get there before someone finds the karaoke machine."

"I'm going in Simon's car," said Vicky, and Simon smiled at her.

"McKenna?" said Naomi.

I hesitated. Normally I'd take my own car without even a second thought, but those four wishes had left me shaky and unsteady and maybe just a little too wired. On the other hand, I didn't want to fight with Naomi anymore. Not tonight, at least.

Then she said, "Actually, you *have* to come with me. I need to stop for Doritos, and I don't have any cash on me."

"Neither do I," I said—and then realized what she was getting at. "Oh. Really? You're sure?"

She shrugged. "You said deal with it or we're not friends anymore. So this is me, dealing with it."

I grinned. "Then count me in."

She hesitated, then made a vague gesture at Oliver. "Parish, you want to come? Technically it's company-only, but the slide-show pictures are mostly yours, so that probably counts."

"Thanks," he said. "But Jamie and I have plans of our own."

"Suit yourself," she said. "Come on, McKenna."

She headed out, and I followed. But when I reached the door, I glanced back, just once. Oliver caught my eye and smiled—and as I watched, he slipped my vessel into the pocket of his hoodie, like a promise made, or a secret kept.

He took Jamie's hand, and they went.

ACKNOWLEDGMENTS

This book was not easy to write. There were a lot of wrong turns, a lot of unintentional detours, and probably more words thrown away than words kept. The process turned me into something of a crazy person—which means that my first big thank-you must go to the people who not only dealt with my crazy, but gave me their love and support instead of backing slowly away. My family—Mom, Dad, Megan—is right at the top of this list, along with the Lovely Ladies of MacDougal Street: Katie Bancroft and Jane Esberg.

And then there's Nina Lourie, who lured me uptown *knowing full well* that she'd have to deal with my crazy—the same Nina who, at this point, probably knows these characters even better than I do. Thank you for being my sounding board, my occasional therapist, my launch party planner, my improvisational publicist, and my favorite Dominion opponent … even if you always win. I mean, just *take* all the platinums and colonies. See if I care!

Speaking of people who know these characters better than

I do—huge, huge thanks to the incredibly talented Alison Cherry, who not only brainstormed half a zillion ideas with me, but read every single draft of this book. All of them. Even the bad ones. Please be my critique partner forever and ever, okay?

Jeri Smith-Ready, thank you for your honest criticism, for telling people to read my stuff, and for being such a freaking inspiration with those amazing books of yours. Andrea Robinson-DiNardo, Miriam Newman, and Corey Ann Haydu, thank you so much for your feedback along the way.

Thank you to the Lucky 13s, the New York City debut crew, all the folks I've met through Teen Author Drinks Night, and especially the Woodstock Wine and Cheese Brigade. I raise a glass (or several) to all of you.

Thank you to the folks at SJGA, especially Matt Bialer and Vanessa DeJesus. Thank you to the amazing Penguin Teen team, especially Anna Jarzab, Tara Shanahan, Regina Castillo, and the illustrious Claire Evans.

One million times thank you to Brenda Bowen, my agent and publishing hero, for talking me off more ledges than I can possibly count.

And Kathy Dawson. I can't even. *I can't even.* Thank you times infinity for your genius, for *Bird By Bird*, for loving my characters even when I wanted to kill them, and for being an all-around awesome lady. Marry me? (Kidding.) (Mostly.)

WISHING FOR MORE MARGO?

Turn the page to see
where her story began in

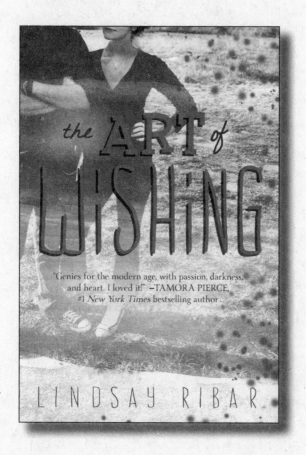

the ART of
WISHING

"Genies for the modern age, with passion, darkness,
and heart. I loved it!" —TAMORA PIERCE,
#1 *New York Times* bestselling author

LINDSAY RIBAR

Prologue

The plan was this: I'd get up on that stage, blow them away with the best damn audition they'd ever seen, and walk out knowing the part I wanted was mine.

And when I was called into the auditorium, that was exactly how it happened.

I walked over to the piano and handed my sheet music to George. "You know this one?" I asked him.

He peered quickly at the title. Nodded and said, "Yup." Of course he did. Silly question.

George flexed his fingers, and I strode up the little side staircase and onto the stage. Bright lights flooded my face, but I was used to that. I shielded my eyes so I could focus on the lone figure sitting in the first row: Miss Delisio, math teacher by day and play director by night. I smiled warmly at her. This was the woman who was going to cast me in my dream role.

"Margo McKenna," she said in greeting. "I do love a straight-A trig student with stage presence. How's calculus treating you?"

I wrinkled my nose. "Straight A minuses this year. Calc is hard. Who knew?"

Miss Delisio laughed appreciatively. "Why do you think I don't teach it?" she said. "All right, what are you singing for us today?"

"I'm doing 'Last Midnight' from *Into the Woods* by Stephen Sondheim," I recited.

"Great song," she said. "Whenever you're ready."

This was it. I took a moment to steady myself, then nodded to George. On my cue, he started playing. I molded my body into the shape of the song, and the lyrics flowed out of me like I owned them. For those few minutes, I became someone totally different from my real self. Someone worldly and manipulative. Someone with very real power.

I'd chosen "Last Midnight" because of that power. And as the song grew in intensity, and my performance grew to match, and the air in the theater seemed to dance to the rhythm of George's piano and my voice . . . . I knew I'd chosen right.

When I finished, a couple of breaths passed before anyone said anything.

"That was lovely, Margo," said Miss Delisio. I couldn't see her face, but I could hear the smile in her voice. "Really, really lovely."

"Yup," said George.

"Thanks," I said breathlessly.

I heard the rustle of a notebook page being flipped. "Stick

around for a little while, okay?" said Miss Delisio. "We'll pair you up and have you read from the script."

"Sounds good," I said. "I'll be in the hallway."

Naomi Sloane, my best friend and Miss Delisio's stage manager, was manning the door that stood between me and the hallway full of nervous students outside. She gave me a thumbs-up as I approached her.

"McKenna, you just nailed that," she said. "Don't tell the masses, but you're the best audition I've seen so far."

I flashed her a coy smile. "I bet you say that to all the girls."

She laughed and held the door open for me, and I floated out into the hallway as she called the next student's name. Sure, I still had to do the reading part of the audition, but that would be a piece of cake. The hard part—the important part—was over. And Naomi was right.

I'd nailed it.

Chapter ONE

Sweeney Todd is a musical about cannibalism. More specifically, it's a musical about a barber named Benjamin Barker, alias Sweeney Todd, who kills his customers and gives the bodies to his landlady, Mrs. Lovett, so she can turn them into meat pies and serve them to people. There's a lot more to it than that—love and obsession and revenge, everything you'd expect to find in a good musical—but for most people, cannibalism is the show's biggest selling point.

For me, though, it was all about the music. Nothing in the entire universe made me happier than sinking my teeth into a really juicy song and performing it for anyone willing to listen—and of all the musicals I've ever loved, *Sweeney Todd* was the ultimate source for juicy songs. Especially if you were playing Mrs. Lovett, which was exactly what I planned to do.

A week after the auditions, Miss Delisio announced that she'd made her casting decisions and the list would be up at the end of the day. So when the last bell rang, I raced out of my last class and up to the theater. There was already a throng of drama club students milling around the door. A piece of light green paper was there, held up with Scotch tape.

I started pushing my way through the crowd, but a hand on my shoulder stopped me before I could get very far. "Congrats, girl!" said Naomi, pulling me into a quick hug. "You got a lead. Told you so, didn't I?"

Naomi had never been interested in acting, but she'd stage-managed our shows ever since freshman year. She was a natural at it, too: level-headed, loud, and popular enough that people actually listened when she told them to do things.

"Really?" I said, returning her grin. "Wait, don't tell me. I want to see for myself."

Call it superstition, but even in a case like this, where I knew beyond a doubt what part I'd gotten, I had to see it in writing before I let it become real. *Margaret McKenna—Mrs. Lovett*. Ever since Miss Delisio had announced that *Sweeney Todd* would be our spring musical, I'd pictured those words in my head, willing them to come true.

I skirted around Naomi and wove through a bunch of guys high-fiving each other, until finally I reached the cast list. It only took a few seconds for me to zero in on my name, about half-way down the green paper. I followed the line that would lead me to the name of my character.

Margaret McKenna—Tobias Ragg.

No way.

The chatter around me dissolved into white noise, and I

blinked a couple times, just to make sure I wasn't imagining things. I traced the line with my finger. No, I'd really been cast as Tobias Ragg. Toby, who only had a couple of songs. Toby, who was young and simple-minded, the exact opposite of the devious and amazing Mrs. Lovett, who I was certain I'd get to be.

Toby, who was a boy.

I mean, sure, I was short and kind of flat-chested, but come on. . . .

"I'm Toby," I said to myself, trying the idea on for size. It didn't fit.

"Yeah," came Naomi's voice from just over my shoulder. Apparently she'd followed me through the crowd. I turned to her, and her congratulatory smile faltered when she saw my face. "Listen, I know you wanted Mrs. Lovett, but Toby's still a really good part. You'll be so awesome."

But her consolation-prize words washed over me, totally devoid of meaning. "Who *is* playing Lovett?" I asked. I hadn't even thought to check. "Wait. Don't tell me."

So she didn't. She just bit her lip and waited for me to find the name. Find it I did. Recognize it, I did not.

"Who the hell is Victoria Willoughbee?"

Naomi went quiet for a moment, her face frozen in an expression that I couldn't read. "You know Vicky," she said at last. "Sophomore? Plays clarinet in the band?" Nothing rang a bell, so I just shook my head. Naomi shrugged. "Well, she's nice."

"But why——"

"Woo-hoo!" came a shout, so close it made me flinch. Just behind me was Simon Lee, looking over my head at the cast list. "I'm Sweeney Effing Todd, suckers! I am the Asian Johnny Depp! I've always said that! Haven't I? Haven't I always said that?"

He punched the air, and a few people yelled out their congratulations and gave him those back-thumping man-hugs. Nobody seemed to begrudge him the lead role, or even the bizarre victory dance he was now doing. Mostly because we all knew he was the most talented boy in the entire school. Not to mention the cutest.

Simon found me in the crowd and gave me one of those lopsided grins that made my chest feel like a tiny hot-air balloon. That was when it hit me.

I wouldn't get to be Simon's costar.

Suddenly, I was absolutely certain I was about to lose it. I had to get out of there. I couldn't let all these people see me cry over a part in a high school musical. Especially not Simon.

"Congratulations," I managed to choke out, and ran like hell toward the girls' bathroom.

I didn't even see the boy coming around the corner until I bumped right into him. My shoulder smacked into his arm with a force that nearly spun me off my feet.

"Sorry!" he said automatically, stepping gingerly out of my way as I looked up in alarm to see who it was. I didn't know him.

But his eyes widened as he looked down at me. "Margo," he said. "Oh. I'm really, *really* sorry."

I gave him a quick once-over—dark hair, light eyes, thin and wiry, cute enough in a nondescript sort of way—but no, I definitely didn't know him. "Sorry about what? Who are you?"

"Nobody," he said quickly, holding his hands up like a white flag. "I'm nobody. Never mind."

I darted past him. Out of the corner of my eye, I saw him turn to watch me go.

The bathroom smelled faintly of weed and cigarettes, and the powers that be had long since stopped scrubbing away the rude graffiti that covered the walls, but at least it was empty. Feeling about nine years old, I locked myself in a stall, drew my knees up to my chin, and shut my eyes.

Miss Delisio always gave the lead roles to seniors. That was how it worked. You paid your underclassman dues in the chorus, or maybe in small roles if you were lucky, and then you got a good part right before you graduated. So why were the rules different for that Vicky Willoughbee girl?

I only allowed myself out of the stall when I'd calmed down enough to form a new plan of action. If I couldn't be Mrs. Lovett, then I would be the sort of person who was totally okay with *not* being Mrs. Lovett. I smiled at myself in the bathroom mirror until it looked real, and then I took a deep breath and headed back toward the theater for the first rehearsal.

Miss Delisio was already sitting primly on the stage when I came in. In addition to being my tenth-grade trig teacher, she'd directed every musical I'd been in since freshman year. I liked her well enough—but sitting next to her, wearing tight jeans, clunky boots, and a black biker jacket, was the real talent: George the Music Ninja.

Even when George was just noodling around on the piano during breaks, it was like listening to some crazy musical genius at work. And that wasn't even counting his other job. When he wasn't musical-directing us, he was the front man of an indie band called Apocalypse Later. He didn't write their music, which probably explained why I wasn't totally sold on their sound, but his vocals and guitar solos were absolutely killer.

"Grab your script and have a seat," Miss Delisio announced in her usual buoyant voice. "We'll start as soon as everyone's here."

One by one, we made our way up to the stage, where there was a pile of scripts, each labeled with the name of an actor and the role they were playing. I watched Miss Delisio closely as I approached, wondering if she would say anything to me. She knew I wanted to be Mrs. Lovett. In fact, last time I spoke to her, she'd stopped just short of outright promising me the role. Would she bother to explain why she'd given it to someone else?

Apparently not. By the time I reached the stage and fished my script from the pile, she and George were engrossed in conversation. I took a deep breath. It didn't matter, I reminded myself. What's done is done. I was okay with it. No, I was more than okay; I was going to kick ass in this role.

Most of the actors with leads had settled in the front row: Callie Zumsky as Johanna, MaLinda Jones as Pirelli, Dan Quimby-Sato as Anthony, Ryan Weiss as Judge Turpin, Jill Spalding as the Beggar Woman. All seniors, of course. But I joined Naomi in the second row instead.

"You okay, McKenna?" whispered Naomi as I sat down beside her.

"Why wouldn't I be?" I whispered back. "Just because Sophomore McWhatserface got Lovett and I didn't?"

Naomi snickered. "You mean Willoughbee," she said, trying and failing to sound disapproving.

I grinned. "That's what I said. Anyway, whatever. I'm over it."

"You don't look over it."

I raised an eyebrow at her. "Perhaps your eyes deceive you."

She looked like she wanted to press the issue, but I was saved by the arrival of Simon, who slid into the empty seat on my other side. "Heya, Toby," he said, grinning.

There was something witty I could say in response to that. I was sure of it. Unfortunately, the best my brain could cough up was: "Actually, it's Margo."

He feigned shock and slapped his forehead with his palm. "Duh. I'm always doing that. Calling people Toby. When will I ever learn?"

Something witty. Something witty. I needed to think of something witty.

But his arm kept brushing against mine as he arranged his stuff on the floor, and that was enough to distract me. I was just about to give up on being witty and blurt out something inane like "Never, I guess," when Miss Delisio began to shush us.

"We've got almost everyone," she said, frowning down at the scripts beside her. "We're just missing Vicky—oh, there she is!"

Her gaze shifted to the back of the auditorium, and everyone twisted around to see who she was looking at. There, at the top of the left aisle, was a girl I was pretty sure I'd never seen before. Clutching a small pile of books to her chest, she hesitated there like she'd been caught in the act of . . . what? Walking into a room?

This was the girl who'd been cast in the role of a lifetime?

"Here you go," said Miss Delisio, holding out a script. Hugging her books closer, Vicky darted down the aisle to collect it. Miss Delisio, beaming, said something I couldn't hear, and Vicky gave her a tight smile in return. Miss Delisio gestured to the front row.

But the front row had already filled up. Vicky hesitated again, and for one relieved moment I was sure she would head toward the back, with the other underclassmen.

Then Simon waved at her. "Saved you a seat over here!" he called, much to my dismay. Vicky slid into the seat on Simon's other side as he gave her his trademark arched-eyebrow smile.

The one that made my heart beat just a little faster when he used it on me. The one that, last spring, had led to an incredibly awesome kiss at the cast party of *Bat Boy: The Musical*. The kiss had never been repeated. In fact, after that night he'd never even brought it up again. But still: awesome.

Vicky, however, seemed oblivious to his flirty look.

"Margo, right?" she whispered to me, across Simon.

"That's me."

"I saw you as Ruthie in *Bat Boy* last year. You were really good."

"Thanks," I said, and smiled at her, exactly like I'd practiced in the bathroom mirror. I was okay with this. I was not allowed to hate Vicky Willoughbee.

Once we were settled, Miss Delisio introduced George, like there was anyone here who didn't know him. He flashed us a grin and settled himself at the piano. We wouldn't be singing today, since we hadn't officially learned the songs yet, but that didn't mean he couldn't underscore us. He began to play the opening bars of the show, and a little shiver flitted up my spine.

With Naomi reading stage directions, we jumped right in. As usual, speaking the lyrics was odd since, without rhythms and melody, lyrics just sound like really weird poetry. But this was the way the first rehearsal always went: just a read-through, so we could all learn the story together. Most of us were used to it. Some people, like Simon, even managed to make it sound kind of good.

Vicky, however, was no Simon. She read all of her lyrics in

an awful monotone, like she couldn't quite figure out what the words meant. And it wasn't just the lyrics, either. The way she read the dialogue was just as bad. It was all I could do not to cover my ears and run screaming out of the theater.

When we finally reached the end of Act One, Miss Delisio called a ten-minute break. I thought about going outside, but when Vicky got up, I decided to stay right where I was. Running into her in the hallway and accidentally punching her in the face were definitely not part of my I'm-okay-with-this plan.

As I skimmed the second half of the script, I saw a student approach Miss Delisio. A student who wasn't in the cast, which was a little unusual. It took me a minute, but I recognized him as the boy from earlier. The one I'd almost mowed down on my way to the bathroom.

He spoke with Miss Delisio and George for a few moments before digging through the pockets of the hoodie he wore, then through the backpack he'd slung over one shoulder. He pulled out what looked like a camera case. I heard the word *yearbook* come out of someone's mouth, and I groaned softly as I realized what was going on. They were starting rehearsal photo shoots this early in the game? Not fair.

When the cast had settled back in their seats and quieted, Miss Delisio took a moment to confirm my fears.

"Guys, this is Oliver Parish." The boy gave a shy little wave to nobody in particular. "He just transferred here in January. He's going to be photographing our rehearsal process for the drama club's section of the yearbook. And maybe, if we're lucky, he'll get enough to put together a slide show for our cast party."

Naomi nudged me and rolled her eyes, which made me grin. I looked at Simon, to see what he thought of this turn of events, but he was busy typing out a text message on his phone. Beside him, though, Vicky was watching Oliver. And she wasn't wearing that timid, deer-in-the-headlights expression from before. She was absolutely beaming.

I looked at the photographer. He smiled back at Vicky, like there was a secret in the room, and they were the only two people who knew it.

The porch lights were already on when I got home that night, and my mom's car sat ominously in the driveway. And the house, as I'd feared, was a mess. There were coats draped over the back of the couch, shoes strewn all around the floor, and four suitcases in the hallway, one of which was open and spilling clothes everywhere. I tried not to think about how I'd cleaned this room just three days ago.

Ziggy was the first to greet me when I opened the door, jumping off her perch on the couch and rubbing herself against my legs. She purred as I bent to scritch her little tabby head. "Did Mommy and Daddy come home?" I whispered to her. "Did they remember to feed you?"

"Margo?" came Mom's voice from the kitchen. "Honey, is that you?"

I rolled my eyes. "No, it's a burglar. I've come to steal all your silverware and jewelry. And your cat," I added, giving Ziggy another scratch.

"As long as you don't steal our daughter," she replied. Emerging from the kitchen with a huge grin on her face and Dad trailing behind her, she gave me a quick hug and a peck on the forehead.

"How was the cruise?" I asked, unzipping my boots and placing them neatly on the shoe rack by the door. I'd deal with my parents' shoes later.

She sighed dramatically. "Absolute heaven. Maybe even better than the last one. I know they say you should wait for summer to visit Alaska, but what's a little cold?"

"Cold schmold," added Dad. "That's what the parkas were for. Not to mention the indoor cabin."

Mom gave him a secretive little smile. "The honeymoon suite, you mean."

"Honeymoon suite, still?" I asked, doing my best to ignore the dewy-eyed looks they were exchanging. "What is this, the third honeymoon you've been on since the wedding?"

Mom thought for a moment. "Fourth, if you count the Grand Canyon trip."

"Which I do," said Dad. "Oh, and we have pictures!" He ran over to the open suitcase and began rifling through it. "Wait till you see these, Margo. Some of the ones your mother took are just, wow."

Ever since the wedding last May, our lives had been one continuous cycle of Mom and Dad planning a trip, Mom and Dad leaving on their trip, a week or two of peace and quiet, Mom and Dad coming back from their trip, and the grand finale, Mom and Dad showing me pictures of their trip. The pictures were always the same, too: Mom pretending to fall over the railing of a cruise ship, Dad wearing another cheesy Hawaiian shirt, stuff like that. Sometimes it felt like they were the teenagers and I was the adult.

"How's school?" asked Mom. "Anything exciting happen while we were gone?"

"Nope," I said quickly. "Same old same old."

I thought about telling her about the cast list fiasco, but this wasn't the time. At best, they'd both go "Aw, that's too bad" and jump right back into honeymoon talk. At worst, they wouldn't even understand why I was so upset. As far as they were concerned, it didn't matter what role I had, as long as their daughter was onstage. These were, after all, the people who'd thrown me a party after I'd played Frightened Theatergoer Number Two in my first-grade musical about Abraham Lincoln.

"Where did I put that camera?" muttered Dad.

"Red suitcase, inside pocket, next to the toothbrushes," replied Mom almost absently, and then turned back to me. "You'll never guess what movie was playing on the plane today. *The Parent Trap.* Can you believe it?"

"Oh, I almost forgot about that!" said Dad, unzipping the red suitcase.

"It was the old Hayley Mills one," said Mom. "The good one, not the remake they did with that awful drug addict girl."

I was about to point out that Lindsay Lohan probably hadn't been a drug addict at the time, but Mom continued, "And we said, take away the twin thing and the summer camp, and that's our Margo! Making us back into one big, happy family."

"It wasn't exactly me," I said, but neither of them seemed to notice.

"Aw, Celia," said Dad. Camera finally in hand, he came back over and enveloped us in a bear hug. Mom hugged back just as hard, so I did too.

If I'd been a character in a musical, this would have been the point where the lights went down on my parents, leaving them slow-dancing in the background like living scenery, as I stepped forward into a lone spotlight for my big solo. It would be a quirky ballad, probably called "I Am Not Hayley Mills" or something like that, and people would applaud when I was done. Maybe they'd even give me a standing ovation.

Of course, people don't usually get standing ovations in their living rooms, but I still toyed with the idea of dashing upstairs, pulling out my guitar, and writing that song. It wasn't worth it, though. I'd tried a million different times to write a million different songs about a million different things, but it was never worth it. My songs always sucked.